I want what I want

Geoff Brown was born in Bridlington in Yorkshire in 1932. His novel *I Want What I Want* was published in 1966 and was made into a film starring Anne Heywood.

I want what I want

Geoff Brown

WEIDENFELD & NICOLSON

First published in Great Britain in 1966
by Weidenfeld & Nicolson
This paperback edition published in 2018
by Weidenfeld & Nicolson
an imprint of the Orion Publishing Group Ltd
Carmelite House, 50 Victoria Embankment
London EC4Y 0DZ

An Hachette UK Company

1 3 5 7 9 10 8 6 4 2

A CIP catalogue record for this book is
available from the British Library.

ISBN (Mass Market Paperback) 978 1 4746 0933 3
ISBN (eBook) 978 1 4746 0934 0

Printed and bound in Great Britain by Clays Ltd, St Ives plc

www.orionbooks.co.uk

Prologue

My name is Wendy. The rain was dreadful this morning. My name is Wendy. Does this bus go to the city centre? My name is Wendy. I am twenty-one years old. I am not married. I haven't got a boy friend. I haven't got a job at present. I am living on some money that my mother left me. She died. Actually, she was killed. She had an accident with an electric tooth-brush. It was a terrible shock. Please don't pull my hair. Would that yellow dress in the window fit me? Have you got the same style in blue? I want to buy a handbag. I want a red cocktail dress with a square cut front. Excuse me, constable, this man is annoying me. He seems to want to pull my hair. I think he's jealous. I can't do shorthand or typing, but I could learn. Could you tell me the way to the Ladies', please? I am Wendy. My mother and I lived in Cottingham. My father was a professional soldier. He was a colonel in the Green Howards—no, he was in the Coldstream Guards. That's why I've grown up tall. His name isn't in the Army Lists—because—because—because I'm a liar. Actually, he was an artist, a painter. He was a most wonderful man, but he never made any money. He was a lamb. My mother never really recovered from his death—she never really recovered from her own death. I'm all that's left. I'm a girl, Wendy, just a helpless girl, alone in the world on high-heels. I love heels. I'm a girl. When I was born the doctor went to my father and said, 'It's a girl.' My father was overjoyed. He always wanted a daughter. I'm his daughter—or I was when he was alive. I often think how lucky I am to be a girl. This is my skirt and my blouse and my shoes and my stockings and all the things I can't tell you about. I'm very prim. That's why I don't want to go on the stage. I'm Wendy. I now have two nightdresses. I now have four pairs of stockings. One of my nightdresses is red and the other is black. I'm going to get them out and have a look at them in a minute. I'm sure they'll be lovely. I love nice things. Tonight I'm going to sleep in a nightdress—the black one, I think. Don't you wish you had two nightdresses like mine? I chose the most romantic ones in the catalogue. They arrived this morning. Would you like to wear a black nightdress? You can't. I won't permit it. It belongs to me. It is mine. A girl has to be careful of all sorts of things. On wash day I have to keep a look out in case some kinky boy comes and steals some of my undies off the line. I think everybody is going mad nowadays. Boys wanting to be girls! I can understand a girl wanting to be a boy, but I can't understand a boy wanting to be a girl. But I suppose there are a lot of things one doesn't understand when one comes from Cottingham. Actually, I used to live in Cottingham. It was very quiet. On Sunday mornings I used to go to church with my mother. I've always believed in God. I think it's best to be on the safe side. Imagine being attacked by a man! My mother and I used to go to church in white gloves carrying white hymn books—we wore the rest of our clothes, of course. I love wearing clothes. Church on Sunday mornings was very nice. They were all very nice people there. It was nice to wear nice clothes and be in church. No one played the trombone in the vestry and I never got my hair pulled. Mother and I lived very quietly after father died. He was the noisy one. He used to get terribly drunk and fight—artists are like that, you know. Once a man came and said something horribly insulting to me—I can't tell you what it was—and my father gave him a fearful thrashing. My father wasn't always terribly civilised. But one has to make allowances for men. They wear such dismal clothes that they have to do violent things occasionally to keep themselves from going crazy. It must be dreadful to be a man. I'm very glad that I'm a girl. My name is Wendy. Wendy Ross.

Part One

NO NAME

1

Dr Strickland said, 'Of course your thinking is still very dualistic.'

I knew what he meant. I could have told him that he should not talk like that to a person who had not been to university, but there was no need for me to pretend about that. I did not really care that I had not been to university. I knew what I wanted.

If I had gone to university, I would have liked to go to Oxford. I had read about it. The only things I liked doing at home were reading and dressing up.

Dr Strickland was a tall man, lounging in his swivel chair. His face was long and pale. It was a face that would have been more suitable for a young man but it had grown middle-aged. His eyes did not look as confident as I thought a middle-aged man's eyes should look. He was like a student.

I was pretty. I sat neatly, small and careful in a black sweater. I was conscious of the stomach in the middle of me. In the beginning there was the stomach that reproduced itself without sex. Now there was the stomach, and below it the sexual organs, and above it the brain. Sometimes it felt as though there were two things, the mind and the body, and the mind wanted to leave the body. It felt like that when I was too pure and intellectual. When those times came I was frightened that my mind might float away from my body. I might be sent to Ward Nine for the rest of my life to live in the dream world with the old men.

Dr Strickland was talking to me.

From where he was sitting he could look out of the window and see the wallflowers growing in their little squares in the lawn and the drive with the sun shining on it and the lodge at the gate and the cars passing on the road.

3

I could not concentrate on what he was saying.

My father had looked ill when he was hitting me. He had dragged me by the collar as though to get me to the sink. Suddenly he had punched me on the top lip. Then he had punched me in the body a few times. If we had been able to stop my mouth bleeding, I would not have had to go to Dr Booth.

I still felt amazement when I thought of that young woman coming to ask for her stolen panties back. But they were her knickers. Perhaps she felt that her vagina had been stolen and she had to have it back. She was a fetishist.

Most people were fetishists. If it was not one thing, it was another.

It would soon be dinner time. After he had finished with me Dr Strickland would go outside and get into his car and go home. His wife would be preparing his dinner. She would be in the kitchen in her clothes. I wished that I were his wife. She had his social position without having to moil with insanity. She did not have to do with all the miserable and hopeless things that crept about in the hospital. She would be cooking dinner. They had a little boy. He might be playing in the garden because it was a summer day. She might go out and pick him up and carry him into the house to have his dinner.

My mother might have carried me into the house once. I could not remember. The main fact about my mother was that she was dead. My sister, Shirley, had taken her place.

Shirley told me that our mother was shouting to the Lord Jesus Christ for forgiveness when she was dying. She died of cancer. Shirley said she was twisted up in the bed through the pain.

Even if I were able to get a lot of money and have an operation, I would never have a little boy. Mrs Strickland did not know how happy she was. It was part of being Mrs Strickland not to know how happy she was. If she did not take it all for granted, she would not be herself; she would be like me pretending to be Mrs Strickland. In her bedroom there would be drawers and drawers and a wardrobe full of clothes. She could choose what she would wear. All the time she was dressed up, but for her it was not dressing up; it was just being herself. There was day after day of being a woman. When

4

she went into a room the gentlemen stood up. When she went to wet she had to sit down. She had no choice. She was always a woman.

If she ever woke up to find that she was Roy Clark, the shock would cause her mind to leave her body, and she would have to be taken to Ward Nine to live with the old men. She would be fortunate if her mind never returned to her body. And all the time I would be Mrs Strickland. I would have her clothes. No one would ever know. I would have to be very careful at first until I learned all about her. I would have to find out about her past life by questioning, without it being known that I was questioning. Dr Strickland would make love to me.

He was saying things to comfort me. He always ended the interviews by saying things to comfort me.

2

The ward was on the ground floor, and at the far end there were french windows that led out onto a square of grass with a hawthorn hedge round it. When one stood at the french windows one could see the cooling towers on the outskirts of Hull. At night one could see the lights of Hull.

After dinner Jim and I took our cups of tea and went out of the french windows and sat in deck chairs on the little lawn. Jim had been determined to be my friend ever since my first night in the ward. His appearance made me think of the White Knight. There was his white hair and his stained grey suit and the brown shoes that he kept telling me he had bought in Australia. His face was sad and his eyes were blue. His hand trembled as he put his cigarette to his mouth. He sucked on it and blew a steady stream of smoke.

'When I was in Australia I got very low sometimes. Do you know what it is to be right down, Roy? No, you don't; you're too young. I got right down. When I got into bed at night I used to want to die. They're such hard people out there. There's no humanity. I went to this coffee bar place kept by this Italian bloke. And he says to me, "They're hard. They've got no humanity." That's Australia. I've been there and I've seen it, Roy. To look at me, would you think I'd been to the other side of the world?' He turned his pale eyes on me for an answer.

I was not sure what he wanted me to say. I said, 'Well, you look like a man who's seen a few things.'

It was the right answer. He made a wink and pushed out his bottom lip. He spoke slyly and confidentially: 'You know, Roy, we're on a good thing here. Three meals a day and as much supper as you want and a good bed to sleep in. That's the main thing: bed and board. You've got to have something in your belly and you've got to have somewhere to sleep. Here we are, and it doesn't cost a penny. "Eat all, sup all, pay nowt." Isn't that the Yorkshireman's philosophy?'

'I understand so,' I said.

He went on talking and started explaining himself to me as he often did: 'You see, my trouble is that I've always been too soft. That's why I've never got married. Women like a man who goes forward and gets what he wants. They want a go-getter. I let other people get in first. It's the money that women are interested in. You've got to have the money. My trouble was that I didn't want any more than would satisfy my needs. I just wanted to go on and have enough. Why do people have to be trying to trample on one another? Tell me that, Roy.'

I told him that I did not know.

He said, 'I'll ask Sam if we can go out for a drink tonight.'

3

I had not liked the hammering in the male occupational therapy room. The female occupational therapy was much more gentle. In the warm summer afternoons it seemed to me to be a civilized place. At three o'clock two of the patients made tea in a great, blue enamel teapot.

The men worked at a table in one corner.

That day I was helping to put a string seat on a stool. The old man I was helping was impatient with me. He pushed me out of his way. At either side of his forehead there were deep scars where his skull had been cut into many years before in an attempt to help him. To him the making of the string seat for the stool was very important. When the sister came to ask him how he was getting on he shook his head as though the job were going badly. I decided that it would be best for me to leave him to himself.

I sat and talked to Larry, who was making a carpet. Larry had been a merchant seaman. He was about forty, small and lively. I only knew him from meeting him at occupational therapy. He was in a different ward from me. Some of the things he told me were very strange.

' . . . The anchor locker is right up in the peak. And these Indians must have stowed away in it. And when we dropped anchor to wait to start getting through the Canal there was blood and bits of arms and legs and gut and all sorts coming out of the anchor port. You see, when the anchor goes down the chain whips round and round. It's lashing about all over. And these Indians must have been sat on the chain. They didn't stand a chance. The old man said there must have been two men and a woman in there. He worked it out from the bits we found. The first mate was badly for a week.'

Having told the story he got his tin box out of his back pocket. He said, 'I've had this box for nearly twenty years. I wouldn't like to lose it.' He always said that when he took the box out for a cigarette. It was a flat tobacco box. All the paint had been worn off or had been scraped off and it was polished bright. He offered me a cigarette. He offered me one every afternoon, and every afternoon I told him that I did not smoke, and every afternoon he said that I was very sensible.

I went and looked out of the window. There was a lawn and, beyond, part of the male wing of the hospital. I could see into one of the wards. I did not know which ward it was. There were people moving about. They seemed to be shifting furniture.

I thought that it might not be a real ward that I was seeing. Perhaps, if I left the window where I was standing and went into the male wing, I might not be able to find the ward where the furniture was being shifted. Perhaps it only existed for me looking out of the window. Yet, if I could see it, it existed as much as it could exist for me. Even if I went across and found the ward, I would only be able to see it, and, even if I tried to get more assurance by touching the walls and the

7

furniture, I could never be absolutely certain that it existed. Even if all the doctors in the hospital came and told me that it existed, I could never be sure.

I thought that, for me, everything might be an illusion. I remembered that I had often thought about the possibility when I was about eight or nine. I had thought that I might be dreaming everything and that I might wake up and find I was really a little girl.

Two rooks came down and walked about on the lawn.

There was no way of being sure what was going on outside myself. Two and two only made four inside my head. Outside my head there was no such thing as mathematics, only in other people's heads—if there were other people.

Everyone lived inside his head. But people who were well and sane imagined that it was possible to get outside. That was how a man could fall in love with a woman.

The rooks could not find anything. They flew away.

I had a picture of my mind as a long tube. It started at the top very thin and almost transparent and went down getting wider and wider and rougher and stronger until it was like the trunk of a tree. At the bottom it was planted in the ground. But when I looked at the top again I found that it stretched up and up, getting thinner and finer so that it became like a strand of cobweb that reached up and up, right into the sky. That frightened me. The danger was that the cobweb part at the top might break off and float away.

I told myself firmly that my mind was not really like that. I told myself not to think about my mind. I should be like a rook, and not know that I had a mind. When people were healthy they did not know that they had minds, just as people did not know that they had kidneys unless there was something wrong with their kidneys. And I remembered that Dr Strickland had once talked to me about the different parts of the brain so that I would know that there was not really anything that could float away. It was all inside the skull, safe and sound.

But they had cut into the old man's head.

They would cut a piece off the brain, but if I asked them to cut a piece off my body they would refuse.

Perhaps Dr Strickland had many patients who asked to be turned into women. He might be sick of hearing it. Probably

8

he became angry with them.

I tried to imagine him getting angry with me. I imagine his shouting, 'Get out, you gruesome creeping thing—you caterpillar!'

I wondered why I had thought of a caterpillar. After a moment's thought I decided that it must have been because caterpillars turned into butterflies. That pleased me.

4

Jim was in the bathroom getting shaved when I got back to the ward.

He strained his chin upwards to scrape his neck. I was glad that I only had to shave two little patches at the sides of my chin where a few hairs grew. He rattled the razor in his shaving mug.

'I'm just getting myself ready for after tea,' he said. 'Sam says we can go out. I thought we'd go to the Greyhound.'

'I don't like going down to the village much,' I said.

'Why not?'

'Well, they know where we've come from.'

'To hell with 'em!'

'Well—'

'To hell with 'em!' He rattled the razor in the mug violently.

'I'd like to go to Hull,' I said.

'I haven't got the money for a trip to Hull. Anyway, we're not supposed to go as far away as that.' He started shaving his top lip, leaning forward to peer into the mirror.

I turned on a tap and turned it off again.

He finished his shaving and wiped his face. He examined himself carefully in the mirror, touching his face here and there. 'Jim's the lad,' he said to his reflection. 'A bit knocked about, but he's still the lad.' He turned to me and held up a fist. 'Look at that. It'd fell an ox!' He grinned.

I thought that it would be a poorly ox that he could fell.

5

The Greyhound was not a village pub. It was a roadhouse that had been built in the thirties. The exterior had an elephantine streamlining. From the car park in front it looked like an Egyptian temple that had been designed to travel at several hundred miles an hour.

Inside it had been modernised. There was unstained wood and creeping plants.

We went in just after six o'clock. The bar was empty.

The manager knew where we were from. He served us and then ignored us.

Jim had a pint of mild. I had a lemonade. We went and sat in a corner.

'When I was in Australia I never had a decent drink. They've no idea. The pubs out there are no good at all. They're more like public lavatories than pubs. You just get in and do your drinking and get out. They close at six o'clock!' He moved his leg out from under the table to show me his foot. 'I bought these shoes in Australia. What do you think to them?'

'They're very nice.'

'It's a long way to go for a pair of shoes!' He laughed. He took a long drink of his beer. Then he said, 'You know, a young lad like you ought not to be stuck in that hospital. You want to get yourself out of it and see a bit of the world. My trouble was that I didn't get out to Australia until it was too late. I was over fifty when I went out. That was too late. I should have gone when I was a young man. You want to get things done while you're young. You want to get yourself overseas or get yourself to a college or something. You're wasting your time in that hospital. There's nothing wrong with you. You know—' He stopped. Then he said, 'If you went away, I wouldn't have anybody to talk to. You won't go away, will you, Roy?'

I was embarrassed. I said, 'I don't know.'

He looked at me intently. I looked back into his blue eyes for an instant. I had to look away.

He said, 'You've made all the difference for me. It's been different since you came.'

I looked at my glass.

Then he was saying, 'I'm an old daft-head. Here I am going on like this. You must think I'm as balmy as I'm supposed to be!' He laughed and slapped his hand on his knee.

He drank his beer and looked about him. After a while he said, 'What do you think to this place, Roy?'

'It's all right.'

'You're not much struck?'

'It's all right. I think it's rather nice.'

'They're all like this nowadays. They get so they're more for women than for men. Everything's for women nowadays. There was a time when they had spittoons in pubs. That was before my time. Would you like that?'

'I don't think so.'

'No, I don't think I would either. Filthy. Tell me, Roy, what would you like the world to be like if you could make it yourself? Imagine you could have everything just as you wanted it.'

'I don't know what I'd do.'

'You should have some idea. What would you like out of life?'

'I don't know.'

'When I was your age I was full of ideas. I suppose I used to spend most of my time dreaming. When you get older you can't get dreams—if you do, you soon find yourself doing things wrong. You get in a mess.' He stopped. 'How old would you say I am?' he asked.

I felt sure that he must be in his sixties. I said, 'About fifty-six.'

He shook his head. 'I'll be sixty next. And what have I to show for sixty years of trailing about? Bed and board in a nut-house.' He took a drink of his beer. 'Once, when I was a lad, I fell in the Albert Dock. I should have drowned.'

He had two pints of mild and I had two lemonades. When other customers began to come into the pub we came away.

We walked back to the hospital. It was a gentle, summer evening.

I was glad that my father would never be in circumstances like Jim's. My father had had some success. He owned a fish-and-chip shop and he had Mrs Wilson. A man had to have a woman. Mrs Wilson could not marry my father because she was a Catholic. Even though her husband had run away,

11

she could not marry my father. It was ridiculous. But she seemed quite happy playing hide-and-seek.

6

I lay in bed. The ward was quiet. Everyone was sleeping or trying to sleep. Half-way down the ward light came from the office. The light fell on a bed and across the floor. I turned over and closed my eyes.

I tried to think of getting ready to go to a party.

I was in a large room with tall windows. It was evening, and heavy curtains were drawn across the windows. Everything in the room was of the best and most feminine. The furniture was light and elegantly made. It was not modern. I did not know about furniture so as to fix on a style and period. The chair seats were covered in striped silk, pink and white. There was an elegant dressing table with a large oval mirror. On the dressing table were expensive jars and boxes that contained creams and powders. There was a big powder puff. It was so big that I thought that it must be only for decoration or as a toy.

I was sitting at the dressing table making up my face. I was wearing a black slip and smoke-thin nylon stockings. On my feet were slippers. The slippers were backless. At the front they had small blue rosettes. The slip I was wearing had lace at the hem and net and lace at the top. In the mirror I could see my black brassière through the net.

I decided that my hair should be down. I saw that it was straight but curled under slightly at the bottom. It was the colour of polished bronze. I had brushed it until it shone. I shook my head, and my hair swung. It was glorious. It was so abundant. I ran my hand into it. It was happiness to have long hair.

I put some cream on my face. I did not know what purpose the cream served, but I understood that it was usual to put cream on before powdering one's face. I wondered whether it was only older women who needed face cream. Then I powdered my face. I was careful not to put too much powder on. I powdered my neck and the top of my chest. I inspected myself in the mirror. It was as I wanted it. It was smooth, there were no patches where the powder was too thick. It did not look as though I had powdered my face at all. That was as it should be.

I took up my lipstick. It was large and heavy, a sheath of pale gold. I took off the top. I twisted it. A pointed torpedo of intense red emerged. I painted my lips with clean, sharp strokes, leaning forward to the mirror, now pursing my lips, now tightening them. I finished and put down the lipstick. My lips were as they should be. There were no smudges outside the edges of the lips.

Next I painted my eyelashes. And then I put on slight touches of eye shadow.

My face was made. It was perfect. I looked extremely pretty. I sat looking at myself for some time, turning my head this way and that and smiling at myself. I was delighted.

I got up and went across to the wardrobe. It was joy to be a pretty girl walking in that room.

I opened the wardrobe. And there was a dress of scarlet watered silk. It was a brilliant scarlet. I took it out and held it up. It was heavy and sumptuous. The skirt was very full. The bodice was simple and looked as though it would be tight. The front was cut square. I hugged it to me. I pressed it to my face.

I went to the wardrobe again. There was a pair of red shoes that matched the dress. The heels were high and at the front they were cut down square to echo the front of the dress.

I would have to take off the black slip I was wearing because of the way that the front of the dress was cut. And I would have to wear a special brassière with the straps coming down to the sides instead of to the front. I might not have a black brassière with the straps coming down to the side. If the brassière I found was not black, I would have to change my panties. And my suspender belt was black. I would have to change everything.

I would not be ready in time. The time would pass very quickly, and I would not be ready. The time would pass, and I would grow old.

I had never been to a party.

13

7

The kitchen was next to the office. There was a sink with draining boards on either side and large cupboards for crockery. There was a gas ring for boiling water for morning coffee and the tea we had at meal times and the cocoa at supper time and the odd cups of tea that Sam, the charge nurse, needed through the day.

Jim seemed very cheerful while we were washing up. He sang and talked nonsense.

'When I was in Australia I used to go shooting kangaroos. I used to go out into the bush and bag a couple of brace of kangaroos and I used to bring them back and sell them to a butcher. I made thousands of pounds. Have you ever tasted kangaroo, Roy?'

'I can't say I have.'

'Very like rabbit, only bigger. Get a good kangaroo steak down you, and you fell like a—you feel like jumping up and down. You can't stop jumping.'

8

We took pills after breakfast and pills after dinner and pills after tea, blue pills and white pills and green pills and yellow pills and red pills and many permutations of parti-coloured pills. I took blue pills. I had just taken my after-dinner dose when a young male nurse came into the ward and called out, 'There's a visitor for Mr Clark.'

I got up.

It was Shirley.

My sister looked as though she was frightened at being in a mental hospital. Perhaps she thought that a lunatic might rush out on her. But when she saw me she seemed reassured.

She was very like me. In heels she was as tall as I was, but if we were both wearing heels, I would be the taller. I was five foot seven. When I had had the chance to wear her clothes they had fitted me, except that I had not been able to wear her

14

shoes since I was about fifteen.

Her hair was the same colour as mine, between fair and brown.

She was wearing a dark grey suit and looking smart. Besides her black handbag she carried a shopping bag of yellow leather.

'I've just come to see how you are. I didn't know you were in hospital till last week. I went round to see Dad, and he told me. I couldn't come before today. I had to get the woman next door to look after Gwen. I didn't want to bring her with me. Dad says you've been in here about ten weeks. I didn't know anything about it till last week. Dad didn't say whether he'd been to see you or not.'

'No, he hasn't been.' I thought, If Shirley were in hospital my father would visit her every week.

'He's been too busy, I should think,' she said.

'Yes, I suppose so. Anyway, he sends me money.'

'That's good. And are you getting any better?'

'I'm all right. It's very nice here.'

'I've brought some things for you.' She opened the leather carrier bag. She gave me three large bars of chocolate and two paper-backed novels.

I thanked her. I took the things and put them in my locker. Then I introduced her to Jim.

They shook hands.

Jim was nervous. 'I didn't know Roy had a sister. He's a very quiet lad.' He grinned foolishly.

I said, 'Would you like to go to the cafeteria, Shirley? We can get a cup of tea.'

The cafeteria had pale green walls. It was in the centre of the hospital, between the male and the female wings. I thought that the room must once have been a large store-room, for there were no windows. Neon lights shone all day. It was like a railway station buffet. Patients sat at small tables drinking tea or coffee out of coloured plastic cups.

Shirley said that the cafeteria was very nice. Then she said, 'Dad's very well. He was cutting fish when I was there. He can cut as fast as ever.'

To me it seemed strange that, though Shirley had married an architect and left the fish-and-chip shop, there was never any stiffness between her and our father. I lived with him and worked with him, but I was never as close to him as she was

15

when she came to see him. It was not easy for me to understand how she could come from middle-class Cottingham to the
part of Hull where we lived and not have any difficulty in
talking to our father.

I supposed I was a snob.

She said, 'You must get yourself a better job, Roy. I said
so to Dad, and he agreed. He said that when you get better
you can go back to working for him if you want to, but he
agreed with me that you ought to try to get something better.'

'I thought that he wanted me to work for him,' I said with
pretended sulkiness. 'That's why I had to leave school.'

'That was a mistake, Roy. But it's no use worrying about
what's past. You're still a boy, you've got your whole life to
make. You can study. You're clever. If you set out to do it,
you could get yourself to a university even now.'

'It's no use. I'm a lunatic.'

'Of course you're not a lunatic. Lots of people have psychological trouble. You've got your whole life before you. You'll
get over this. What you did wasn't so shocking.'

'Did Dad tell you about it?'

'Yes, he told me.'

'All about it?'

'Yes.'

'About his hitting me?

'Yes. He said he couldn't help it. He said he was sorry that
he did it. You must try to understand how he felt, Roy. He
was brought up in a hard world.'

'Did he tell you about what I did?'

'Yes.'

'What did you think?'

'I thought that you had been very foolish. But I did think
that you must have been under some kind of strain and had
a breakdown. I suppose it just came over you. It isn't unusual
for a young person to have trouble of that kind.'

I said, 'Do you mind if we go for a walk outside? I'm feeling
a bit sick all of a sudden.'

Behind the hospital there was a rose garden with gravel
paths and rose beds enclosed by grass verges. The red and white
roses climbed on rustic frames. Here and there along the
paths there were park benches. The roses were well trained
and the grass verges were closely shaved and cleanly edged.

It was a place for visitors to see. The less reliable patients were kept out, lest they pick the roses or lie down on the grass. It was a formal garden for formal people.

Shirley said that the garden was very nice. She asked me if I was feeling any better. I said that I was. We sat down on a bench.

'Don't you think you ought to get yourself a better job?' she asked in a tone that made the question mean that she was convinced that it was my duty to find myself better employment.

'I don't know,' I said.

'Of course Dad had the idea that you'd take over the shop after him. But I think that he understands now that that wouldn't really suit you. There's a good living to be made out of fish-and-chips, but I don't think that you ought to spend your life in the shop. I think that the cause of your trouble is lack of opportunity for self-expression. You're too much shut in on yourself. Don't you think that might be the case, Roy?'

'I don't know.'

'Working with your father is all right, but you don't meet anybody. And you're very different from Dad.'

'I don't punch people in the face.'

'That's not fair.'

'It's true.'

'You mustn't feel bitter against your father. He lost his temper. It's not easy for people of his generation to understand things. You must realise that some people are very afraid of anything that might seem abnormal. He was very upset. After all, it could have been worse. If that woman had gone to the police. . . .'

I did not say anything.

'What's the food like here?' she asked.

'Not too bad. It's all rather heavy stuff. I think they want to fatten us up so that we look well-cared-for.'

'What treatment are you having?'

'Pills.'

'Is that all?'

'I go to see Dr Strickland sometimes.'

'Is that doing any good?'

'I don't know.'

'You must have some idea.'

17

'I don't think it's doing anything.'

'Why not?'

'Because it's not possible for it to do anything.'

'You mustn't talk like that. I understood that they could cure trouble like yours quite easily. If you cooperate, they'll be able to help you.'

'I don't really want to cooperate.'

'Why not?'

'I want what I want, not something else.'

'I don't understand.'

'I want what I want, not what other people think I ought to want.'

'But you have to behave reasonably.'

'Why?'

'We all have to behave reasonably.'

'Nobody behaves reasonably.'

'Of course they do.'

'Of course they don't. If everybody behaved reasonably, everything would stop.'

'That's just talk, Roy.'

She had always been able to dismiss my arguments before they were developed.

She went on, 'Of course you should never have left the grammar school when you did. It was bound to upset you. But you know, Roy, you could still catch up. There's that money Mother left you. You'll soon be twenty-one, and then you can use the money to do some private studies. I'm sure that Bill would help you in any way he could. With the interest that's built up, you should get well over five hundred pounds. You can do quite a lot with five hundred pounds.'

'It would cost nearer five thousand pounds.'

'What would?'

'Nothing.'

'It sounds a very expensive nothing.'

'It is. It's a very expensive nothing.'

'Well, I think that five hundred pounds spent on your education would do more good than five thousand pounds spent on nothing.'

'You think I ought to be like Bill.'

'No, you don't have to be like Bill.'

'You think I ought to be like Bill and smoke a pipe.'

'You don't have to be like Bill—and you certainly don't have to smoke a pipe.'

'Thank you for that.'

'I don't understand you, Roy. What have you got against Bill?'

'Nothing. I like him. But I don't want to be like him.'

'You don't have to be.'

'Yes, I do.'

'Am I upsetting you?' she asked.

'No. I'm sorry. Don't pay any attention to me.'

We did not speak for a while. Somewhere around the male side of the hospital a motor mower was droning about its business.

I said, 'They're always cutting the grass here.'

'They keep it very nice.'

We sat without speaking again.

I said, 'Does Bill enjoy smoking his pipe?'

She was surprised by the question. She smiled. 'Yes, I think he does. Why? Are you thinking of getting one?'

'No. I just wondered if he enjoyed it.'

'He seems to.'

'Perhaps he only pretends to enjoy it.'

'What on earth for?'

'Because he thinks he ought to enjoy smoking a pipe.'

'Instead of cigarettes, you mean?'

'No, because he thinks it's the moral thing to do.'

'You're being silly, Roy.'

'Then I'm in the right place.'

'I didn't mean anything like that.'

I said, 'Were you upset when Dad told you what I'd done?'

'Naturally I was upset.'

'Didn't you know I was like that?'

'Like what?'

'Like that.'

'I don't know what you mean.'

'Didn't you know I was mad?'

'You're not mad.'

'Yes, I am.'

'No, you're not, Roy.'

'I've been mad ever since I was little, ever since I can remember. Do you know what Dr Strickland said to me?'

19

'No.'

'He said, "We are born mad, we grow old and miserable, and then we die." It was what some German had said.'

'That doesn't sound very well calculated to cheer anyone up.'

'I was born mad.'

'Don't be ridiculous.'

'Yes, I was. I've always been the same as I am now. And I don't see why I should have any desire to grow old and miserable.'

'We all have to grow old.'

'But we don't have to pretend to like it.'

'I don't know what you mean.'

'I mean that I don't want to be cured. I want what I want, not what other people think I ought to want.'

'What do you want?'

'I want to be a woman.'

'That's just your illness, Roy.' Her voice was at its most soothing.

'That's what other people call it.'

'That's what they must call it. Obviously it's an illness.'

'But I've always wanted to be a girl, ever since I can remember.'

'I'm sure you're mistaken. You haven't always had that thought. It's just come on because you're not very well.'

'I've had that thought ever since I can remember.'

'But you won't think like that always. You'll get over this trouble and you'll meet someone and fall in love with her.'

'I don't think so.'

'Don't you like girls?'

'Yes—but not like that.'

'You're not a homosexual, are you?'

'No, I'm not. I would never do the horrible things they do. I hate homosexuals. The thought of them makes me feel sick.'

'Then, if you feel like that, you'll certainly be cured. It's just a phase you're going through. I'm quite sure you don't want to be one of those revolting creatures that change sex.'

'Yes, I do.'

'I don't believe it.'

'It's true.'

'It can't be true. Everyone regards them as a joke. You can't seriously mean that you want the whole of your life to

20

be a dirty joke?'

'I don't care.'

'Well, I care.'

'I can't be respectable just for your sake.'

'There is such a thing as self-respect.'

'How much self-respect can I have as I am now?'

'I'm sorry, Roy, but I was rather taken aback. You mustn't feel too badly about being in a psychiatric hospital. Lots of people have psychological illnesses.'

'I didn't mean that.'

'What did you mean?'

'I meant that, if I were a woman, I wouldn't be stealing women's clothes.'

'Oh, I see.'

'Did you know that I used to wear your clothes when you and Dad were out? And I've stolen things of yours.'

'Yes, I knew. I didn't say anything because I thought it would pass off.'

'You can never hide things from people. What you mean by self-respect is only trying to hide things.'

'No, it isn't. You ought to be able to see your illness as an illness. I don't believe that people with sexual peculiarities should be punished, but it's impossible to pretend that they aren't ill. The trouble is that these things are glamourised nowadays. The cheap Sunday papers get hold of a story, and they make out that somebody who ought to be confined in a place like this has done something wonderful. It's sick. But, anyway, you're not like that. You'll get better. And then you'll go on and get married and settle down, and you'll forget all about this nonsense. Because it is nonsense, Roy. . . .'

She went on for some time telling me that it was nonsense. But I was thinking that, all the time she was telling me, she was a woman. I thought how much sweeter her life was than her husband's. I thought of Bill's pipe. How harsh and dull his pleasures were, and how tender and bright her pleasures were. As I sat there I could not feel that there was no sense in wanting what I wanted. I thought that every man, in his heart, must wish that he were a woman.

I went with her to the front gate to say goodbye. She said that she would come again.

I knew that she was right in the way that I knew that Dr

Strickland was right. But their right was outside of me.

Shirley was sure that the world was as orderly as the rose garden. For her a system of behaviour had brought desired results, and thus she was secure in the illusion that two and two made four outside her head.

I felt that, if I could be a woman, I could believe in the world. I would be part of the world, like Shirley.

When I got back to the ward Jim said, 'It's easy to tell you're brother and sister.'

He was busy setting out the tea things. I helped him.

The hospital lumbered on with me inside it.

9

The end of my stay in hospital started one night when Jim and I went to the Greyhound.

Jim spoke of the Australians.

'. . . wide open spaces and narrow minds, cold beer and ignorance. . . .'

He drank his beer and smoked his cigarettes. He seemed to be his usual self.

He never had more than three pints. He had told me that in his young days he had been able to drink six pints without noticing much effect. That evening he had two pints and then half a pint.

We were walking back to the hospital. The fields were silent. We walked where a row of great trees, heavy with summer, lined the way. The air was soft and cool.

'Isn't it a beautiful evening?' said Jim. Then he said, 'How would you like to stay out all night? We could sleep in a wood.' He put his hand on my shoulder.

I became tense. I said, 'Do you think there'll be enough milk for the cocoa?'

'You know, Roy,' he said confidentially, "you are very like your sister. If you were dressed as a girl, you'd be just like her. Have you ever been dressed as a girl, Roy?'

I felt dizzy. I struggled on, trying to pull away from him.

'Are you a girl?' he asked.

22

'No, I'm not. Come on. We have to get back.'

'I think you are a girl, Roy.'

He dropped his hand from my shoulder and put his arm round my waist. I struggled to get away from him. He tried to put his head against mine. I wrenched myself free and broke from him.

'Roy!' he shouted. He sounded as though he was hurt.

I turned. 'What's the matter? Stop it, Jim.'

'I want to hold you, Roy.'

'I don't want you to.'

'Why not?'

'Because I don't.'

'Why not?'

'Look, Jim, stop it.'

'But you're a girl, Roy.'

'I'm not. Leave me alone.'

'Just let me put my arm round you.'

'No.'

'Just for a minute.'

'No.'

'Why not?'

'Because you can't.'

'I want to.'

'Stop it, Jim.'

'But I love you, Roy.'

I started walking away from him. I felt unsteady on my feet. It was as though I could not judge the distance to the ground.

He caught up with me. 'Don't you like me, Roy?'

I kept walking. 'I like you. But you can't do this.'

'Why not?'

'You can't.'

'I'm fed-up. I want to kiss you.'

I started to run.

He shouted after me, 'I'm not like that. Don't think I'm like that. It's you, you little pansy!'

I went straight to the kitchen when I reached the ward. For some reason I got hold of a cloth and started rubbing the bottom of the sink as though it were dirty.

Things had happened to me before, but it was worse this time because I knew Jim and liked him.

I got the kettle and filled it and put it on the gas ring and

23

turned the gas on.

The male nurse who was on duty came in. 'Are you trying to do away with yourself?' he asked. 'It's a good idea to put a light to the gas after you've turned it on.' He struck a match and put it under the kettle. The gas ring thumped into flame. 'We'll have to get you down on the suicidal list.'

I could see that Jim had come into the ward. He was standing by the side of his bed with his hands in his jacket pockets. Somebody spoke to him. He did not answer.

I hoped that he would not come into the kitchen for a cup of cocoa. He did not often want cocoa after he had been to the pub.

He did not come.

I washed up after all the cups had been brought back. Then I cleared everything away. When I looked out again Jim was in bed.

10

I lay in bed thinking about what had happened.

Jim was not a homosexual. If he had been, it would have been noticed and he would have been kept away from me. It was just loneliness and beer. Anyone could have had such a fit. He was only a poor old man. He would not do it again. It would soon be forgotten.

I said to myself, 'He said that I was a girl.' I put out my hand and took hold of the rail at the top of the bed. I smiled to myself in the darkness.

11

Next morning Jim did not sit next to me at breakfast. He sat at the far end of the table and did not look at me. After breakfast we worked together at the washing up, but he did not speak to me. I asked him a question about Australia to show him that I wanted to talk to him. He did not answer me.

When I had the coffee made I took him a cup. He was sitting in one of the arm chairs at the end of the ward reading a newspaper.

'I've brought you your coffee, Jim. Tell me if you want any more sugar in it.'

He looked up at me and said, 'Bugger off, you bloody little pansy!'

I put the cup and saucer down by his chair. I went back to the kitchen and stood at the sink. I put my hand across my eyes and pressed. I stood with my hand pressed over my eyes trying to prevent myself from crying. I kept saying to myself, 'Jim isn't well. Jim isn't well.' Then I sat down on a chair by the draining board and started crying. Someone came into the kitchen. I did not see who it was. He went out again. When I stopped crying I went to the sink and put cold water on my eyes.

12

I sat in a deck chair on the little lawn outside the ward and thought about getting into the female nurses' quarters and putting on clothes there.

I thought that I would like to wear a nurse's uniform. I imagined myself being a nurse, proceeding neatly down corridors and remaining neat and calm in the midst of mental and emotional confusion. I would like to clip a fountain pen at the front of my starched, white pinafore.

I imagined that if I could get into the nurses' quarters and dress myself up, I would immediately turn into a woman. The instant I finished dressing my body would change. I would be able to walk out and not get into trouble. If I were stopped, I would be able to say that I had put on the clothes because I had suddenly turned into a woman, and that, unless someone provided me with other women's clothes, I would stay dressed as I was. I could not be expected to go back and put on my own clothes, they were men's clothes. What did they think I was, a transvestite? A peanut?

I started to laugh. I laughed and laughed.

13

Jim asked to sweep the floor instead of washing up in the mornings. When Sam asked him why he did not want to wash up Jim said, 'It's a job for a Mary-Anne, and you've got a Mary-Anne to do it.'

We avoided each other in the ward, planning our ways in the restricted spaces to keep from meeting.

I thought that a few moments of embarrassment should not be allowed to become permanent. I would have liked to go to him and say that I wanted to be friendly again. I wished that the cause of the trouble was that I had done something to offend him so that I could apologise.

Sometimes I talked to myself about him: 'I can't help it if I don't want him to touch me. If I was a girl, I wouldn't want him to touch me. Anyway, he should have a wife. He's not homosexual, he just thought that I looked nice. He can't blame me for that. He's a neurotic. He blames the Australians for being as they are. He wanted to go to the other side of the world and find a place just like England, except for the sunshine, and when it wasn't as he wanted it he blamed the Australians. He's a fool.'

But I knew that I was angry at what had happened and not at Jim.

14

Without Jim the days were not the same as they had been before.

I considered making a trip home. I could have got permission to go home for an afternoon. I thought about it, but decided that I did not want to face my father.

And Mrs Wilson would be staying on after helping in the

shop.

Statues of the saints stood round in the church where you put sixpence in a box and took a pamphlet on Papal Infallibility or the Rhythm Method, and Mrs Wilson was lying in bed waiting for my father to get his trousers off.

15

It was late one evening that I first thought that Jim's behaviour was becoming odd. He was standing at the bottom of the ward looking out of the french windows at the lights of Hull in the distance. I realised that he had been standing there every evening for some time.

He stood with his hands in his jacket pockets as he had stood by his bed on the evening of the incident. He was still standing there when the rest of us were getting into bed.

The next evening he was standing there again.

He moved about the ward with his shoulders hunched and his head forward. His tread seemed to have become heavier. At meal times he did not talk about Australia anymore. At breakfast one morning, when it was raining hard outside, someone asked him whether he wished he were back in Australia.

'I bloody do! I wish I was out of your way, and all you balmy buggers in here! And don't think I went out for ten pounds. I paid the full fare both ways.' His eyes caught mine. 'I can see you looking. You know what I think about you!'

When I was clearing away after the morning coffee he came and stood at the kitchen door. 'You think you're very clever, don't you?' he sneered.

I continued putting the cups away in the cupboard and tried not to look at him.

'You think you're very clever, creeping about. I've seen you creeping about, you bloody little pansy. I've seen you trying to get out of the way. . . .'

He went on for some time. When I had finished putting the cups away I pretended to be wiping down the draining board.

He stopped quite suddenly and went away.

I knew that I had caused his illness. The fact that I had not done it by any action made no difference. I had caused it. I thought that it might be right for me to leave the hospital. It was possible that my being in the ward was disturbing Jim day by day. I could not tell anybody about it, but I could ask to be discharged.

16

One afternoon there was a tall nurse in the occupational therapy room whom I had not seen before. She was fair and athletic looking. I could imagine her in Sweden leaping about with a hoop in her hands. In her hands she carried some skeins of blue wool and she was looking for a place to sit.

I indicated to her that there was a chair empty next to me.

She came across. 'I'll come and sit amongst the men.' She sat down and put the skeins of wool on the table and started winding very fast to make a ball. She pushed the wool away onto the table after each burst of winding to prevent it being pulled to the edge and falling off.

I asked her if I might hold the wool for her.

She thanked me.

I took up the skein she was winding from and held it stretched between my hands.

She said, 'I had to bring it up here. You can't do anything on the ward, they're always wanting something.'

She was a few years older than I was. I thought that if I were very fair and athletic, like her, I would want to play tennis.

'Do you play tennis?' I asked.

'Yes. But I'm not very good.' She smiled. 'Do you play?'

'No. I just thought you might.'

'Do I look the type?'

'Yes, you do. I can imagine you playing at Wimbledon.'

'You haven't seen me play.'

'Have you a nice uniform?'

'I've got the uniform I've got on.'

28

'No, I mean tennis things.'

'Do you call that a uniform?'

'Well, it's smart and neat, like a uniform.'

'I see what you mean. Is that what they call it now?'

'I don't know. It might be. They're always changing the names of things. What's your tennis outfit like?'

'Just a white slip thing. It's very plain.'

'You don't believe in frills and pink pants?'

'No.' She lifted high the ball of wool she was making to clear a tangle. 'When you play like me you don't want to draw too much attention to yourself. My forehand isn't too bad, but I haven't any backhand at all. I have to run round everything.'

'Has your tennis slip any decoration on it?'

'There's a sort of small rose-thing at the side. Here.' She put her hand to her left shoulder. 'It's done in black and red silk.'

'Is the skirt pleated?'

'There's just two box pleats at the back.'

'It sounds very smart. What's the neck like?'

'It's just circular.' She drew it on her chest.

'Do you like square cut necks?'

'Sometimes.'

'Would you like to have a cocktail dress in red watered silk with a square cut neck?'

'It might be very nice.'

'With a tight bodice and very full skirt?'

'It might be very nice indeed. Do you know somebody who's giving one away?'

'I'm afraid not. I just imagined it. Would you like to wear a dress like that?'

'Yes, I think I would. But I never get invited to cocktail parties.' She put in a fierce burst of winding. 'You seem very interested in clothes,' she said.

'I am a bit.'

'You'll like it in a fortnight's time then. There's the fancy dress ball. There's one every year. Everybody gets dressed up. Last year there was a man from Male Ward Three in a full suit of armour made of cardboard. It must have taken hours to make.'

'What did you go as?' I asked her.

'It's only for the patients. I was on duty. I could have gone

29

as a Dutch girl. I have a pair of wooden shoes that my brother brought me back from Rotterdam.'

I said, 'You'd have needed a long full skirt made of heavy material with lots of petticoats underneath to fill it out and a white cap with wings at the sides and a little shawl round your shoulders and crossing at the front.' I was drawing the things on myself. I put my hands to my face. 'You'd have to have your face made up with two round patches of rouge on the cheeks so that you'd look like a Dutch doll.'

'It would look lovely!' she exclaimed. 'You could dress up like that.'

'I meant you.'

'But you could dress up like that. I'd lend you the shoes.'

'I'd look awful.'

'No, you wouldn't. I can just see you. You'd have to get a blonde wig. A lot of Dutch girls are blonde.'

'I don't want to dress up.'

'Why not? You might win a prize.'

'I'd feel silly.'

'Nobody bothers about that. You might win a prize. You'd make a lovely Dutch girl.'

'Do you think so?'

'Yes, I'm sure you would. I'll bring the shoes tomorrow and you can try them on.'

'But where could I get the other things I'd need?'

'You'll have to go and see Sister King. She's in charge of the things for the fancy dress ball. There's lots of costumes that they lend out every year. She has some blonde wigs that she lends out to the men. Some of them come dressed as women—they look terrible! She might have a Dutch girl costume, and if she hasn't, she's sure to have some things that can be made into a Dutch girl costume.'

'She might not want to lend me the things.'

'Why not?'

'She might think I shouldn't dress as a girl.'

'Why not? A lot of men come dressed as women.'

'But that's only in fun.'

'Some of them are a scream!'

'But I'd be trying to look nice.'

'It doesn't make any difference.'

'It does.'

'How?'

'People might not like it.'

'Nobody would mind. Why should they?'

She had not seen my father looking ill when he was punching me. For her there were no rats racing on a treadmill.

As her body was cool in her clothes, so her mind was cool and comfortably in place. I wished that I were like her.

I wanted my body to be cut into until I was emptied. Then I would be bandaged and wrapped in white sheets, quiet and empty. I would be unable to move. I would have become part of the world.

That night when I thought of going to the fancy dress ball as a Dutch girl I realised that I would not be happy doing it. I would have to wear my own things underneath, and there would be no happiness in looking like a girl if I did not feel that I was a girl.

I wondered what surprise the nurse would have shown if I had told her that I wanted pretty things to wear underneath and some sticking-plaster to fix myself up. She would have remembered at once that I was a patient.

The next afternoon she brought the shoes to the occupational therapy room.

I told her that I had decided not to dress up for the fancy dress ball. I said that I was afraid that the people in my ward might make fun of me.

'Oh, you don't want to care about that. You're probably too sensitive.' She addressed Larry who was standing near, 'I want him to dress up for the fancy dress ball. Don't you think he ought to?'

'I'm going as a pirate,' said Larry.

She turned to me. 'There, you see, a lot of patients dress up. If nobody dressed up it wouldn't be any good.'

'What do you want him to dress up as?' asked Larry.

'A Dutch girl. I've brought these clogs for him to try on.'

'I should think he's a bit shy of dressing up as a lass.'

'There's no need for him to be.' She turned to me. 'Is that it?' she asked.

I said that it was.

'I know how he feels,' said Larry. 'You wouldn't get me to put a dress on.'

When the nurse had gone Larry spoke to me as an older to a

31

younger man. 'You don't want to be dressing up as a lass,' he said, 'you might give folks the wrong idea. I've seen 'em when I was at sea. You get a lot of queers in the merchant navy. I remember one night I was on watch, and this big queer came up on deck in a baby-doll nightdress and pissed over the side. Great big bloke in a baby-doll nightdress pissing over the side! I thought, Bloody hell! He was a decent bloke, but he was as queer as buggery. You get 'em like that sometimes. Folks who haven't been to sea don't know nowt.'

17

My discomfort at what was happening to Jim increased.

It was wrong that a weakling should have damaged a man who had survived for so many years; who, through private and common difficulties, had struggled on day after day and maintained a dignity.

I shut my eyes tight and bent my head. But when I opened my eyes and raised my head again I found that I had done nothing to help Jim.

I had not done wrong. I was wrong. I had no more intent to be loathsome than had a jellyfish, but, like a jellyfish, I was loathsome. I had seen them lying on the beach at Bridlington, blots of bloody jelly, like the phlegm of some giant consumptive.

Men were as wholesome as sunlight and singing in the morning. And women were as gentle as evening and as perfect as sleep. But I had no time of day.

Male-hipped trawlermen were nimble on the deck. And mothers held helpless babies to the breast. But all I could do was to cause illness in a poor old man.

Mr Allsop, a handsome man who was a commercial artist and an alcoholic, spoke to me about it. 'Poor Jim has gone right off. They'll be shifting him out of this ward. God knows what's gone wrong with him.'

'I suppose he's just relapsed,' I said.

'Yes, I expect so. Mental illness is very strange. What are you in here for, Roy?'

'I was run-down—worried.'

'I had to come in here because I couldn't get in the house for empty bottles.'

18

I must leave the hospital. I must go home and leave it behind• My father would have me back to work for him. I would take the eyes out of potatoes and swill the yard and stand by the chip pan again in my white coat.

The young woman in the next street might have talked to people about my stealing her panties off her line, so that the customers in the shop might know about me, and they might know that I had been away in a lunatic asylum, but they would not be able to harm me. They would not climb over the counter to punch me and kick me. And if they laughed at me, I could pretend that I did not know what they were laughing at.

However long I stayed at the hospital Dr Strickland would not be able to do the right thing for me. Nor could I do the right thing for him. He could not send me for hormone treatment and operations, and I could not alter my mind to please him.

I told myself that, beneath his kindness and beneath everything he said, he must surely despise me.

Perhaps one day I would come back to him as a woman. He would have to stand up when I entered his consulting room. He would want to touch me, and then I would be able to despise him in return. I would say, 'Had you done this for me, I would have let you touch me. But you failed me. I despise you. If you try to touch me, I shall scream for help.'

At my next interview with him I would tell him that I wanted to be discharged.

19

I was to see Dr Strickland on a Tuesday morning. The fancy dress ball was in the evening of that Tuesday.

On Monday after tea Sam came into the ward carrying what looked like a pile of old clothes. He was followed by a young male nurse with more things.

'This is the stuff for the fancy dress ball,' Sam announced. 'I want all you lot dressed up for tomorrow night. You're supposed to be just about fit in here. I want you to set an example to the rest of the hospital.'

It occured to me how fantastic was the idea of a fancy dress ball in a lunatic asylum. Before I came to the hospital I believed it would be a place filled with Napoleons and popes and kings and queens. I found that I had been mistaken. But now the patients were going to dress up and pretend to be madmen and madwomen.

Sam and the young male nurse had put their loads on the table.

'There it all is,' said Sam. 'You can pick where you like. Look, here's a three cornered hat.' He picked out a battered cardboard hat and put it on his head.

Most of the things on the table were old and worn. It looked like the wardrobe of an amateur operatic society of extreme poverty. There was a faded red tunic with many buttons missing and a policeman's helmet that appeared to have been trodden on.

Mr Allsop held the helmet up. 'This probably happened down Hessle Road on a dark night.'

There was an imitation Elizabethan ruff made of muslin that was grey with dust. There was a sailor's hat with H.M.S. TASKER on it. There were many old jackets and trousers of no particular interest and some women's dresses.

Sam said, 'There's more stuff to come. Sister King has some beards and things. Anyway, sort out what you want from that lot there, and if there's anything that anybody wants, I'll get it before she goes off duty. It'll be no good tomorrow; she'll have nothing left. I want to see every one of you in some sort of costume tomorrow night. We've got to enter into the spirit of things.' He took off the three cornered hat and went away to his office.

The young male nurse felt that it was his duty to be encouraging. He kept pressing things on people. 'See if this'll fit you.'

'I've got a jacket. I want some black trousers to go with it.'

'What are you supposed to be, Mr O'Brien?'

'A concert pianist.'

Mr O'Brien, who was a small, round, balding man, had put on a tail coat that was much too big for him.

'But that jacket doesn't fit you,' reasoned the young male nurse. 'Look at the sleeves. And the tails are nearly touching the floor. You'll hang yourself in it'—which was tactless because Mr O'Brien had once attempted to hang himself. 'Give it to Mr Allsop, he's the concert pianist type. Can you play the piano, Mr Allsop?'

'Like a fish.'

The nurse picked up the three cornered hat and put it on my head. 'It suits you,' he said.

'Who am I supposed to be?'

'I don't know—but it suits you.'

I took it off and put it back on the table.

Jim had joined the group. He stood gaping with his hands pressed hard down in his jacket pockets. 'What's all this?' he asked.

'It's for the fancy dress ball, Jim,' said the young male nurse. 'Do you think you'll feel well enough to go?'

'I don't think so. I've felt lousy today.'

'You can go and watch, Jim.'

'I don't want to watch anything. What do you think I am?'

'Well, go and sit down, Jim. You need to take it easy when you're not up to the mark.'

Jim began to move away. But then he stopped and came back to the table. He took hold of one of the women's dresses, a cotton thing with red and yellow flowers. He pushed it towards me as though he were trying to see if it would fit me. 'Here, this is for him,' he shouted. 'Put this on him! Put this on him!' He laughed. 'Here, this if for you, Roy petty. You can dance and kick your legs up.'

The male nurse took him by the arm. 'Come away, Jim, and sit down.'

Jim thrust his head forward and glared at me. 'You're neither nowt nor summat. I know you. You're a bloody little pansy!'

Sam had come out of the office. 'What's the matter, Jim?'

'Do you know what he is?' demanded Jim pointing at me.

'It doesn't matter what he is,' said Sam. 'Come on, Jim, I

think we'll have you in bed. You're overwrought.'

'He's a dirty little pansy!' shouted Jim.

Sam and the young male nurse took him away to his bed.

I heard him saying to them, 'What do you think to a bloody little pansy that gets himself dressed up in his sister's clouts?'

I wanted to wrap my arms about my head and shut everything out. I wanted to roll up like a hedgehog.

Mr Allsop turned to me. 'My God, you look sick!'

When Jim lay quiet in his bed Sam came away. 'He'll have to be moved from here. He'll need electric treatment. I can't think what's come over him. He was doing so well, and then he just started going down hill'.

Somebody said, 'It makes you wonder how he managed in Australia.'

'If he ever was in Australia,' said Sam. 'I should reckon he's always been the same. I should think he's been in this sort of place before, but he'd never let on.'

20

While I was making the cocoa that night Mr Allsop came into the kitchen.

I wanted to tell him that Jim had been wrong about me.

I said, 'Jim's very ill.'

'Yes,' said Mr Allsop, 'poor old chap, he's gone right off it.'

'What do you think is the matter with him?'

'I don't know. I expect he's a schitz.'

'He was talking nonsense after tea. I couldn't understand him. Could you understand him?'

'No.'

'It was just rubbish, wasn't it?'

'I expect so.'

'It's just because I'm not very big and I'm a bit pale.'

'I expect so.'

'You don't believe I do anything like that, do you?'

'Of course not.'

'But I don't.'

'Of course not.'

'I don't.'

'What you do is your affair, Roy.'

'But I don't, Mr Allsop.'

He went out.

They all knew.

I stood holding on to the edge of the sink. I thought that, if I did not move at all, I might be able to disappear.

21

On Tuesday morning I kept my eyes on what I was doing while I worked. I tried not to look up so as to avoid meeting anyone's eyes.

Jim was taken away.

I thought that perhaps he had guessed about me because he was once like me himself. I wondered if he had a sister.

I went to see Dr Strickland at half-past eleven.

He did not want me to leave the hospital. He said that he did not think that I was well enough to go home.

But I had decided. I was calm and I kept saying the same thing. 'I want to go home.'

'Why?'

'It's no use my staying here, I can't be cured.'

'Cured of what?'

'I want what I want, not what I ought to want.'

He picked up a sheet of paper from his desk, looked at it for what seemed like a whole minute, and then screwed it up and dropped it over the edge of the desk into the waste-paper basket.

He looked at me. 'I don't want to keep you here if you really want to go home. This place isn't a prison. I suppose I can only hope—for your sake—that you'll behave sensibly. You're not a fool. Try to remember that you won't prove anything by behaving like a fool. Do you think you'll start stealing women's underclothes again?'

'No.'

'If you do, you might find the police tramping all over you. Would you like that?'

'No.'

'Neither would I. Very well, you can go home tomorrow. But I'd like to see you at the Wilberforce Hospital in Hull sometime. You'll get a card through the post.'

I said, 'I hope it doesn't seem that I'm ungrateful for the help you've given me.'

'Why should it? If you want to go home, you want to go home. There's no point in your staying in hospital for the rest of your life.'

I said, 'I'm sorry I couldn't cooperate properly. I've been wasting your time. I've read about people like me. They go to psychiatrists but it's never any use.'

He told me that when I got home I ought to go to see the local doctor, Dr Booth, who had sent me to the hospital. He also said that the psychiatric social worker, Mrs Turner, might visit me.

The interview ended. He could go home to his dinner. His wife would be waiting.

Whenever he had been talking to me he had been waiting for dinner time to come so that he could go home. Nothing he had ever said to me had been real. I was only a sickening boy with a sickening madness. I was not a girl. The bright coloured dream that I could see was to him a filthy abscess. Certainly he must feel contempt for me. He was a man, and what I was must be contemptible to any man.

I would not go to see him at the Wilberforce Hospital.

22

After tea those who were dressing up were busy with their costumes.

Mr Allsop appeared in heavy black boots topped by red socks, black football shorts, a long green pullover with a polo neck and a very flat cap. The cap was geometrically level on his head and had been pressed to its thinnest and flattest. His white legs coming from the boots looked as though they were stretched upwards to his body rather than supporting his body. In his hand he carried a wooden spear, which had once been the staff of a large but cheap flag.

'Ask me what I am,' he said to Sam.

'What the hell are you?'

'A prehistoric Yorkshireman.'

Mr O'Brien was wearing the guardsman's tunic and the policeman's helmet, both of which were too big for him.

'Mr O'Brien,' explained Mr Allsop,' is a ceremonial Black-and-Tan.'

David, a powerful, good humoured man, with a hunch of shoulder and a strong, pugnacious head, was dressed as a woman. His large mouth was painted red, and the black he had put on his eyes added to their boldness. On his head was a yellow wig. The tresses were dry and without any likeness to human hair. His breasts were enormous and lumpy, bulging out in the red woollen dress that was strained across the shoulders and empty about the hips and buttocks. His legs were hard and muscled and blackened with hairs. I thought of a savage islander of the Pacific who had killed and eaten a lady missionary and then put on her clothes.

There was laughter as he thudded about on the floor of the ward.

Mr Allsop said, 'You look ravishing, David.'

'Chase me, sailor, I'm the last bus home!' shouted David, and he swung round grinning, showing a breadth of shoulder and a strength of arm, a massive, cheerful obscenity.

'I think I'll walk,' said Mr Allsop.

Others had done what they could to make costumes. Nothing seemed to fit. There were pieces of string holding things together.

A middle-aged man who was always very quiet was wearing the dress with red and yellow flowers that Jim had thrust at me the night before. He held a yellow wig in his hand. His head was bald. He smiled a gentle smile. I thought of middle-aged transvestites living their harmless lives. I imagined a Hindu gentleman wearing a sari and hoping that he would be a woman in his next existence. I pictured a successful Japanese business-man dressed as a geisha girl drinking tea behind paper blinds; a middle-aged German, who had once been a Hitler Youth, long-faced in an expensive blonde wig; an Italian gentleman sweating in a tight skirt; a worried American gentleman putting off painful high-heeled shoes as he sat writing to a mail order company for a rubber bosom. It was sad. They were all growing old and they would never be women.

Sam reviewed the costumes and approved: 'A very good effort. I've never seen such a crew. A very good effort.'

23

The ballroom was a great, stark hall that was reached by a corridor in the female wing of the hospital. There was a stage at one end, and on the stage the members of the small band that had been hired for the entertainment were sorting out their music and tuning their instruments. They were worldly looking men in dinner jackets. The drummer was a small, cruel-faced young man with a pointed beard.

Round the hall were rows of chairs, which male nurses were pushing and shoving and rearranging. Other male nurses stood in conversation, smoking and self-assured.

A convoy of old men arrived escorted by two male nurses. None of them was in costume. They were from one of the wards for people who were almost beyond participation in any activity. Some of them would be completely insane. They were made to sit on a row of chairs at the back. The male nurses placed themselves at either end.

People were arriving in all kinds of costume. There was a butcher with a striped apron and a straw hat carrying a cardboard meat axe. There was a lady in a crinoline having difficulties with her parasol. There was a tough old woman dressed as a witch with a pointed black hat and a broomstick trailing from her fist. Larry came in with a red and white cloth tied round his head and a black patch over one eye. He brandished a cardboard cutlass. There was a ghost bobbing along in a white sheet. There was an undertaker in a tall hat with black crepe round it. His face was painted yellow. There was a man dressed as a cook with a huge white hat and a frying pan. Mr Allsop talked to a sorrowful John Bull who had a toy dog on a string for a bulldog.

I sat and watched the dancing. I could only dance in my dreams.

Many odd couples moved and revolved over the floor. David, a ghastly, bright red woman, danced with a tiny pale girl dressed as a milkmaid. Two women dressed as men danced affectionately. A queen in a crown danced with a man in a sou'wester and oilskins. A schoolmaster in cap and gown danced with a girl in a paper grass skirt. Two pretty nurses dressed as nurses danced carefully together to encourage the others.

The Chief Male Nurse went up on the stage and announced that Dr Toeman and Mrs Toeman would judge the costumes. He directed that all the people in costume should form themselves into a procession round the hall. Then Dr Toeman and Mrs Toeman went up onto the stage to be in a position to make their decisions.

The people in costume began to form up into a column. There was some jostling. Suddenly a man in a kilt was set upon by a red man with a single green feather in a band round his head. Male nurses rushed in, and both men, the innocent Scotsman as well as the violent Red Indian, were taken away and out of the hall.

The band attacked 'Sons of the Sea' with gallantry. The head of the column went forward round the hall and joined up with the tail. And then the whole procession was revolving. There was lurching and walking proudly and laughing and waving to the uncostumed who sat watching. Mr Allsop came past with his flat cap level and his spear held perpendicular. Mr O'Brien staggered past under his policeman's helmet. John Bull had his dog trodden on and the string broke. The lady in the crinoline was still having difficulties with her parasol. She thrust it about, endangering eyesight. A party of Arabs marched past in robes that had once been bed linen. The man in the sou'wester and oilskins held up a string of cardboard fish for display. A plump lady skipped past dressed as a French sailor. A girl came along dressed as a drummer boy. Her drum was a real drum and she rattled on it bravely with drumsticks. She wore a red tunic that fitted her tightly to show that she was not a boy, and white knee breeches and white stockings. On her shoes were silver buckles. She had tied her hair back with a bow of black silk and she wore a black three cornered hat.

On they rumbled. They were more real than men and women

in the world outside. In the sober world there were illusions of choice. But at this fancy dress ball there was consciousness. The French sailor was a volunteer, not a complaining conscript. The queen with a cardboard crown was a queen by choice, not by accident of birth. Here was no pretence. Or so it seemed to me.

If I had not been a reasonable person, I would have liked to join them, dressed perhaps as a can-can girl, vulgar and blatant. I might have shouted, 'This is what we have become! Once only our stomach and our sex had desire, but now our brain has desire! Madness is the lust of the brain!'

Dr Toeman and Mrs Toeman had picked out the winner of the first prize. It was the girl dressed as a drummer boy. She received a large box of chocolates and some stockings. To me it seemed unjust that she should be allowed to dress as a boy and be given stockings.

The procession marched on again. The lady in the crinoline received the second prize. It was another box of chocolates. One of the Arabs received the third prize. He was handed a box of cigarettes.

There was a fourth prize and a fifth prize and a sixth prize—I lost count. Nearly half the people in costume got something. The last prizes were packets of cigarettes. Finally Dr Toeman held up his hand and said, 'I'm sorry, that's all there is. But I can see some people I would have liked to have given prizes if we hadn't run out. It's a pity. We'll have to have more prizes next year.'

Tomorrow I would go home.

Part Two

—

ROY AND WENDY

1

The yellow sun of late summer shone on the fronts of the terrace houses and on the flagstones before them. It was nearly dinner time. A Shell tanker bulked in the street. Children ran and shouted. A girl with a headscarf over her curlers slouched along, antagonistic, female unfeminine and heavy-legged in the middle of the day.

My father would be battering fish and dropping them into the pan and wiping his hands on the damp cotton cloth. Mrs Wilson would be wrapping and serving.

It was not a very poor district. The houses had inside lavatories and most of them had had baths put in. But in the sunshine the streets looked their worst.

The men of these streets would have to laugh about me because they had to be as bluff as the next man.

And the women would have to despise me for wanting to be like them—though they felt themselves to be sacredly superior to men.

I knew them.

I wanted to be far away from this street of bricks.

I saw the board sticking out, rectangular: FISH and CHIPS.

I stopped. I turned round and walked away. I would go to Cottingham and see Shirley.

I walked back the way I had come. My case and my raincoat were becoming burdensome. I caught a bus to the city centre. When I got to the railway station I handed my case in at the left-luggage office. I wondered if the man who took the case thought that I looked effeminate and that the case might be full of women's clothes. I wished that it were. I asked for the case back and opened it and put my raincoat into it and gave it back to him.

On the train I thought about Jim. I hoped that he was

getting better. I thought that I would like to send him some money. Perhaps I could send him a pound in an envelope so that he would not know from whom it had come. It would buy him some cigarettes.

The train took about a quarter of an hour to reach Cottingham.

Most of the town was on the side of the station on which I got out. On the far side were some allotments doing well in the sun and a wood that looked as though it would be interesting to walk in—but was probably privately owned and protected.

The summer afternoon was pleasant in the countryside. A breeze turned the leaves of a sycamore tree. Privet hedges were neat and firm. On a lawn a sprinkler went round and round. A woman of about thirty, slim and smart, came out of a house and down the garden and got into a small car to drive away. Perhaps she was going to buy clothes. Her husband might worrit and smoke in Hull's working afternoon, but he could never wear the nice clothes. He could only have clean collars and pressed trousers. As long as he was healthy he would be expected to work. He was not free in the afternoon.

A young girl walked on the footpath. Her hair was black. The breeze folded her summer dress as she walked. She walked along pretending to be unconscious of her happiness. There was something intelligent in her movements. Perhaps she was down on the long vacation from Oxford. Perhaps she was a clever model, come home for a rest from London. The first was possible. The second seemed unlikely. She was not tall enough. I was tall enough.

Perhaps she had once been a boy. Did she know that there was a street with a fish-and-chip shop in it, that there were bluebottles flying about round the empty fish boxes in the back yard? No. The gardens and the trees and the summer afternoon had always been hers.

She was carried along by the pleasant afternoon and by the money of her parents and by the money-getting young man who would come for her and by her children and by all the pleasant summer afternoon of her life.

She would have to be married in a white gown with a headdress of spraying net. How excited she would be, dressing on her wedding morning. When she was dressed and ready she would be weak with nervousness.

Sweating like a June bride.

I wished that one day I would sweat like a June bride, sweating weakly and femininely from nervousness and happiness in white satin.

First there had to be money. Money bought the houses and the gardens and bought the clothes that the women wore. Only money could buy the female hormones and the cunning surgeons.

Before I could make enough money I would be old and thick-faced. Nothing could be done.

The only way to get to Cottingham was the way that Shirley had done it.

But the homosexual daddies would pretend to have more money than they really had. I would not find one who had five thousand pounds to give away. And, in any case, I might not be able to make myself go through the horror.

I wondered if Bill was good at thinking up new things to do to Shirley. An architect ought to be imaginative.

Shirley's house was a cube with a roof of green tiles on top. It had a picture window and a garage door that swung upwards. It stood alone in its own garden. Bill's father had paid four thousand pounds for it. There was a tree in the garden near the gate. Its branches were lopped but it had covered itself with leaves that shook in the breeze. It was a beech tree.

All this Shirley had achieved by being as she was. Men had built the house by laying bricks with their rough hands, by sawing wood and bending pipes and putting in electric cables. But, now that it was complete and part of the world, Shirley lived in it. She had got what she wanted by being, not by doing.

Shirley and Bill might have an argument, and Bill might say the more intelligent things, but always Shirley would be the woman. Bill might lose his temper and strike her, but she would still be the woman.

I pressed the bell. A double note sounded inside the house. I pressed again. The double note sounded again.

Shirley was wearing a dress of mustard coloured cotton. She had been out in the sun on previous days. Her face had an even, pale tan that made her grey eyes look lighter than usual. My eyes were grey. She looked fresh and happy.

'Hello, Roy! What are you doing here? Come in. I'm busy

47

just now. I'm going to make some pastry.'

I went in upon the carpet in the hallway.

'Gwen's gone to a party,' she told me as I followed her into the kitchen. 'I'll have to fetch her at four o'clock.'

The kitchen was white paint and formica tops and aluminium pans shining. The two wooden chairs were painted red.

'You've left hospital, have you?'

'I was discharged this morning.'

'Have you been home?'

'No.'

'What have you been doing till this time?'

'I decided to come and see you.'

'Have you had any lunch?'

'No.'

'Would you like some egg and chips or something?'

'It doesn't matter.'

'You must have something. Haven't you had anything since breakfast?'

'I don't feel hungry.'

'I'll fry you two eggs. Would you like that?'

'I don't really want anything, thanks.'

She fried me two eggs and mashed a pot of tea. While I was eating she started making pastry in a large bowl.

'How are you now, do you think?' she asked.

'I'm a lot better.'

'Have you got rid of those peculiar ideas?'

'I don't know.'

'You mean you're not sure?'

'Not really.'

'Well, I suppose these things take time. But do you feel that they did you any good at the hospital?'

'As much good as it was possible for them to do, I suppose.'

She looked up from what she was doing. 'Really, Roy, you are dreadfully apathetic!'

'It's the way I'm made.'

'But you can't go on like this. What's to become of you?'

'I don't know.'

'Why don't you make an effort? You must be a lot better or they wouldn't have discharged you. Can't you try to make something out of your life?'

'I think they discharged me because they lost interest.'

'Of course they didn't. I can't believe that. They don't do things like that.'

'They know when they're up against a brick wall.'

'You don't still have that crazy idea about wanting to be a woman, do you?'

'I don't know.'

'Anyway, you won't start stealing things again, will you?'

'No.'

'Are you sure?'

'I'm not sure of anything.'

'It's no good being like that, Roy. You must pull yourself together. Life isn't easy for anybody. What would happen to Bill and Gwen if I gave way to every ridiculous idea that came into my head?'

'They wouldn't get any home-made pastry.'

'Exactly.' She smiled.

She told me at length that I ought to get myself better employment than helping in the shop. I listened to her and wondered if I would ever make pastry for anyone.

When I said that I would have to be going she asked me to find my own way out because she had her hands in flour.

I had an opportunity. I said, 'May I use your lavatory?'

'Of course. You know where it is. First right at the top of the stairs.'

I went up the stairs and saw that the door to the front bedroom was standing ajar about a foot. I moved stealthily with my weight on my toes, and pressed against it. It did not make any sound in opening. The room was still and silent. There was pale blue wallpaper. On the bed the cover was of peacock blue. There was a wardrobe and a chest of drawers and a dressing table all in limed oak. At home Shirley had always kept her underwear in the chest of drawers. The carpet I trod on was pale blue. It was thick and soft. I made no sound. I went to the chest of drawers and opened the top drawer, easing it carefully open about two inches. I could see that it contained Bill's shirts, clean and pressed. I closed the drawer. I tried the second drawer. It creaked as it came open. I stopped. My hands were beginning to sweat. I opened the drawer further. It was empty. I pushed it back. It creaked again as it went home. I opened the third drawer carefully. It moved easily. It was full of Shirley's underwear. There were things in pale orange and in blue and in black and in white. The scent was exciting. I took out a black slip and then searched about until I found a pair of black panties. I was on the point of putting them into my jacket pockets when I told myself that I ought not to take anything that I did not need. What I needed was a suspender belt and some stockings. The girdle that was hidden in the attic at home was old. And I thought that I might feel more feminine in a suspender belt. But perhaps Shirley did not have a suspender belt. Perhaps she wore a girdle all the time now that she was older. I did not need a girdle. If I had treatment, I might become softer. I put the black slip and the panties back. I searched and touched what I thought was a suspender belt, but when I drew it out I found that it was a yellow brassière. Then I found a suspender, but it was attached to a girdle. Finally I found a suspender belt in the far corner of the drawer. I was very glad to get it. It was yellow. The suspenders struck the edge of the drawer as I got it out. They rattled on the wood and jingled. The noise made me cringe with fear. I got it into my pocket. Then I decided that I wanted the yellow brassière to match it. The one I had at home was pink. I found the yellow brassière again and put it into my pocket. I thought of looking for a yellow slip and knicker set, but I did not want to steal too much from Shirley. There were several rolled-up pairs of stockings in the front of the drawer. I took two pairs. The stockings I had at home had ladders or holes in them. When I was taking the stockings I saw a pair of blue panties decorated with a lacework of white flowers. They were very pretty. I wanted them. I had three pairs of knickers at home—but ordinary people had lots of pairs. It was necessary. I wanted these. I took them and put them in my pocket. Then I tried to straighten out the things in the drawer so that it would not be obvious that they had been touched. I closed the drawer. I tiptoed out of the bedroom.

I went into the lavatory and turned the handle so that there was the sound of flushing. I ran down the stairs. As I got to the door I called out:

'Cheerio.'

Shirley called back from the kitchen: 'Cheerio, Roy.'

I was outside in the summer afternoon. I had a suspender belt and a brassière and two pairs of stockings and a special pair of knickers.

I wished that I had found a yellow slip and knicker set to match the suspender belt and brassière. The Have-nots had to take from the Haves.

All the things I had in the attic had been stolen from Shirley before she left home. She had things that I was not allowed to have. And so I was forced to steal from her.

If it were not for my father, I could send away for things that could be delivered by post. But there was right-mindedness. I was forced to steal.

I had to have women's clothes because I was a woman in the head. They could oppress me, but they could not get into my head. It was as impossible for anyone to make me believe that it was better to be a man than a woman as it would have been for them to make me believe that the streets where I lived were better than Cottingham. In their hearts, they must know the truth themselves, but they had to keep pretending for the sake of decency—while all the time they knew that men, with their grotesque sexual organs, were always indecent. To be a man was to be horrible. It was ridiculous that I should have been sent to a mental hospital. It was perfectly sane for me to want to be a woman. It was my body that was wrong, not my mind.

I had stolen clothes again. I was myself despite everything. In the end they would learn that they could not change my mind.

I had stolen a pair of blue and white panties.

I wished that it had been possible to steal a nice dress—or the suit that Shirley had been wearing the day she visited me in hospital. I would have liked to wear that suit very much.

I hurried on. I was sweating.

At the station I was told that there was nearly a hour to wait for a train to Hull.

I hated men's lavatories. They always seemed dank and, however clean they might be, one always imagined the strong amber tang of the male. I hated homosexuals most when I thought of them doing things in such places. I remembered the joke about the lavatory attendant who was told that he could take his holidays at his own convenience.

I walked up and down the platform and worked up anger about what I had read about the sinking of the *Titanic*. Boys had dressed themselves as women to try to get into the boats.

51

They had been discovered and thrown out and they had been called cowards because they did not want to die. But women who were dressed as women had been helped into the boats. A woman of middle-age who had had the best of her life could be saved, but a boy who had hardly had any life at all had to be left to die. It was possible that some of the women who got away from the *Titanic* became suffragettes and paraded about demanding equal rights with men, until the war started in 1914.

I concluded that women were adults on calm waters, but when the ship began to sink they wished to be counted with the children. They thought it right that any boy should die so that there would be a place in the lifeboat for some stupid, selfish, moral-minded, parasitic woman.

2

My father was a strong man. He was three inches taller than I was, but he did not look tall. Mostly his head was thrust forward from the shoulders. It was an aggressive look. He had been a handsome young man. There was a photograph of him that officially should not have been taken when he was in the East Yorkshire Regiment in Normandy. He was a sergeant. The others were sprawled on the grass grinning at the camera. He was resting on his elbow, withdrawn, as though he knew that time would pass and Normandy would be a summer long ago. His face was lean and virile then. It was heavier and softer now. He had helped to win the war. People might walk in Paris and in Oxford and talk of this and that as though the future would wait forever, and a beautiful woman might move in a spacious and elegant room with yellow roses in a bowl upon the table; and all because my father had struggled from the sea on the first morning of Normandy. Evil had not been broken by considered words and the accepted indignation of the well-educated, but by men like my father, by my father himself.

When he opened the shop door to me he was surprised. Then he seemed pleased. But he did not touch me. He could never touch me in affection. He had struck me in anger, but it was not possible for him to put out his hand to touch me because he loved me.

He could kiss Shirley.

I had some of Shirley's clothes in my pockets, but he did not know that.

'I've been discharged,' I explained. He might have thought that I had run away from the hospital.

'I'm a bit surprised. Come in. Why didn't you write and let me know you were coming? Give me your case. Have you had your tea?'

We went through the shop and into the kitchen.

'When did you leave the hospital?' he asked.

'This afternoon.'

'Did you have any dinner?'

'Yes. I had my dinner at the hospital.'

'You'll be ready for your tea. Get yourself sat down.'

He seemed to be glad to see me. It was as though he had forgotten what I had done.

I said that I would take my case upstairs to my bedroom.

I slept in the back bedroom. It had been Shirley's room. I had a double bed to myself. My father slept in a double bed in the front bedroom without Mrs Wilson.

There were no material shortages. Always there was enough food and enough money. And there was enough time in which it was not necessary to work so that he could go to visit Mrs Wilson and I could dress up. We were well off. If I had wanted a motor cycle, my father would have bought me a motor cycle, and if he had been willing to be taught to drive he could have bought himself a car. Mrs Wilson often told him that he ought to buy a car. I could spend ten pounds for a new pair of trousers—but I could not spend five pounds for a skirt in blue poplin, a skirt that would swing as I moved and make me happy. I sometimes thought that my life was like a forced march on rations of corned beef and tinned spinach.

I took the things I had stolen from Shirley's out of my pockets and put them at the back of the bottom drawer in the big chest of drawers. After tea I would take them up to the attic and put them with my other things.

My father was pouring out the tea when I got back to the kitchen. 'I didn't come to visit you because I thought you might be better left alone. I thought you needed to be away

53

from things for a bit.'

'I was all right. Thanks for the money you sent.'

'You have to have something. Are you all right for money now?'

'Yes. I've got about fifteen pounds in my back pocket. I haven't spent much.'

'You don't spend enough, and that's a fact. You want to enjoy yourself a bit more, instead of mopping about and reading all the time. I think you spend too much of your time stuck in the house. When I was your age I was out every night.' He went to the mantelpiece and found a ten packet of cigarettes. He got one out and lit it.

I realised that he was tense. I thought that he must have been having Mrs Wilson in to sleep with him while I was away.

He said, 'Our Shirley came to see you, didn't she?'

'Yes.'

'She said she was going to. That was a bit ago. I haven't seen her since then. She was upset when I told her you were badly. She thinks a lot about you. And Mrs Wilson has missed you. She's had to look after the chip pan and run the chipping machine as well as serving. I gave her a hand when I could. We were falling over each other on Friday dinner times and Saturday nights. I thought of getting somebody in to help out, but I didn't know when you'd be coming back. We did well this dinner time. I went through three trays of fish. Haddock's a bit pricey just now. Mrs Wilson has been staying on Wednesdays and making tea. She'd have been here tonight, but she's sitting in with a woman in her street whose husband has just died.'

Now that I was back Mrs Wilson would not be able to be alone with him in the house. When she did come in the evenings we would all have to watch the television.

I would have liked to make a bargain whereby Mrs Wilson came to live in sin with my father in exchange for my being allowed to send away for clothes and dress up when I wanted.

Such a bargain was impossible. We all had to play hide-and-seek. I thought that it was not unlikely that my father had punched me in the face because of a build-up of annoyance at the times that I had been in the house when he wanted to make love to Mrs Wilson.

It was difficult to keep calm about hypocrisy. I had to try to remember that I was very intelligent, while my father and Mrs Wilson were only ordinary people.

Considering that I was a nuisance, my father was managing to seem glad to see me.

After tea I went up to my bedroom and got my bedding out of the wall cupboard where it had been stored while I was away. The bedding was quite dry and fresh. There was no dampness in the house.

When I had made my bed I went to the big chest of drawers and got out the things I had brought from Shirley's. I took my shoes off and went upstairs to the attic. There was a front attic and a back attic, both with sloping ceilings and fanlights. I had slept in the back attic before Shirley had left home. There was a little catch on the lock for locking the door from the inside. I closed the door behind me and slipped the catch. If a man came and put his weight against the door, the catch would snap at once. The floor was bare. The single bed was bare. The room had looked bigger when I had slept in it. There had been lino on the floor and furniture. All that was left of the furniture was a wickerwork chair with its seat burst through. In the corner, under the slope of the ceiling, was the wooden fat-box that contained the dozens of pieces of the electric train set I had not particularly wanted one Christmas. I had liked playing with Shirley's doll's house until my father had got rid of it. One could play a story with a doll's house. On the far side of the bed there was a wall cupboard between the flue that ran up the wall and the corner of the room. I went across and opened the cupboard. On a shelf there was an old copy of a children's book, *Chatterbox*. Some of the stories in it were intended for boys and some were intended for girls. The girls' stories were mostly about the boyish adventures of schoolgirls. I had supposed that the heroines wore the navy blue knickers that the little girls wore at the school I went to. It had been after I had gone to the grammar school that I had stopped wanting to wear the navy blue knickers and be a little girl and started wanting to grow up to wear knickers of silk and nylon and have breasts. I fixed my finger nails on the end of the floorboard at the bottom of the cupboard. It was difficult to move the board. But as soon as it moved it came up. The pillow case was there. In it were all the women's clothes I had. Underneath the pillow case I kept some copies of *Vogue* and *Harper's Bazaar* and all the cuttings I had been able to collect about people who had changed into women. I pulled the pillow case out. It was heavy. It was tied at the end with a piece of string. I took off the string and stuffed the things I had brought from Cottingham into the pillow case. I retied the string and pushed the pillow case back under the floor. I replaced the floorboard and closed the cupboard door.

Tomorrow was Thursday. My father would go to Mrs Wilson's. I would be able to dress up.

I went down to the kitchen and presented myself to my father as though I were an honest boy.

We watched the television.

3

Always the slowest job was preparing the potatoes. They had to be put through the potato machine and then every one had to be looked at and any eyes or bad patches taken out with a potato knife.

It was with a feeling of the beginning of long labour that the first bucketful of rough potatoes was lifted up and poured into the machine. The potatoes thumped and rumbled round in the machine and the water hissed and swished. Then muddy water started to come out round the edges of the hatch at the front. The rumbling and hissing continued, and soon the water was coming out clean. After about a minute the hatch was opened, and the potatoes came pouring out, white and pale yellow. The hatch was closed, and another bucketful of potatoes went into the machine.

Each skinned potato had to be taken in hand and picked before it could be thrown into one of the galvanised dolly tubs filled with water. In winter one's hands lost feeling in the cold water and the cold from the concrete floor came up through the soles of the rubber boots and through two or three pairs of socks to make one's feet agony. And in winter the potatoes had more eyes and more rotten parts in them. In summer the work was only tedious.

It was Thursday morning. We were doing the potatoes for Friday dinner-time opening.

Because of the weeks I had been away from the job I noticed the alkaline smell of the potatoes. The din of the machine and the background noise of the big refrigerator running was violent after the quiet of the hospital.

'The spuds have been a hell of a job single-handed,' my father shouted.

By eleven o'clock he had sung all his songs and we had two dolly tubs full of potatoes.

'I think that should do. You go and make a cup of tea, Roy, and I'll swill down. They won't be delivering the fish till tomorrow. But I have nearly enough cut in the fridge. I want to change the fat in the fish pan this morning.'

While we were drinking our tea he said, 'You want to get yourself to Anlaby Road this afternoon. Yorkshire are playing Kent. It's a nice day. You want to get yourself down there.'

'I don't like cricket much,' I said.

'You want to get to like it. You want to get yourself interests.'

After we had had our tea he changed the fat in the fish pan and I cleaned the inside of the shop windows.

At half-past twelve I went to make the dinner. We had boiled potatoes and a tin of peas and a tin of corned beef followed by tinned apricots and tinned cream. I made everything look as nice as possible. I often thought that I would like to dress up to get dinner ready. When Mrs Wilson cooked our dinner for us she always made Yorkshire pudding. She could make very light Yorkshire pudding. Shirley's Yorkshire pudding had always been too heavy. I had once tried to make Yorkshire pudding—it was like lead.

My father went up to change after dinner. He came down to the kitchen in his best suit and took three pound notes out of his wallet and laid them on the table. He pointed at them. 'Go out and spend that, Roy. Don't sit in here all afternoon. It's a lovely day. Get yourself out. Get yourself off to Bridlington or somewhere and see what's going on.'

57

4

As soon as he had gone I went out into the back yard and got my bicycle out of the lean-to shed. The tyres were down. I went back into the house and found the pump in the drawer of the sideboard in the kitchen. I pumped the tyres up. It was to be expected, in accordance with the contrariness of the world, that one or both of them would have developed punctures since I had last ridden the bicycle. But, to my surprise, the tyres stayed hard.

I set off to the city centre.

There was no effort going up hill and there was no enjoyment going down hill. Hull was all quite flat. So many turns of the pedals caused so many yards to be covered along the road. Cars passed me. Blue and white buses passed me.

I came under the shadow of a grain silo that stood like a Norman keep, but bigger than any keep built by the Normans. When there was fog its heights were lost in the sky. I rode amongst the girders of the drawbridge that spanned the barge-laden River Hull. Between the bridge and the Humber there was a warren of warehouses and narrow lanes. Merchants might seek to bring ships safe home by witchcraft. The big docks along the Humber were of modern times, but this place was medieval.

When I crossed the bridge as a child I thought the warehouses might provide hideouts for gangs of criminals. Kidnapped girls might be taken there bound and gagged. Sometimes I liked to imagine a splendid ballroom, hidden inside one of the dark old buildings. I pictured limousines, under cover of darkness, bringing beautifully dressed women to dance in the secret ballroom with sophisticated criminals. The criminals of my imagination were hard handsome men in dinner jackets, each with an automatic pistol slung out of sight beneath his left arm. The women were so beautiful and beautifully dressed that they were near to fainting with the mere ecstasy of being themselves. But I was the most beautiful. I would be going to the ballroom in a long Rolls Royce, softly lit. I would be poised and self-assured in a sheath dress of black satin with a stole of black chiffon about my shoulders. The chauffeur would be my body-guard as well as my driver, a silent man, as ruthless as he was loyal, ready to cut down anyone who caused me even the slightest annoyance. I would arrive at the secret ballroom and everyone would gasp. I would dance with the most successful of all the criminals, Max, cruel and handsome like a tiger.

Now I smiled at what I had imagined. Certainly there was not a secret ballroom in any of the warehouses. And the criminals of Hull were not noted for their sophistication.

I went to a chemist shop and bought the sticking-plaster I would need. I bought a bottle of aspirins. I needed the aspirins because fixing myself up always caused me to have a painful throbbing in the front of my head. Then I went and bought a large tube of rubber solution at a cycle shop.

The man behind the counter could not suspect why I needed the rubber solution, just as the girls in the chemist shop had not suspected me. If the girls had known, they might have expressed contempt. They would not have accepted the flattery of imitation.

As I rode home I told myself that, since women believed themselves to be superior, and men were expected to respect the notion of that superiority, there could be no reasonable objection to the way I behaved. I wanted to improve myself. What I did must be natural because it was done. The unnatural was that which was not done. I had as much right to be a female as anyone else.

By the time I was riding down the ten-foot to the back gate I felt that I could be as sure of winning in a debate as I could be of losing in an argument.

I always had a bath before I dressed up on Tuesdays and Thursdays. When I had dried myself I went to my bedroom. I had all the things I would need to make myself right set out on a chair. Also there was the bottle of aspirins and a glass of water.

I stood by the chair and began work on myself.

Everything had to be done methodically. I had evolved my technique over the years. My first attempts had been unbearably uncomfortable and unconvincing in appearance. But I had invented better ways of getting the results I wanted.

I worked slowly and with concentration. It had to be right. The pain I caused myself while I was working did not matter, but when it was finished it had to look right and I had to be able to live in it. It had to last four weeks before it was changed.

The noise of the traffic in the front street seemed louder. I could hear my watch ticking on the dressing table. My head was beginning to hurt. I worked on.

The afternoon light from the window was moving round. There were men's voices in the front street. It must be after five o'clock. I was finishing.

It was done. I was like a female. I could wear knickers.

Now I was exhausted. My head was thumping with pain. I took four aspirins.

It was necessary to lie down. I got into bed and lay naked between the sheets. My head was marking time with a measured thumping. I drew my knees up and pushed my head forward. I saw elephants marching round and round a circus ring, heavy and imperturbable, marching round to *Colonel Bogey*. All performing elephants were females.

When I awoke my headache was over. I was comfortable and beginning to feel happy. I went and looked at my watch. It was a quarter to seven.

I put on my everyday clothes and went downstairs and drew the curtains over the kitchen window so that when I was dressed up I would be able to go down and have my tea.

Then I went up to the attic and got the pillow case out and took it down to my bedroom. I took off my everyday clothes.

I got the yellow brassière out of the pillow case. I had some difficulty getting the hooks into the eyes. It was several weeks since I had put a brassière on. The cups were empty. I had read about transvestites whose breasts had begun to develop without hormone treatment. But sexual deviants were often liars.Mine had not developed. I had had to make my breasts from the sponge-rubber stuffing of a cushion. I found them and put them into the cups of the brassière. That felt better. I got the suspender belt and put it on. The suspenders dangled down. An unattached suspender looked unfortunate. I had a yellow brassière and a yellow suspender belt. I wished that I had stolen a yellow slip and pantie set. But the blue and white panties were very nice. Now I was going to put them on. They were mine. I was going to put them on. I was careful to hold them the right way round. I took them and stepped into them. They were on my legs. I drew them up. The suspenders got outside them. I pushed the suspenders in and drew the panties right up. The white flowers rounded on my tummy prettily. I had only two slips, a white one and a pale blue one, both of which I had taken when Shirley had lived at home. They were both tired looking. I chose the pale blue one and put it on. There was some lace round the hem. Now I was wearing a skirt. I was feeling happy. Putting stockings on was my favourite after putting knickers on. It was not so significant, but it required ladylike skill. The activity of getting the suspenders and fastening the stockings was busy and self-forgetting, yet feminine. When I had both stockings on I admired my legs. I had very good legs. They were not at all hairy. They were long and shapely and the knee-caps were small.

I was dressing up. Everything was better than it had been. The clothes made me feel more real and alive. They felt nice and I felt more like myself.

I had two dresses that had belonged to Shirley, one was pink with white flowers and the other was chocolate brown. And I had a quite wearable blue cotton dress that I had found in a sack of cleaning rags my father had bought. There was also a black skirt that Shirley had worn for work when she had been a typist. The black skirt showed my legs off well because it was tight and it made me feel secret.

I pondered between the pink dress with white flowers and the black skirt.

I decided on the black skirt because the pink dress needed pressing.

I put a pink cotton blouse on with the black skirt. The buttons of the blouse were at the back. Nothing that a man wore buttoned at the back. I was glad of the difficulty of fastening the buttons. I wanted all the difficulties that women had. Being female was having the limitations of the female.

I was not glad when I thought about shoes. I had a pair of slipper shoes that could be either a boy's or a girl's shoes, but I liked things that were only for women. I always wanted heels. I had not worn heels since my feet had outgrown Shirley's shoes. My feet were not big, but they were long. I thought that they would look excellent in heels. Heels made one feel smart and gave one more sex.

I had some cosmetics. Shirley had always had more little boxes and pots than she knew. I had four old lipsticks that she had half lost and I had found. And I had two lipsticks that I had bought myself. I had gone into shops and bought the most expensive lipsticks in stock, and the assistants had thought that I was buying presents. One had cost me a guinea and the other had cost me thirty-five shillings.

I found the thirty-five shilling lipstick. It was a heavy metal cartridge in black and gold.

When I looked in the mirror I wished that I could let my hair grow or buy a wig. If I bought a wig, it could be blonde. I might make a brilliant blonde. For a moment I wished that I had blue eyes. Blue eyes were thought of as very feminine. Once I had seen a picture of a man who had been turned into a woman but the eyes that were looking out of the face were a man's eyes. It was strangely frightening. When I saw pictures of people who had changed into women I always looked at the eyes. My eyes were soft. I had noticed that they became softer when I was dressed up. They were a woman's eyes. A person with eyes like mine could tend a baby.

Whatever happened, I would never have a baby—unless the doctors became much more clever. If I did have a baby, he would rule the world—unless it was a girl. I would like to have a little girl. I might have two children, John and Ellen. Then I would be as much a woman as any other woman.

The lipstick made my face more feminine, but it made my hair seem shorter. I thought I looked rather like a lesbian schoolmistress. But I did look like a woman. If I had the courage to go out, I could pass for a woman. I wished I had more courage. I was a very prim girl.

My hips and rump filled the skirt well. I was very slim, but I was a better shape than any boy.

I was fixed up perfectly underneath and I was dressed altogether as a woman. I felt like a woman. Certainly I could not behave like a man even if I wanted to. I was a woman.

'I am Wendy,' I said, and I stretched with the physical pleasure of being myself. It was good. I was happy. I sat down on the chair and crossed my legs. It was pleasant to be crossing my legs in a tight skirt and nylon stockings. Now the world was as it should be. I was myself.

My anger at the shop girls had been foolish. I was the same as they were. I was forced to sit down whenever I used the lavatory. I could affect disdain for the masculine as they could.

I wanted to suffer the special discomforts that a woman had to suffer. I wanted in everything to be a woman.

Women could be happy, because their sexuality was part of them. They had their bodies, and their lives went forward to real, physical conclusions. A man could never be happy, because his sexuality lived a life of its own and ran in front of him. A woman carried hers in her body.

The river flowed to the sea and the city was full of well-intentioned activity. The world was an existence and did not need meaning. I was. The top of my mind and the bottom of my mind were one, and there was no way of dividing my mind from my body. My mind was my body. I was part of the world. All things had come home. I was Wendy. I was glad that I had been born to be conscious. I was sitting there being myself. I was happy. The resentment and the tension were past. I was myself. Now I was not mad.

I thought that Dr Strickland would like me. He would not be able to stop himself seeing that I was pretty.

Roy was someone else. Roy was insane, but I was well-balanced and calm. Roy had been in a lunatic asylum, but I knew nothing of such places. Poor Roy had abnormal desires. I was a real girl sitting in a real bedroom in a real house in a real street in a real city.

If I could go on wearing the right clothes and not be stopped by the return of my father, I could go on being sane. But when my father returned I would have to be mad Roy again.

While I was eating my tea in the kitchen I told myself that I must send Shirley some money to pay for the things that I had brought from her house. Roy might claim some insane justification for stealing things, but if a girl meant to keep her sister's clothes, she ought to pay for them. I decided that I would put three pound notes in an envelope and send them to Shirley.

Poor Roy was a fetishist. He had that common obsession with knickers. Poor boy. I wished that I could help him. But it would not be correct to help him by letting him wear my clothes. That would be to encourage vice. I did not want the house full of boxing gloves and whips and extraordinary apparatus. I was a normal woman.

It would be best if Roy could be kept away.

Near the time of my father's return I would have to go

upstairs and put on Roy's clothes. Underneath I would still be fixed up and I would put on one of my other pairs of knickers and the pink brassière. But I would not be able to put the breasts in the brassière and I would see Roy's clothes on my body. I would have to wear trousers all day and male pyjamas at night.

After tea I washed the things I intended to wear under Roy's clothes. I got out the electric fire and put the things over a chair as close to it as I dare. I wanted them to be dry before half-past ten. If they were not dry, I would have to wear them damp.

Everything had to be so furtive. I ought to go away and try to live as a woman. One could not hide oneself forever.

I had read that men who wanted to be women but were too dishonest to admit it to themselves often developed cruel personalities. They became rigidly determined to excel and dominate.

I moralized: It was better to do what one wanted and take the consequences than not to do what one wanted and make other people take the consequences.

But women often liked men who were determined to excel and dominate.

The knickers and brassière were dry enough after I had ironed them.

I decided that on the following Tuesday I would iron all my things. Washing in the early afternoon, ironing after tea. I would be busy. It was something to look forward to.

5

When I came back from posting the envelope to Shirley on Friday morning Mrs Wilson had arrived for the dinner time opening and was sorting out the white coats. She was a very clean woman. Her appearance suggested a Protestant conscience. It was difficult to imagine her going to the mass and hearing Latin and smelling incense.

She seemed pleased to see me. 'How are you now, Roy? Are you feeling better?'

No doubt my father had told her what I had done. He told her everything. He told her about Uncle Arthur having been in prison for getting credit without disclosing that he was an undischarged bankrupt. I was sixteen before I knew that Uncle Arthur had been in prison. Perhaps she had given my father advice about me. I remembered once she had been talking about a boy who lived near her who had stolen clothes off a washing line. She said that the thing to do was to catch him wearing the clothes. She said that always cured them. She had not said it with any moral vindictiveness but simply as a statement of the way in which a cure might be obtained, in the same way that she might have recommended a cure for a cold in the head.

I said, 'Yes, I'm all right now.'

'I thought you would be. I told your dad that they wouldn't have sent you home if you hadn't been cured. The main thing is not to think about it anymore.'

'I don't.'

'You don't want to. What's passed is done with, I always say.'

I wondered if she would be allowed to say that when she got to the Roman Catholic next world. Probably she would have to go to Purgatory to be made to forget her love. I thought that places where people were operated upon to make them into women were rather like Purgatory. One went in as a pervert, and one came out entitled to use the Ladies' lavatory and get married.

'The great thing,' she said, 'is to get out and see the world. You're too much stuck in the house.'

It would have been incestuous for me to want to be Mrs Wilson. The best arrangement would have been for her to be my mother and me to be her daughter. She would have given me advice about my periods and told me many frightening things. I might have become Irishly Catholic and lit candles and prayed to Mary. I might have been a young girl with a body like an autumn pear and a mind like the window of a shop where devotional objects were sold, all wine red and pale blue and cluttered and piled up with sanctity and bad taste. At worst it would have been better than having to be a man. And, whatever ideas I might have about religious matters, my knickers would have been modern.

65

Mrs Wilson had once had a baby. But it had died. I wished I could have a baby.

Before the shop opened we always washed ourselves and scrubbed our nails even if they were clean. My father and I combed our hair carefully before the mirror over the fireplace in the kitchen. Then like surgeons we put on our white coats and went into the shop.

The gas burners under the pans were lit and the fat in the pans began to melt. I watched it melting in the chip pan. It was like sand-coloured ice turning into dark brown water. As soon as the fat was melted my father went and unbolted the shop door and fastened it open. I put the first lot of chips into the pan. They did not cause a boiling as they would have done in a hot pan. They sank with lazy, oily bubbles. Mrs Wilson looked in the pan and said that it was not hot enough. I agreed. I looked to see if the gas was full on. It was. We always had the gasses full on for Friday dinner time opening. Mrs Wilson said I should have waited because the chips would be soft if they fried slowly. I said that I thought that some people might like soft chips. I closed the lid of the chip pan. My father told Mrs Wilson that he had put five pounds worth of floater in the till but that there wasn't as much copper as he would have liked. She opened the till and had a look and said that she would be able to manage.

The first customer arrived, a little woman putting a basket on the counter and asking for four times a haddock and sixpennyworth. My father told her that he was waiting for the fish pan. The little woman praised the weather. My father said that the nights were drawing in.

I told myself that I was as much a female as Mrs Wilson and the little woman with the basket. But I did not believe myself.

My father started battering fish and putting them into his pan. I opened the chip pan and found that it was boiling. I lifted out a scoop of chips and tried one with my fingers. It was very soft. I wondered whether some people did like soft chips. I started getting the chips out of the pan and putting them in the chip box. Mrs Wilson started filling grease-proof bags for the little woman's order.

Another woman arrived. She wanted three fish-and-sixpennyworths. Then a little girl came in. Mrs Wilson asked the little girl how her mother was. The little girl said that her mother was a lot better.

Soon a queue was growing. I had to go and fetch bucketfuls of potatoes to put through the chipping machine. Mrs Wilson was serving and giving change at her best speed. My father was tossing out fish and arranging them cleverly.

Some of the customers in the shop must know what I had done. The young woman whose panties I had taken must have told every woman she knew. I had demonstrated that her clothes were desirable.

People were looking at my back while I was standing at the chip pan.

I told myself that it did not matter. I should not care what was going on in their heads—there was enough going on in my head to keep me busy. No doubt they talked about Mrs Wilson. Yet she could face them and give them their change. There was no need for me to blush. But I was blushing. I called myself a fool. If Mrs Wilson could face them, I should be able to face them. Most judgements on sexual behaviour were nonsense. Even when people were so feeble that they never misbehaved themselves there were always their thoughts trotting about in their heads doing the things that their owners dare not do. And if there were people with no lascivious thoughts, those people were the same as dead, and thus beneath contempt.

I was happy when I was dressed up. I knew what I wanted. Many people became so confused through telling each other lies that they did not know what they wanted.

And yet, if I could get onto the other side, I would live happily with inhibitions in me because they would be the inhibitions of a woman. I wanted to be one of them. I did not want to stand apart and see them as fools, I wanted to be foolish with them. I wanted to suffer everything that they suffered. I wanted to be limited and mistaken. I wanted to be part of the world that was wrong instead of being shut in with my meaningless mathematics of thoughts that were right. A woman's body was a better place to live in than a man's brain. All real stuff was woman stuff. Mother and daughter and mother and daughter were one flesh going back and back in time to the female stomach creatures that needed no male. The male was outside. He might master the world, but he was not part of the world. When the sadist tortured the bound woman his cruelty was his anger that he was not the woman. She might have pleasure in pain, she might be bound and helpless, but she was still the woman, the centre. Her helplessness emphasised the truth that she did not need to act in order to exist. A man might make his gentlest love to a woman and serve her powerfully and well, and in the moment of the orgasm he might feel that they were one. But two had not become one. The moment was gone, and he knew that it had been an illusion. He knew that he was still outside, still not a woman.

I felt pity for men.

Mrs Wilson was most jolly when the shop was most busy. She jollied me. 'Come on, Roy. We want some more chips. What are you thinking of?'

Some of the customers would know that I had been in a mental hospital. I could dismiss them easily. There could be hope of a cure for a mental illness, but for stupidity there was no cure.

My father had to go to fetch some more trays of fish. I went to look after the fish pan while he was away. I battered fish and dropped them in. They bobbed up in the fat, frying and bubbling. Frying fish was more entertaining than frying chips. With fish one felt that one was cooking. Chips were just a process.

After a quarter-past twelve the queue had disappeared and by half-past twelve the shop was empty. My father closed the shop door and we took fish and chips for ourselves. Mrs Wilson always had her dinner with us after a dinner time opening.

In the afternoon I cleaned down the pans and swept and tidied the shop while my father was cutting the fish for the evening opening.

Friday evenings usually began quietly. Many people in the district had had enough fish-and-chips at dinner. Sometimes my father would say that it was hardly worth the gas and electricity to open on a Friday night. But after the pubs had closed it was as busy as a Saturday night. Then talkative men would arrive flushed with beer. Just before the pubs closed on a Friday night there was a period of about a hour in which there were hardly any customers at all. We would stand about in our white coats. My father would tell about the war, and

Mrs Wilson had stories about her girlhood that wandered on and gave the impression that she had been a girl for about a hundred years.

I settled down to be as I had been before. I did my work with that useless conscientiousness of people like me, as though I thought that, if I behaved myself extremely well, in the end I might be allowed to be a woman. On Tuesdays and Thursdays I dressed up, and all the time I was fixed up underneath. I hoped that the physical pretence might lead to real physical changes. Almost every night I inspected my chest to see if anything was happening, and often I persuaded myself that there were signs of the beginning of an alteration. But, when I was honest, I could see that nothing was happening. The real changes that would come would be changes that I did not want. My beard would grow stronger and my shoulders would begin to spread. I supposed that what successful transvestites reported about changes that had taken place before treatment began were lies told to make themselves more acceptable.

6

A card came from Dr Strickland. I could go to see him at the Wilberforce Hospital. I tore the card up. I could think anything that he could think. And thinking was no use.

7

We opened on Monday nights but did not open on Monday dinner times. Monday dinner in the district was usually made of what was left of Sunday's joint.

On a Monday morning I sat down to breakfast and my father handed me a letter. It was on a large sheet of thick notepaper. The small handwriting was Shirley's.

Dear Dad, I have been meaning to come to see you but I have not been able to get round to it what with one thing and another. I have sat down to write because there is something that you ought to know about. I did not know whether to tell you at first, but I have come to the conclusion that I must tell you. It is that Roy came round here on the day he was discharged from hospital and stole some of my clothes. I was very much surprised because he told me that he was better. It would seem that they were not really able to help him at the hospital.

I don't know what ought to be done, but obviously this sort of thing mustn't be allowed to go on. Please don't lose your temper with Roy. We ought to feel sorry for him rather than be angry with him. I am worried because I feel if he does not stop this sort of thing he will get into all sorts of trouble and perhaps end up by ruining his life. I don't really know what we can do, but we must find a way of getting him away from his strange ideas. I thought you ought to know. Please don't be angry with him. I'm sure he can't help what he does. It is an illness that he is suffering from. Perhaps he could be taken to a really good psychiatrist. It might mean a lot of expense, but I think we must do all we can to help him.

A few days after he had been here he sent me some money. I expect he must have had some idea of stopping me telling you what he had done. I enclose the money with this letter. Please give it back to him.

'I know that he has had the illness he is suffering from for a very long time, and it may be difficult for him to be cured, but we must do all we can. I do not believe that Roy is bad at all. He just has an obsession about wanting to be a woman. It may have something to do with his mother dying. Please don't be angry with him. I am sure that nobody would be like he is if they could help it.

Your loving daughter Shirley

My father was angry. His eyes were bright. I could tell that he would lose his temper. I was frightened.

'Where have you hidden Shirley's things?' he asked very quietly.

I sat silent. I did not want to give up my new things.

'Where have you got them?' His voice was louder.

'I threw them away.'

'You're a bloody little liar! You'll come upstairs with me

and take your clothes off. Mrs Wilson noticed your back last week, but I wouldn't believe her. She said she thought you were wearing a brassière. Come upstairs and take your clothes off.'

'I won't.'

'Then you are wearing women's things underneath.'

'Yes.' I was in a state of disorganization and truthfulness.

'You balmy little bugger! I've heard about people like you, but God knows I never thought I'd rear one! Get upstairs and get those things off. Are they Shirley's things?'

'No.'

'So you've been pinching some other stuff. Where did you get it from?'

'They are Shirley's things, but I've had them a long time. I got them when she was at home.'

'Daft bugger! Where have you put the things you've just pinched from Shirley's?'

I did not answer.

'Where are they? I'll smash your bloody face in—'

'In the attic.'

'Whereabouts in the attic?'

I was silent again. I had my head down. I was staring at the table cloth.

His voice was quieter. 'You're round the bloody bend. That's your trouble. You're balmy. If you were a kid I could understand it, but you'll be twenty-one before very long. Have you no bloody pride in yourself? You want to get yourself to London if you're a bloody pansy. They're all bloody pansies down there. There's pubs in Hull where there are people like you. I'll take you if you like. You can get some bloody dirty old man to muck about with you. You disgusting bugger! You look like a big tart sat there. It makes me feel sick to look at you. You'll finish up going after little lads. You haven't been doing owt like that, have you?'

'No. I'd never do that.'

'By God, if you did, I'd kill you with my own hands! That I should have a bugger like you for a son! You'll either pull yourself together or you'll get out of this house. If you go on like you are doing, you're no son of mine. You can get to hell out of it! How do you think I felt when that woman came round here and said that you'd been at her washing?

71

By God, I clouted you, and I did right! I don't care what our Shirley says, a bloody good hiding wouldn't do you any harm at all. You need some sense knocking into you. And for God's sake hold your head up and try to look like a man even if you aren't one!'

I raised my eyes and fixed on the wall behind his head without seeing. It had become as though he were talking to someone else. I had shut myself in. If he had punched me in the face, it would not have hurt me very much.

Suddenly he changed to kindness: 'Look here, Roy, we'll have to do what we can about this rotten business. I want to know where you've got those things hidden in the attic. We'll have to get rid of them. The things you got from Shirley's will have to go back. You can make a parcel of them and post it. The rest of the stuff you can burn. We'll get rid of it, and then you can make a fresh start. I don't want to see you finishing up in trouble with the police—and that's what it might come to, Roy. We'll get rid of that stuff this morning. And after dinner we'll go to Dr Booth and see what he can do. I'll come with you, and we'll see if we can't get some sense out of him. We'll have to see what's to be done. I'm giving you one more chance. But this is your last chance. Now go upstairs and take off anything you've got on underneath and come down and have your breakfast. Then we'll get things sorted out.'

His kindness made it possible for me to think. I was thinking that what was happening to me could not happen to Shirley.

I said, 'It's no good.'

'What do you mean, it's no good?'

'It's no good.'

'Don't be a bloody fool. You've got to pull yourself together.'

'I'd pull myself together if I could. I can't.'

'Don't talk like a pansy.'

'I'm not, I'm just telling the truth.'

'I don't want to hear it.'

'Then what's the use?'

'You'll just have to pull yourself together. If the doctor knows of anybody who can do anything for you, I'll pay the bill. I'll have you cured no matter what it costs.'

'I can't be cured.'

72

'Don't talk tripe.'

'It isn't tripe. There are people like me, and they can't be cured.'

'They can if they want to be. A man can do anything he wants to do.'

'I —'

'A man can do anything—if he is a man. How do you think I felt sometimes in the war? I'll tell you. I was damn near shitting myself. But I had to get on. That's what you'll have to do.'

'I don't know how to try.'

'Don't talk tripe. What the hell do you think you're going to do? Do you reckon you want to finish up like one of those mucky buggers that change sex?'

'Yes.'

'You balmy little bugger!'

'I'm only telling you the truth.'

'What sort of truth is that? What the hell on earth is the world coming to? If you were really crackers, I could understand. But it's just this one balmy idea you've got hold of. We're having no more Sunday papers in this house! Did they teach you this stuff at the grammar school? It's a bloody good job you didn't stay there! You should have been working when you were fourteen, like I was. That's what you want, some damned hard work. You get it too soft here. I bring you up and give you everything you want, and how do you repay me? Pinching women's knickers! You filthy little bugger! You bloody louse! You bloody well ought to be a woman. You look like a big, stupid lass sat there. You filthy bugger! The Germans used to stick people like you in concentration camps. They used to gas buggers like you. Do you know you can go to prison for reckoning to be a woman? That's where you'll finish up. They'll have you inside.' Then suddenly he became lyrical. 'You've got to be a man. It doesn't matter whether you're rich or poor, if you're a man, you've got something to be proud of. You've got to stand up like a man and take what's coming in this world.'

Being a man never sounded pleasant. The expression 'Be a man' was always used in connection with something painful or disappointing.

He went on, 'It's all right men dressing up as women for a

73

bit of fun. There's a time for everything. Men get dressed up as women in pantomimes. It's just for a laugh. There's no harm in it. But people who want to dress up as women all the time are touched in the head. They're sex mad. You want to get yourself out and find some lass. I'd rather you got some lass into trouble than messed about dressing yourself up. In fact, I'd be pleased if you did put some lass in the family way. At least it would show that you were all right. Don't you like lasses?'

'Yes.'

'Then why don't you get after one? You'd have a hell of a sight more fun getting up some lass's skirt than messing about like a ninney. You want to get out and see what you can do.'

'I don't like them like that,' I explained.

He exploded. He started on me again. It seemed as though he were trying to beat me to the floor with his words.

I heard him, and I believed him. I was filthy. Women, with their white, sluggish bodies and painted faces, were filthy. For a man to want to be a woman was a filthy desire. There was the stink of the grave in it. It was a desire for death. The male was the sun, the father star, the skilful hunter, the staunch warrier. The female was the moon, the satellite, the hand to get what it had not killed, the accommodating slave.

As my father punished me with his words I loved him.

It was not until I went upstairs to take off the things I had underneath that I started crying. My eyes were full of tears, and it was difficult for me to see what I was doing. I told myself that it would be impossible for me to unfix myself. It always took a long time to get it all off. And I wanted to keep it as it was.

When I went down again and he saw my eyes he said, 'For God's sake pull yourself together. Have you taken those things off?'

I told him that I had.

'Right, you can have your breakfast. Then we'll get all that stuff burnt. For God's sake stop bluthering!'

I said that I did not want anything to eat.

'You'll eat your bloody breakfast if I have to ram it down your throat!'

It was difficult to swallow.

After I had eaten what I could he said, 'Come on, you'll show me where that stuff is.'

74

At the foot of the stairs he put his hand on my shoulder and took hold of my sweater like a policeman making an arrest. He held on all the way up the stairs, coming up behind me, so that I felt that he might pull me over backwards. It seemed ridiculous.

The knickers and the brassière that I had taken off were lying on the floor in my bedroom. My face felt very hot.

He said, 'Pick those up.' He let go of me.

I picked them up.

He said, 'Come on, we'll go up to the attic.'

I went up first and he followed me.

When we got to the landing he said, 'Where are they?'

I motioned to the back attic.

He pushed me in. 'Whereabouts?'

I said, 'I don't want to tell you.'

He hit me across the face with the flat of his hand. It made a sharp crack. I thought that he had broken my cheekbone. I shut my eyes and put my head against the wall. He hit me very hard at the back of the head. It was just as it had been before.

He got hold of my sweater at the neck and pulled me away from the wall. 'Do you want any more?' he asked very quietly.

I said, 'No.'

There was a jumping sensation in my face.

He let me go and I went across and opened the cupboard door. I got down. But I could not raise the floorboard because I could not see what I was doing and I could not get a hold with my finger nails.

'They're under here,' I said, 'but I can't get the board out.'

'I'll count ten, and if you haven't got it out, I'll kick your bloody face right in.' He started counting.

In a panic I got my nails on the end of the board and got it up. I lifted the pillow-case out.

'Good God!' he exclaimed, 'how much stuff have you got in there? You balmy little bugger!' He came and looked into the space under the floor. 'What's this! Women's magazines. You poor creep!' He pushed the pillow-case with his foot. 'Are our Shirley's things in there?'

'Yes.'

'You'd better get them out, and then we'll take the rest of

the stuff downstairs and get rid of it. Let's have a look what there is.'

I started to try to untie the string at the neck of the pillow case. I could not untie it. I had to pull it off the end. I began getting the things out.

Amongst the things I brought out there was a sanitary towel. When it came out my father said, 'Stand up straight.'

I straightened up.

His hand came up before I saw it and struck my face. I stumbled sideways and went down on my knees. I was stunned. I heard my voice saying simply, 'Don't hit me again. I don't want you to hit me again.' It sounded as though I were weak-minded. I looked up at him.

Our eyes met.

He said, 'Get up, you gutless little bugger.'

I took the clothes and the magazines and the newspaper cuttings and put them in the fireplace in the kitchen. My father had the two expensive lipsticks in his hand. He put them on the floor and stamped on them until they were flattened. Some of the lipstick was squeezed out of the black and gold one that had cost me thirty-five shillings. He picked them up and threw them on top of the pile of clothes and papers that filled the fireplace. Then he brought a can and poured out paraffin. He struck a match and set my things alight. They burned quickly. The flames made a roaring sound in the chimney. He stood watching the blaze with his head tilted on one side like a man who has made a satisfactory solution to a problem. When the fire was dying down and my things were gone he told me to wash my face.

I washed myself at the kitchen sink. I said to myself, 'He doesn't know that I'm fixed up.'

After I had washed myself I made a parcel of the things I had stolen from Shirley and addressed it. While I was doing it I felt I hated Shirley. Everything seemed so perfectly unjust.

By the time we set off to see Dr Booth in the afternoon my face was no longer red, but it was still rather swollen. We walked along in silence. I was worried that my father might ask Dr Booth to give me a medical examination. We sat in the waiting room side by side in silence. I felt like laughing. My father's face was set with determination. I thought, 'All that seriousness to crush me!' I knew that our outing was completely futile. Dr Booth would not be able to do anything, because there was not anything that anybody could do to stop me wanting what I wanted. Other patients sat round us, containing themselves, thinking about what they would say when they got into the surgery. Some of them would have self-curing ailments, but some were obviously suffering from age and misery. There might be one sickening for cancer. I thought that being a doctor and dispensing cheerfulness and confidence to all the inevitably dying must require an inborn talent for dishonesty.

I did not think about the coming interview.

I began to wonder how I could get some women's clothes to replace those that had been burnt. I decided that I would not steal anything again. I would have to get the courage to go into a shop and buy what I wanted. This led me to thinking about the things I would like to buy.

It came to our turn and we went into the surgery. Dr Booth was sitting at his desk. He was a small dark man who wrote with a rapid pen and seemed more efficient than sympathetic. I had seen him once in the city square driving a red sports car. But when he saw my face he looked sad to show that he understood what had happened and appreciated that it must have hurt.

There were only two chairs in the surgery. I had to stand. I felt like a specimen when my father began to tell about me.

At first my father had difficulty getting out the words to explain that he had discovered that I was the same as ever.

Dr Booth nodded as though nothing my father told him was surprising. Then he got out a letter. 'Dr Strickland says that Roy responded to treatment quite well.'

'I can't see that,' said my father; 'he still does it.'

'Well, actually,' said Dr Booth like a man who is about to embark on an explanation that he does not expect to be understood, 'sexual matters are very difficult. Very often there is not a lot that can be done. People come up with new ideas and new methods that are supposed to bring about cures, but, when you get to know more about them, these supposed cures often leave a lot to be desired. A human being can't really be trained like a dog. You see, it's really impossible to pin down the sexual drive. Men have been struggling with these problems for thousands of years, and there are about as many opinions as there have been men expressing opinions. You've got to remember that our sexuality begins as soon as we come alive, and for a long time at the beginning of our lives we don't know which sex we are. . . .' He told my father at length that there was nothing that could stop me wanting what I wanted.

I could see that my father was not listening. He had made up his mind and he was only waiting for Dr Booth to stop talking. I expected that, when he did say his piece, he would suggest that something drastic and painful should be done to me. I had a picture of myself having a false moustache sewn onto my top lip.

Dr Booth was saying, 'Roy might go into the theatrical business. . . .'

My father cut across him: 'That'd make him worse, if anything. It wouldn't do him any good to get to know a lot of people worse than he is.'

'Your son has his life to lead,' said Dr Booth.

'He'll live it like a man or he'll not live it at all,' boomed my father.

I wondered if my father's statement sounded dramatic to Dr Booth. It seemed not. Perhaps, as a doctor, he was case-hardened to rhetoric.

They argued, but in the end, despite his efforts to impose his working-class-noble view of human nature, my father understood that Dr Booth thought that I was as I was.

I felt joyous. I had heard it admitted that I was myself. I would always want to be a woman. I was a real transvestite. There had sometimes been the fear that I might be merely a sneaking fetishist like everybody else.

When we got outside in the street my father said to me, 'They all know you're no bloody good.'

I thought, 'I'll dress up whenever I can. And if I ever have enough money I'll have treatment. I know who I am. He might just as well try to stop Shirley wanting to dress as a woman. He ought to go and hit her in the face for wearing women's clothes.'

When we were nearly home my father repeated himself, 'They all know you're no bloody good.'

We spoke only a few words during the rest of that day.

78

8

That night when I lay in bed I cried because of my things being burnt. Then I started thinking that it was nice to be able to cry, and I felt better.

I thought I should leave home. If I did not, my father might end by killing me.

I would wait until I was twenty-one, and then I would get the money my mother had left for me, and I would be able to go away and try to live as a woman. People had done it before. I could do it.

I imagined going away and somehow getting enough money to have treatment and then coming back home. It was pleasant to think about that. I pictured myself coming into the house very well dressed and very pretty. I would be his daughter. He would be amazed when he saw how lovely and how delicate I was. The pictures were very clear. They made me glow. But then they stopped.

I did not want to go down to London. London was full of homosexuals. And I did not want to go on the stage. Everything would be made cheap on the stage. I wanted to feel that I was a real woman. There was need for formality. Without formality one knew that one was only pretending. That was why it was necessary to be dressed correctly in detail when one was dressed as a woman. If one left one's back suspenders unfastened, one started thinking. I must be conservative because women were conservative.

I could get into reality.

9

On the following morning my father came into my bedroom and woke me. He had never done that before. If I overslept, he called me from the bottom of the stairs. But that morning he was standing over me when I opened my eyes.

He said, 'I'm going to watch you get up and get dressed to see you don't put anything on. I'm going to do it every morning.'

I was afraid. I could not think what to do. I must not let him see that I was fixed up. I said. 'I've got nothing to put on.'

'I'm going to watch you just the same.'

I said, 'Then I won't get up.'

'I'll have you out of there,' he shouted. He took hold of the bed clothes.

The horrible thought came into my mind that he was sexually interested in me. I shut it out. I could not think what to do. 'Leave me alone,' I wailed. 'You'll kill me if you don't leave me alone.'

'I will bloody well kill you, and I'll be well shot!' He wrenched at the covers.

I held them down as best I could.

'You're not bloody well dressed up under there, are you?' he demanded.

'No.'

'Well, get out.'

I slid my legs out on the far side from him and sat up. I unfastened my pyjama jacket and took it off. Soon he would see that I was fixed up. I wished that I had not made myself look so real. He would get more excited. He might keep hitting me until he killed me. I sat on the edge of the bed quite still. I decided that I would not take my pyjama trousers off. I would just sit there, and he could do what he liked. I looked at the wall and stopped thinking.

Then I heard him going downstairs. It was over. I did not know why he had relented. Perhaps I looked as frail and helpless as I felt, and he had pitied me.

At breakfast he seemed to want to be kind. As we were finishing he said, 'I don't suppose you can help it, you poor bugger.'

It was Tuesday.

After dinner he said, 'I want your keys.'

I asked him why.

'I'm going to lock you out of the house when I go. You can take yourself off to the pictures or somewhere, but you're not staying in here.'

When it was time for him to go he took me out the back door with him and locked it. 'You can go where you like,' he said, 'but don't come back here until after eleven tonight.'

80

I wandered to the city centre.

There were crowds of women. They could go into any shop and buy what they wanted. Here were shops full of women's clothes, dress shops, shoe shops, hat shops, shops where cheap but pretty frocks hung in parties, stores where dresses hung in regiments. There were shoes and coats and skirts and night-dresses and slips and bras and panties and girdles and belts and stockings and blouses and gloves and suits. There were fur coats. There was silk and chiffon and satin and cotton and nylon and wool and linen and poplin and suede and ribbon and lace. None of it was for me.

I went into a coffee bar and sat over a milk shake. In the sunshine the women were passing; young women in high-heels, complete and self-loving; older women going about the pleasure of looking after their families so as to get the most love for themselves; all intent on happiness either through pride or self-sacrifice, their skirts moving as they walked, swinging or creasing to and fro, confident in their superiority or cunningly humble. I played a game in which I tried to pick out girls who could be boys dressed up.

I left the coffee bar and walked to the city square. Opposite the Civic Hall there was a pigeon-whitened Queen Victoria standing on top of public lavatories. I always thought that the Civic Hall looked like a cinema where nothing but epics about the Roman Empire were shown. There was the tomb-like art gallery. But dominating all was the Dock Offices building, a work of imagination in the Italian style with domed turrets and high, rounded windows. To look at it one might have supposed that Hull was a Mediterranean city that had sent ships to fight at Lepanto. On the same side as the art gallery there was a long railing through which one could see part of the Albert Dock. There were two big trawlers moored side by side, fitting out, garnish with patches of orange paint.

I went round behind the Dock Offices and into Queens Gardens. The gardens had once been Queens Dock, but the dock had been filled in. There were paths and pools with cultivated reeds and there were fountains playing. At the far end of the gardens was the massive block of the new technical college with the Wilberforce Column in front of it. I remembered that William Wilberforce was a drug addict. I was a drag addict. Along the side of the gardens was the central police station.

81

It was a rather temporary looking piece of modern-shoddy work. One felt that a violent drunk might knock it all down while he was being got inside. I hoped they would never get me inside.

The old buildings enclosing the gardens had once been dock-side warehouses. Some of them had been turned into shops or offices, but most of them had remained as warehouses, but now they were filled with the attractive things that were sold in the shops. Perhaps one of them was full of nylon stockings.

Hundreds of men had worked at digging the dock. Then men had worked hard, year in year out, unloading cargoes. Then hundreds of men had worked to fill in the dock. Now there were gardens with flowers and fountains, and a young woman might walk there with the pleasure of being herself.

I sat for some time watching a fountain.

When a patrolling policeman looked at me I got up and started walking.

I reached the river. The Humber was sliding along with a fast ebb tide. Some big ships were anchored down river. The Lincolnshire side looked very green. Down at Saltend the oil storage tanks were shining in the sun. It was all as it was expected to be.

I thought about throwing myself in.

I supposed many people thought of it. Occasionally people actually did it.

The summer was ending.

I had my tea at the café in Hammond's store opposite the railway station and then I went to the pictures.

When I got back home I had to stand in the back yard for about half-a-hour waiting for my father.

He was cheerful when he arrived. 'What sort of time have you had?'

'All right.'

'Anyway, it got you out a bit.'

On the Thursday it rained. I went to the reference room of the public library and looked up everything there was about Sporus/Sabina. Then I studied a book on anatomy that I had often studied before. I considered how much fat there was on the female: fat at the back of the neck, fat behind the deltoid muscle, fat on the flanks, gluteal fat, sub trochanteric accumulation of fat, fat of breast, fat of abdomen, collection of fat in front of pubis, fat on the fronts of the thighs. The rain streamed down the windows. I looked at the collected poetical works of Housman. The pane was blind with showers.

He continued to lock me out of the house on Tuesdays and Thursdays.

Sometimes while we were doing the potatoes he would talk in an attempt to persuade me of the advantages of manliness. He told me how he had once solved a difficult problem by the use of his fists when he had been a young man. He spoke about the intricacies of cricket and the excitements of football. All that he said reinforced my view that I would make a poor man. I wanted to tell him that I did not doubt that the male was stronger and faster and more intelligent and more intense than the female—but I knew what I wanted.

I would have to leave home. We could not go on living together. There was no reason why he should have to endure me. I was not a son. His efforts to change my mind embarrassed me. I felt that I was humiliating him. I felt as a mongol child might feel if it knew that it was a mongol child.

Once I saw him put his hand to his forehead with a movement that suggested despair.

On the morning of my twenty-first birthday he called upstairs, 'Many happy returns of the day, Roy!'

I hated myself. I felt ill with unhappiness.

When I got downstairs he said it again: 'Many happy returns of the day.' He smiled as well as he could. It seemed like the smile of a man greeting a Martian to whom he was determined to show a friendly face despite the Martian's repulsive strangeness.

On the table next to my plate was a small rectangular box. It was a wrist watch.

He said, 'Go on, open it.'

I opened the box. There was a slim gold watch. I thought that it must have cost about fifty pounds.

He said, 'My father bought me a gold watch for my twentyfirst. Many happy returns. You're a man now.'

I put my elbows on the table and pushed my face into my hands.

I heard him ask me what was the matter. I did not answer.

Then I told myself that I must behave myself decently no

matter what I felt like. I took my hands away.

He was looking out of the window gloomily.

I thanked him for the watch and said that I would save it for best.

He was encouraged. 'I bet there isn't a better watch in Hull than that you've got there. It's shock-proof and water-proof. It's not gold-plated. It's gold metal right through. It's a self-winder y'know. You don't have to wind it up. It winds itself up when you move your arm. It's absolutely water-proof. The man said that it was so well made that you could wear it in the bath.'

'I'll save it for wearing in the bath,' I said.

The joke pleased him.

He was in good spirits while we were working that morning. He told his favourite war story about how he had taken a prisoner: '. . . so we crept along this hedge, dead quiet. And there was this young lad sat there. He was just sat in this slit trench. And he had this bit of stick in his hand and he was drawing on the side. He was just sat there drawing with this bit of stick. So we just reached in and grabbed him and pulled him out. God, was he surprised! It was the shock of his life. He wondered what the hell had happened to him. Then he started yelling his head off in German. So I just stuck my sten gun in his ribs, and he went as quiet as a lamb. He was a Panzer Grenadier. He had one of those black, double-breasted jackets. And then we found this tin in the trench with holes punched in the lid. And inside there was a little mouse. He'd been feeding it with bits of bread. We didn't half laugh. But he starts near begging for us to give him this mouse. So we gives him it. And he puts it in his tunic pocket real careful. I reckon he'd been in the line too long and he was going a bit balmy. I reckon all Germans are a bit balmy. They must have been. Anyway, after Caen, we just went forward smashing everything.'

Mrs Wilson came at tea time bearing a birthday cake that she had made. It was iced in white with twenty-one in pink icing on the top. I had a desire to run out of the house.

While the tea party was going on I started laughing and got a piece of cake stuck in my throat. My father slapped me on the back and I recovered. They asked me what I had been laughing at. I said I did not know. I felt I needed to wear

84

women's clothes very much.

My father said, 'When you're twenty-one you have to have the key of the door.' He gave me back the keys he had taken from me. He said, 'Now that you're a man I have to trust you, Roy. I'm sure that you won't ever let me down.'

Mrs Wilson said, 'I'm sure he won't.'

I told myself that I must get away from these people before they ate me like they were eating the cake.

Mrs Wilson asked me what I would be doing with my mother's money that I would be receiving.

I said that I did not know.

'Five hundred pounds is a lot of money,' she said. 'You must use it sensibly.'

I said that I would use it sensibly.

I told myself that I would use it to go away and live as a woman.

10

A drunk came into the shop one night just before we were going to close. He was a big, beery-looking man of about fifty with a grubby collar and a tie that had got pushed to the side. He leaned on the counter, his eyes watery, and said to my father, 'Hey, is it right?'

My father turned from the fish pan. 'Is what right?'

'Is it right that your lad there has to sit down to let go of his maiden's water?'

11

Mrs Ford gave the impression of being extremely materialistic. She was about fifty. She was slim and her hair was dyed black and lacquered so that it looked rather Japanese. She wore spectacles with heavy black frames and smoked one cigarette after another with her painted lips. Her femininity depended on making money from her lodgers. She needed money to buy smart clothes. Her clothes had to be more expensive than those that would suit a girl. I thought that I would like to be something like Mrs Ford when I was fifty. She seemed compact and unsentimental—though when I arrived a dog barked hysterically. It was an old terrier on stiff legs.

The boarding house was on Beverley Road, a main road that ran to the centre of the city. Sections of it looked prosperous and other sections were delapidated. There were chapels, dance halls, hostels, shops, cafés, boarding houses, bowling alleys, fish-and-chip shops, churches, cinemas, laundrettes, pubs, trade union offices, coffee bars, second-hand motor dealers, men carrying ladders, women pushing prams, unemployed men walking purposefully, heavy lorries shaking the ground, cars, buses, trolley buses, girls on scooters, leather-bound youths on motor-cycles.

It was an old house, a unit in a block of tall, well-built properties. There had been gardens at the front but they had been concreted over and cars were standing where once there had been respectable flower beds. It seemed to be a place where people would be too busy to take any notice of me. Once the house might have been ruled by a sound father, patriotic but liberal, provident but generous. Now it was amoral—or seemed so. The walls in the hallway and up the stairs were painted grey. When I saw them I was reassured. It seemed a house for strangers to live in. Parcels could arrive and nobody would ask what they contained. Strangers allowed freedom. When Mrs Wilson had brought the birthday cake the feeling that I would be helped to pretend that I was a likeable person had been almost unbearable. The kindness made me feel too ashamed.

Mrs Ford told me that dinner was at six o'clock. I had come to a place where dinner was not the main meal in the middle of the day. Surely, I thought, in this place people would not expect to know all about each other.

She showed me a room at the front of the house on the second floor. It was simple and clean. The single bed had been made up geometrically and firmly so that it looked as though it had never been slept in. By the bed was a small table with a bedside lamp on it. The lampshade was of an oatmeal colour decorated with large interlocking circles of red and black.

There was a plain oak wardrobe and a plain oak chest of drawers and a modern easy chair with wooden arms. It was an easy chair to sit in but not to go to sleep in.

The room would do until I was ready to leave the house.

As soon as Mrs Ford left me alone I went to the wardrobe to find out whether there was a mirror on the inside of the door.

It was a long mirror. I could manage to see myself full-length in it.

A small picture hung on the wall. I examined it. It was a reproduction of a painting of a waterfront. There were no figures, just ornate white buildings and a promenade and the blue sea. The scene appeared to be under oppressive heat. I decided that it must be siesta time and everybody was indoors. Inside, the men were sitting about in white suits, drinking whiskey and arguing about politics. They were sweating and working up nasty tempers. Upstairs, in a cool bedroom, a girl, tall and dark with dark eyes, cool in a midnight blue negligee, was lying on a couch upholstered with dove grey silk, thinking dreamily about clothes and sipping a cool green drink from a tall glass. In the afternoon the promenade would be thronged with people. The girl would put on a red bikini and swim in the sea with other rich and beautiful girls. The men in the white suits would watch slyly from the sea wall and use carnal words to one another to pretend that they liked being ugly. But the girls would be swimming superbly in the sea, happy and pretending to be unconscious of being seen. The men could do nothing but think, trousered and congested with viciousness.

I had a plan.

I was going towards the morning when I would walk on the pavements in high-heels. Then I would have broken through and escaped. It was impossible to know how long I would be able to go on living as a woman. In the end I might be caught and punished. But for a time I would have a holiday. I had not enough money to have treatment so that I could escape forever, but I had enough money for an outing that I would be able to remember whatever was done to me or however old I might become. After I had done what I wanted to do no punishment could change it. Not all the policemen in the country could break into the past. No magistrate, however pompously indignant, could make a court order to stop what

87

had already happened. No stupidity or dishonesty would be able to touch what I remembered. Sabina had been Empress of Rome, and the miserable Christians who came after could not alter that with all their lies.

I hoped that I would not be caught on the day that I set out.

12

Dinner was served in the front room downstairs. The boarders called it tea.

I sat at a table with two worn, middle-aged, clerkly men and a young man who had wavy fair hair that I hated. He had two pens and a propelling pencil in his top pocket. The middle-aged man opposite me kept pushing against the front of his top set of false teeth with his index finger as though to fix them further up into his head. The middle-aged man next to me had a folded copy of the Hull Daily Mail in his jacket pocket.

At the other table in the room there were two middle-aged men and a gaunt, self-satisfied man of about thirty. I did not like him.

The young man with the wavy fair hair asked me my name.

'Brian,' I said, 'Brian Wilson.'

'My name's Peter,' he told me. 'You'll know me because I'm always cheerful.'

Mrs Ford came in and leant on the back of the gaunt, self-satisfied man's chair.

'What did they say to you at the City Hall?' she asked him.

'They said I'd have to wait for at least three weeks.'

'That's a nuisance.'

'I'm not going to bother.'

'You men,' said Mrs Ford, 'you're all the same. If you aren't suited, you go into a sulk straight away.'

I realised that Mrs Ford was very fond of men. I altered my opinion of her.

She rested on the back of the self-satisfied man's chair as he sat forward over his meal. The way she held herself made me think of a she-cat putting itself up against a tom-cat. As soon as the tom-cat took notice she ought to walk away.

The self-satisfied man was serious with his rice pudding.

'You're a strange lad, Jack,' she said in an attempt to get his attention.

I wished that she would stop.

'I'm not as strange as some,' said Jack preoccupied with the pudding. 'There's bits of soot in this rice.'

'There are not.' She straightened up, the scandalised woman of the house. 'I'm sure there's no soot in it. Are there any bits of soot in your rice pudding, Mr Dixon?'

Mr Dixon peered up at her through pebble lenses and said if there were any bits of soot he had not seen them.

'I wasn't complaining about Mr Dixon's pudding,' said Jack sarcastically, 'I was complaining about my pudding.'

There was an inspection that ended with Mrs Ford exclaiming, 'One little speck! You men, you're all the same.' Then she said, 'Give me a cigarette, Jack.'

Without looking up he said, 'You can smoke your own. You're always after my cigarettes.'

She tossed her head and went out of the room.

I would not have behaved as she had behaved. I did not think that Jack was attractive at all. She was a smart woman—even if her hair was somewhat overdone. She probably had some very nice clothes. I would not have allowed myself to be humiliated by the self-satisfied Jack.

Peter with the wavy hair continued to be friendly. He told me that he was a clerk at a firm of timber importers: 'Everything has to be checked and double checked.' He was a clown. I wondered how a woman could make do with such a man. But many women had to have such men. Many women had to make do with men like the middle-aged men in the room. It was impossible to imagine getting into bed with any of them.

Then it occurred to me that nobody was getting into bed with them. They were living in a boarding house.

13

That night Peter took me to a bowling hall. Young men were mincing in soft shoes and putting down big balls along the tracks at the crowded skittles. They would hop on one foot as though they were professional sportsmen anxious to win prizes of thousands of pounds. There were some girls bowling. They seemed more sensible, they did not do so much posing. Pop music came out of a loudspeaker and howled round the hall.

Peter showed me how to bowl. He took hold of my hand and put my fingers in the holes in the ball. At first I was frightened that they might get caught and broken as I released the ball.

After some attempts I got the ball to go almost in the middle of the track and knock all the pins down. I decided that bowling was a sport that flattered people of negligible dexterity and no athletic endowment into thinking themselves games players.

Several times Peter asked me what I thought about different girls in the hall. Other young men would have talked of failure or success with girls and so made a connection, but Peter only asked for my opinion. When I had a conversation with the girl in the next alley he became very interested in wiping his hands with his handkerchief.

We bowled for some time, and then he took me to a part of the building that was a café and bought me a cup of coffee.

He talked about the injustices and jealousies in the office where he worked. There was a woman at the office whom he particularly disliked. From what he told me I understood that she was efficient and neurotic and regarded him as uncouth and unreliable.

He did not seem uncouth to me. Probably he was unreliable. His best characteristic seemed to be an indefinite enthusiasm. It was as though he felt that something wonderful might possibly happen but had no idea what or when.

I thought that some empty-headed girl might find him bearable. I was sure that I would not like to have him for a boy friend. He had wavy hair and a shiney nose and he was a fool. I thought that a person as silly as he was might have been better as a girl. But he could not have been made into a girl. He was one of the negative intersexes. He had neither the presence of a man nor the appearance of a woman. There were so many of them that they went unremarked.

I felt sorry for him.

90

He became sad on the way back to the boarding house. He put his hand on my shoulder and told me about some trouble he had had with his step-father.

14

I lay in a strange bed. It was harder and much narrower than the bed I had got out of that morning.

Tomorrow I would start making preparations. I would have to buy a foam rubber cushion to make breasts. It would be possible to buy a false bust, but I could not be sure that it would be right for me. I must start thinking about my voice. And I must start thinking about my walk.

Mrs Ford turned out to be different from what I had first thought. She seemed foolish when she kept saying, 'You men are all the same.' I had not suspected that she could be like that when I had first seen her.

I wondered what I would look like in thick-framed spectacles.

Mrs Ford's behaviour at tea-time had shown how stupid a lack of self-confidence could make people. I supposed she got affection from the stiff-legged terrier dog, but she wanted Jack to show her that she was still a woman. I hated Jack. Or perhaps Mrs Ford wanted a man very much, not to prove anything, but to hurt her. I supposed that, if one had a woman's body, one could want a man very much—one could want and want and want. When one wanted something from another person one was most vulnerable. One could easily be driven to stupidity.

If Mrs Ford wanted to be hurt, I forgave her with all my heart. She had a right to be foolish. A woman was a woman.

And I forgave her if all she wanted was evidence that she was still attractive. When I started to live as a woman I would want evidence as soon as possible that I was attractive.

I was attractive as I was—but not to real men, only to queers —and poor old Jim.

I hoped that Peter would not bother me too much.

15

In the days that followed I observed that Mrs Ford was continually humiliated by Jack. It became a bore. And from what the middle-aged men said I gathered that he had been going to her room regularly for almost two years.

I got a catalogue. Looking through it made me very excited. There were women's clothes of every kind, and now I could get them for myself. My hands shook. I kept seeing things that I thought I would like to wear. On one page there was a three-quarter length evening dress in cherry red shantung with a large fold-over bow at the hip. I wanted it. There was a grey-blue jersey suit. I wanted it. There was a blue slip with black lace. I wanted it. There was a belted raincoat that I wanted and a topless bra that I wanted and an ankle-length dress in red and white that I wanted and a choir-boy jacket that I wanted and a tweed coat with big pockets that I wanted . . .

I stopped myself. A topless bra would not be any use to me. I told myself coldly that I must only order what I would need to make the break-through. I did not want to have a lot of stuff to carry with me when I left the house. And it would be much more enjoyable to buy things from shops as a woman than to pick things from a catalogue as a boy.

In the catalogue it said, 'Hold tape snug but not tight when measuring.'

I was busy and interested and happy in my room, making lists and measuring myself with a tape measure and filling in the order form.

I ordered a black skirt, a pair of black slacks, two blouses and two pairs of shoes—one pair had flat heels for wearing with the slacks and the other pair were high-heeled court shoes—two brassières, a suspender belt, two slip and pantie sets, two pairs of briefs for wearing under the slacks, two nightdresses—one black and one red—and four pairs of nylons. I had difficulty in choosing a coat. Finally I decided that the belted black raincoat that I had liked would cover me well enough in most weather.

That was enough.

I thought of crossing out the slacks. Another skirt would

be better. But I decided to leave it so as to keep the order form neat.

I wrote my name on the order form: Mr B. Wilson. The people who dealt with the order would know that I was a pervert—but they would send the things because they would want to keep my money.

My only worries, I told myself, were whether the things would fit me and whether they would be of the quality that they appeared to be in the catalogue. It would be much better when I could buy things from the shops.

The next day I bought a foam rubber cushion and started making a pair of breasts. It took me three days to complete them. I did not make them too big because I would be a tall girl. I would not be heavily feminine.

I was progressing.

16

Mrs Ford began to want to know what kind of creature I was and what my employment prospects were. She embarked on friendly conversations to pump me.

It would have been bracing to tell her to mind her own business.

I told her that I had left a fish-and-chip shop home in Bridlington after an argument with my father. It was a story in which my father wanted me to remain frying chips but I wanted to go out into the world and improve myself.

She seemed satisfied with my explanation of myself, and when I made it clear that I had enough money to pay for my bed and board for any conceivable time to come she was sympathetic about my employment difficulties.

'It's all certificates nowadays. If you haven't been to college, you haven't a chance of getting a really good job. You're either in or you're out, that's what I say. My niece's boy is doing very well. He's going to be a university lecturer. He's got brains.'

Despite her smartness and her well-preserved figure, she was a vulgar defeatist. She enjoyed feeling inferior to people with 'brains', just as her grandmother might have enjoyed feeling inferior to the gentry.

My judgement was proved correct when she talked about a 'brilliant' coloured doctor. The servile kind always knew of a 'brilliant' coloured doctor somewhere.

To placate the desire in the house to see me in employment I began to go out to imaginary interviews from which I returned disappointed. Peter gave me advice and Mrs Ford found vacancies in the evening paper.

One morning while I was thought to be trying to make myself a clerk at the offices of a building company I bought myself a suitcase. It was of red leather and lined with pink and white silk. I had not intended to buy such an expensively feminine case, but when I saw it in the shop window I wanted it very much. I told the assistant that it was a present for my sister and asked her to wrap it for me. It was wrapped with difficulty, and I bore it away and got it into the house without Mrs Ford seeing it.

17

The parcels came on a morning of steady autumn drizzle. Mrs Ford called upstairs, 'There's some parcels for you, Brian.'

When I saw the four parcels I was dismayed. I had expected one big, brown, meaningless lump. These were wrapped in blue and white striped paper and the name of the order company was prominent four times. Brown gummed tape had been used to make them strong, but I thought that they looked as though they could not contain anything except women's clothes. There was a dull rattle inside the parcel that contained the shoes. It was easy to guess that it was two shoe boxes wrapped together, and I thought that it was easy to guess that the shoes inside were women's shoes.

For a moment I thought of walking out of the front door and not coming back. I avoided Mrs Ford's eyes.

I took the parcels upstairs and put them on the bed. I called myself a fool for not sending instructions that they should be put in plain covers.

But then I became calmer, and I saw that really they were not at all obvious. They were simply well-made parcels in blue and white paper strengthened with brown gummed tape. They were quite workmanlike.

Perhaps Mrs Ford would come up to find out what I had received. I got the parcels off the bed and into the wardrobe.

She knocked as I was closing the wardrobe door. 'Can I come in a minute?' she called from outside. 'I'd just like to have a look at the pillow-case I gave you yesterday. I think it's torn. I think I gave you the wrong one. Can I come in?'

I muttered, 'Gruesome bitch!' and called out, 'Yes, come in, Mrs Ford.'

She came in and went to the bed to turn the pillows over.

'What was in the parcels?' she asked, sounding more friendly than curious.

'Just some things I sent away for.'

'Some clothes?'

'Yes. A jacket and some sweaters and some shoes.'

'Aren't you going to look at them?'

'I haven't time just now. I have to go for an interview about a job.'

'Do you like sending away for things? I always think that you can't be sure you'll get what you want.'

'They seemed cheap, so I thought I'd get them.'

'What's that parcel you've got under the bed?'

She meant the suitcase.

'It's a present. I bought it for my brother. It's for his birthday. It's a case.'

'I didn't know you had a brother.'

'Yes. He lives in Cottingham. He's married.'

Mrs Ford seemed to be on the point of becoming suspicious of me. I wished that my hair would grow quickly so that I could get away. I could send for a wig—but I did not want to wear a wig. I wanted to have my own long hair.

Why had I turned Shirley into a brother?

Mrs Ford might tell her Jack about the parcels. He might understand that they contained women's clothes. He seemed perceptive enough to have identified me as the kind of person who dressed up.

It was necessary to go to the interview I had invented.

Outside the drizzle was coming down as if forever. I looked

95

down at my raincoat and thought of the raincoat that was in one of the parcels in the wardrobe. I wanted to open my parcels, but instead I had to tramp about the streets getting wet.

I thought about how thrilling it would be to open the parcels. My throat began to feel tight with anticipation. I would lock my door and spend the afternoon trying on the things, and if Mrs Ford came creeping about, I would tell her that I could not open the door. She could think what she liked.

I had lunch at a café and arrived back at the house just before half-past one.

I met Mrs Ford in the hallway.

'How did you get on at the interview?'

'They said they'd let me know.'

'I'll be out this afternoon,' she said.

I would be alone in the house. It flashed in my mind that clothing of hers would be in the house. But there was no need to think like that now. I had clothing of my own.

Clothes.

I went past her and took the stairs two at a time.

I went into my room and locked the door after me. I got the parcels from the wardrobe and put them on the bed. At first I could not break into the large, square parcel that contained the shoes. I was so excited. I took hold of one corner in my teeth and made a tear. Then I got my fingers in and tore the paper off. An account sheet slid to the floor. I got the lid off one box. There was a smell of new leather. I took out the tissue paper. There were the flat-heeled shoes, brand-new-black and mine. I took one shoe in my hand. It was lightly made and girlish. I took the other shoe out. They were my shoes. They were shoes for a girl and they belonged to me. I put them down on the bed and opened the second box and took out the tissue paper. There were the court shoes, my high-heels. They were women's shoes, my shoes, elegant black leather outside, soft grey leather inside, gold lettering stamped on the inside, hard slender heels that would click and tap on the pavement. The shapes of court shoes were civilised as the shapes of a violin were civilized. My heart seemed to be forcing itself into the base of my neck. I had to sit down on the bed.

The excitement was pounding inside me. I could not go on examining the things. I must get dressed up as quickly as possible.

I went and drew the curtains and then got out of the clothes I was wearing at comically high speed. When they lay on the floor I despised them. They kept me male. I kicked them all under the bed and out of sight.

I burst open parcels and got the things I needed.

There was a white brassière and a black brassière and a black suspender belt. The breasts I had made were hidden in my old case. I put on the black brassière and found that they fitted perfectly. I congratulated myself on my work.

I was putting on my suspender belt. I was fixed up and I had a bust, so already I looked like a woman.

One of the slip and pantie sets was black and the other was slate blue. I chose the black set. For the first time I was stepping into a pair of knickers that had no possible owner but myself. And as I cast the slip over my head I felt how luxurious it was to be putting on clothes that had never been worn before. I eased it down over my shoulders and bust. It was as tight on my body as I had wanted it to be. The black lace made me love myself. New things were heaven.

I was very careful not to catch the new stockings with my finger nails. I fastened them so expertly, quickly yet gently. I ran my hands over the stockings to feel the sheerness, and told myself that not every girl had such long legs as I had.

I was ready to put on my high-heeled shoes.

They were tight. I wished that I had a shoe horn. But then my foot was in. It was firmly held. I put on the second shoe. The fronts of my feet looked just as I had wanted them to look. Mine were women's feet in high-heeled shoes.

I stood up and walked. The tip-toe feeling made me light and feminine. The consciousness of my feet and legs delighted me. I moved with a step instead of a tread. It was a wonderful sensation.

I lifted the hem of my slip to consider my legs. The stresses caused by the new position of my feet had made improvements. It was impossible to imagine that they could ever be male legs. They were not merely props for supporting my body and moving it about. They were a dramatically important part of my personality. If a man could see them as I was seeing them, his eyes would widen.

I dropped the hem of my slip and swung round on my toe

in a spontaneous dance step. To be myself was joy. After years of wasted time, shuffling about dressed as a boy, I had come to this. I was alive in actual time, wearing my own clothes, standing on my own heels.

I would not need to worry about my walk. The heels and my own feeling about myself would make me walk properly. I told myself that, since I felt so like a woman, I could behave as a woman unconsciously. I was sure that I would not make any mistakes.

I went across and opened the wardrobe to look in the mirror. I saw that I was a tall girl in a black slip. The straps of the slip and the brassière made my shoulders look very white. I straightened the straps.

My hair was still damp from the morning's drizzle. Its shortness made me boyish, but it was getting longer. My father would have told me to get it cut. I pushed my hair forward with my hands. That made it seem more. When it was long enough and I was ready to set off I would cut it into a fringe. I wanted my hair to be about my shoulders, curled under slightly at the bottom. It would be some time before it was that long—Christmas. But it would soon be long enough for me to pass as a girl.

I wished that I had a lipstick. My lips were rather pale. I always lost colour when I dressed up. There always seemed to be less blood in my face. I was pale and gentle-looking and there was the softness in my eyes. It was as though my body ran at a lower pressure when I was dressed up. I was cool and poised. My mind was calm and limpid—and happy. I supposed that my mind gained dominance over my chemistry when I was dressed as a woman. When I began to wear women's clothes all the time my chemistry might undergo a decisive alteration. I hoped so. Surely nobody, however jealous, could expect me to dress as a boy if I developed a bust.

But there was no knowing what the police-minded might expect. They might try to force me to have plastic surgery to make me flat-chested again. The police-minded could be senselessly brutal. They were ugly and unpleasant and cruel and dishonest. They would say that I was unnatural. Yet there was seldom anything good of nature in them. Their persistent emotion was envy and their central quality was cowardice. Even that which was supposed to be their courage was a manifestation of their cowardice. They could endure because they were afraid to rebel.

Still, they were necessary. One day I might go up to a policeman as a girl and ask the way. He might say 'Madam'. That would be delicious.

I got out the black skirt. It was simple and sharp. I had picked a black skirt and black shoes and black raincoat because I did not want brightly coloured clothes that would make me conspicuous. I could buy flashy clothes after I had gained confidence. Black was a safe colour—much favoured by lady spies. Ordinary green and ordinary brown were the colours to be avoided. Lamp-post green looked like nothing, and fawn gave the impression that a girl was courted by a man who wore bicycle clips.

I stepped into the skirt and drew it up. Putting my slip into it as I got it up was pleasant. There were many small sensuous pleasures in being a woman. It was tight at the waist and I had to pull to fasten the button at the side. I pulled up the zip. It fitted me smartly.

The two blouses were brightly coloured. One was vermilion and the other was deep pink. The pink one had a large rounded collar. It was more feminine than the red one. It smelt fresh and new as I was putting it on. I fastened the buttons behind me and tucked it into my skirt, running my fingers round to make it smooth.

I was dressed completely and correctly as a woman.

The pink of the blouse was a warm colour. My black slip did not show through. Perhaps it would in a strong light. I I had not thought of that. It was getting dark in the room with the curtains drawn. I went and switched on the light.

I returned to the mirror. I wished that I had a lipstick, and some eye shadow, and a pair of ear studs, and a bracelet for my wrist.

But I had money and I could buy the little things I wanted. Everything would be perfect. When my hair grew I would be able to pass for a girl. I had no doubt that I could do it. The difficulty would be in overcoming the nervousness. Setting out would be like walking on a narrow plank over an abyss. Yet other people had walked over that abyss on high-heeled shoes. I could do it.

I said, 'My name is Wendy. Wendy Ross.'

I would have to speak softly and sound my voice from the front of my mouth.

I tried again, this time attempting a Cottingham accent. 'My name is Wendy. The rain was dreadful this morning. . . .'

I stood before the mirror for a long time, talking all sorts of nonsense to myself to practise my new voice. It sounded feminine enough—if a little deep—but I could not be sure.

It was after I had looked at the nightdresses and started to clear away the wrappings that were strewn about that I discovered a parcel that I had not opened. It must be the raincoat. I decided to leave it.

I undressed and put on the white brassière and a pair of the briefs that were for wearing under my slacks. Then I dressed myself up as a boy, flat chested and ordinary. Wearing an empty brassière was not pleasant.

On the landing I met Peter. He was going into his room but he stopped when he saw me.

'What have you been doing today?' he asked. 'Have you been out looking for a job?'

'I went for an interview this morning.'

'How did you get on?'

'They said they'd let me know.'

'That doesn't sound too good.' Then he said, 'You're looking very pale. Do you feel all right?'

'Yes, I'm fine.'

'You don't look it. You look washed out.'

18

At bedtime I had a look at the black raincoat. I tried it on over my male clothes. When I pulled the belt tight the coat stood out at the hips. It was a short coat. Two or three inches of my skirt would show below it. It was a coat for getting about in, a handy coat. The pockets were large. It would do very well. I would look confident and capable in it. It would make me into a girl who knew her way about.

I undressed. It was necessary to put the black brassière on

because the white one would have shown through the black nightdress. I slipped the breasts in.

The nightdress produced a feeling that was a stillness. Its femininity was my femininity. I was real and desirable. It was beautiful to be gently alive and conscious of myself. The door was locked and I was safe. I had become the centre, still and alone. The nightdress was the truth about me. Whatever might be written on the birth certificate that was amongst my father's papers at home, I knew that I was female. The nightdress was correct. It was my nightdress. I had chosen it. The error of nature was not my error.

Now there was tranquillity. It was time to go to sleep. The day had been a birthday with presents. They were my presents to myself. No one else could have given them to me because no one, except myself, would admit that I existed.

I had been like a ghost watching the body being made to move. Now that I had clothes to wear my ghost could go into the body again and move it with real life.

It was exquisite to lie in bed in a pretty nightdress. I wondered whether I would lie in my coffin in a nightdress. In the end, would I be buried as Roy or Wendy?

I thought of a man coming into the room.

He switched on the light. He was cruel-faced, with a small, pointed beard. He wore a dinner jacket and a black bow tie.

I sat up.

Out of his pocket he brought a stubby revolver and pointed it at me. 'Don't make a sound or there will be an unfortunate accident with this gun. Get up.'

I had to obey. I was careful with the skirt of my nightdress as I got out of bed.

'I have something here that may help you to control yourself.' From his pocket he took a piece of wide sticking-plaster folded on itself. He drew it open, having difficulty because of the gun in his hand. 'I'll just put this over your mouth.'

I had to submit because he was a man and he had a gun.

He fastened the tape over my mouth. 'Is that comfortable?' Of course I could not answer.

'Now I think I had better tie your hands behind your back so that you won't be tempted to try to get that off.' He took a length of white cord from his pocket. He turned me round and tied my wrists behind me very tightly, so tightly that I wanted to cry out. I could feel him looping the cord round my wrists and pulling tight and tying knots. It was so tight that my hands felt quite useless. I knew that when he had finished there would be no hope of my being able to free myself.

'One can never be too careful,' he said, and I felt him take another piece of cord and start binding me above the elbows. He pulled my arms so that my elbows were pressed together. The cord cut into the soft flesh. I screwed my eyes shut with the pain as he wrenched at me to make a girl into a funny, trussed chicken. I felt that I would hardly be able to breathe. My arms were paralysed.

He finished my arms and turned me round. He could do what he liked with me. He had me bound and gagged. 'Hop into bed,' he said. He pulled the covers right down.

I wobbled and sat down on the edge of the bed.

He took my legs behind the knees and swung them onto the bed.

I struggled to sit up. My efforts made me feel as ridiculous as I was helpless.

He took another length of cord from his pocket. 'Now we'll have to tie your feet. You mustn't go running about and getting into trouble. Would you mind crossing your ankles?'

I did as he told me. He had put the gun down after he had tied my wrists, but now he did not need a gun to make me obey him. With two pieces of cord he had made me unable to do anything for myself.

He tied my ankles together.

I wanted to tell him that there was no need to tie them so tightly, but the plaster over my mouth made me unable even to appeal for mercy.

'Lie back.'

I fell back so that my head was on the pillow. I was only in a nightdress and strong cord bit into me and pinioned my arms behind me. My wrists were tied and my hands were helpless. My ankles were crossed and tied.

He brought the covers up and tucked them in round me as though he were trying to make me comfortable. I was helpless and in pain, and he was making sport of my condition.

He got out a gold cigarette case and opened it. He held it towards me. 'Do you smoke?' He smiled. 'Not just now, perhaps?' He took a cigarette himself and lit it.

102

I cringed as I thought that he might be going to torture me with a lighted cigarette. He could torture me for hours before he killed me.

He went to the door. He was leaving me. 'Goodnight,' he said. He switched off the light and went out.

I was alone. It was his most cunning cruelty to leave me alone.

I was alone and helpless and in pain. The cords above my elbows were like steel.

I struggled in the darkness. I tried to get the plaster off my mouth by rubbing it against the pillow. It was useless. I tried and tried to get at the knots on my wrists. My hands could do nothing. The cords seemed to be cutting deeper into me. I twisted and writhed and sweated in the darkness. I was in agony.

I was completely helpless. I lay still.

Suddenly I was in a frenzy, a fury of hysterical striving, a madness to break the cords. I strained at my bonds with all the strength I had. My female body contorted itself in sweat and pain. I strained and suffered in the darkness, tears of frustration filling my eyes. I tried and tried until I was exhausted.

I could not get free. He had tied me up too cleverly. He knew how to tie a woman up. I lay still again. The man had made me so that I could not get free. He had been merciless. I could only lie in the darkness, brutally tied up, waiting. That was all I could do. I was a thing.

19

When I woke up next morning and discovered myself in the black nightdress I was pleased with myself.

I wished that I had not imagined what I had imagined the night before. I did not approve of that kind of thing. It seemed inhuman, because it did not fit to the rest of my thought. There was something religious about it.

I felt annoyed when I had to take the breasts out of my brassière in order to disguise myself as a boy to go to the

103

bathroom.

I washed and shaved the sides of my chin.

It would be necessary to buy a large stock of razor blades. I did not want to have to go into a shop to ask for razor blades when I was dressed as a woman.

It was hateful to have to shave. There were just the patches on the sides of my chin, but they would have to be gone over every morning. Hair remover would have no effect. The hairs grew because I had been born a man child.

'Let the day perish wherein I was born, and the night in which it was said, There is a man-child conceived.'

I had read that even hormone treatment could fail to remove the beard. Masculinity was a hideous disorder.

That morning I went to the bank and drew all my money out.

I went to a chemist shop and bought three large packets of razor blades and three sticks of shaving soap. It was a supply that I estimated would last me more than two years. I did not try to estimate how long my five hundred pounds would last me. It looked a lot of money in ones and fives and tens. I must be very sure not to lose it or have it stolen.

Seeing a lot of money in cash made me determined. I had to be myself. In the afternoon I made an expedition to a chemist shop to buy cosmetics. It had to be done whether I liked it or not.

There was only one assistant in the shop, a woman of about thirty-five. Her duck-egg blue coat was starched and crisp and she was well-groomed. She looked a nice woman. I was relieved that I was not going to be served by a girl. If there had been a man behind the counter, I would have asked for aspirins or barley sugar. As it was, I could not start speaking.

She asked me what I wanted.

I said I wanted a lipstick.

She asked me what shade I wanted.

I thought that she must be able to see that I was a pansy and that I wanted the lipstick for myself. But it was true. I was a pansy and I did want the lipstick for myself.

In a daze, I bought a lipstick and some eye shadow and some black for my lashes and a compact. The woman served me impersonally and politely. It was dream-like. I could have stayed with her all afternoon, she was so understanding.

No doubt she would tell about me afterwards. Probably she

104

would laugh. But afterwards did not matter. She served me as though I had come for a toothbrush. I would have liked to think that she was extremely kind and tolerant and knew that what could not be cured had to be endured.

I was out in the street again and on my way. The woman I had left behind me could not send for the police to pursue me. The money I had paid her was legal tender.

But I did feel rather ill.

I told myself that I must stop being ashamed. It was a dishonest feeling. Really I was glad that I was as I was. It would have been best to be a woman, but it was better to be a transvestite than to be a man.

I decided against buying a pair of ear studs. In my black coat I would be emphatically unsentimental. Ear studs might look unnecessary.

Perhaps the woman in the chemist shop had thought that I was a girl dressed as a boy. The thought lightened my tread.

I went into a hardware shop and bought a small plastic bowl so that I could wash my face in the bedroom after my experiments with make-up. I would leave it behind me when I set out. It would puzzle Mrs Ford.

20

One had to have a woman's National Insurance card to get employment as a woman. But Wendy Ross had no official existence. I would have to live on the money I had and on hope—simultaneous fires destroying all government records.

I had heard that London was as expensive to live in as it was depraved.

I would go to Leeds.

But then I began to think that there would be no danger of my being recognised in Hull. I saw that when I was dressed and my face made, I was 'quite different from Roy—or Brian. As a boy I was small, but as a girl I was tall. And when my face was made it looked far better than the mask I wore as a boy.

It was one evening after rain, while I was out walking to get

105

through the days until my hair was long enough, that I finally made up my mind to stay in Hull.

Pavements were washed clean. It would be cold later. Now the air was fresh and mild. Not many people were about and the traffic had slackened. Cars went past travelling fast. It was shortly after tea time. The buses came past almost empty.

I turned off Beverley Road and went along towards Spring Bank. Some minutes of walking brought me to a district that was called The Avenues. I had strayed into this district before. I liked it. There were wide streets with very wide grass verges with old and well-grown trees. Once it had been a quarter where moneyed people lived, but now money took people out to Hessle and Kirkella and Willerby and Cottingham. The houses of The Avenues had been turned into flats that sheltered schoolmasters and social workers and local government officials. Inside there would be art teachers painting pictures and English masters writing novels. People who had passed examinations came to this district. The air was soft with literacy. The cars were small, but the Sunday papers that went through the letter boxes would not contain the life stories of people who had changed into leg-showing girls. In the Sunday papers that were delivered in this district most matters were problems.

This was where I would come to live.

I would say that I had been at home in Cottingham until my mother had died, and I had come to Hull, untrained for anything, knowing nothing of the world, a demure rentier. I would let them explain everything to me. There might be some interesting people to get to know.

21

Peter became concerned about my hair: 'You know, you ought to get your hair cut, Brian. You'll never get a job looking like that.'

At tea he told Mrs Ford that I ought to have my hair cut. She agreed, and then asked her Jack if he agreed. His gaunt face was then turned in my direction. His hard, male eyes looked at me. He said, 'You want to get your hair cut. What do you think you're on?'

'Don't be so rude, Jack,' said Mrs Ford.

'Well, I reckon he ought to get his hair cut. This is supposed to be a men-only boarding house, but it isn't that kind of men-only boarding house.'

'What kind's that?' asked Mrs Ford.

'The kind where they have long hair and they don't know whether they're coming or going.'

'You really ought to have it shorter, Brian,' said Mrs Ford. 'It can't be any help to you when you go about a job.'

'I wish I had as much hair as him,' said a bald middle-aged man.

The man next to me lowered his Hull Daily Mail and looked at me point-blank. He said, 'He looks like that lass on BBC television who does a bit of chat between programmes. What do they call her?'

I was pleased with him. I knew the woman announcer he meant. I had often thought that I looked rather like her.

Peter said, 'Making personal remarks is bad manners.' He leant towards me. 'You can come with me on Saturday. I go to a very good man.'

The voice I had been practising came from the front of my mouth. It said, 'I don't want to have my hair cut. Actually, I want it much longer.'

They stared at me.

I would have to leave sooner than I had intended. I had told them that I wanted to be a woman.

But Peter, who had become engrossed in jam pastry and custard, was unaware that anything had happened. He went on, 'I always go every other Saturday afternoon to get my hair cut. I used to go on Wednesday nights—'

'You can save it,' said Jack, 'he doesn't want to have his hair cut. His voice is changing. I reckon he knows an easier way of making a living than we do. That's why he doesn't get a job.'

'I wish I knew an easy way of making a living,' said Peter.

'You want to go out with Betty there some night. He'll show you.' He said Betty as though he had named me in that way before.

I got up and went out of the room.

I would have to leave. People hated effeminacy. I was effeminate. People hated me because they had to. They could not choose. As soon as they realised what I was they hated me. It was automatic.

22

My rent was a week in advance. I would depart at the next sunrise.

I dressed up.

Surely the person in the mirror was a girl. Surely I could not be mistaken. She was tall. The brow was smooth. The superciliary ridges were just apparent. The nose was small. The hollow between the brow and the bridge of the nose was very shallow. The jowl was not heavy and the chin was small. The lips were full and the mouth was large, but it was a well-shaped mouth. The ears were small and flat to the head. In the full-face position it was only possible to see the lobes. The neck was right. The thyroid showed but it did not bulge. There was no Adam's apple. The shoulders were not wide. In the black raincoat the shoulders and the bust looked very compact and feminine. I held up my hands. They were long and decisive, capable hands, but not at all bulky. There were no hairs on the backs of them. But I should have bought a pair of gloves. I put my hands on my hips. The waist was small. The hips were boyish, but the pelvis seemed to be wide enough. The distance across the hips was obviously more than the distance from armpit to armpit. I turned round and twisted myself to see the backs of my legs in the mirror. The form of the calves was good. My legs would be admired.

There was no reason why the girl I could see in the mirror should be suspected of being male.

But I was still afraid.

And yet the fear would make the experience more intense. When I set out the fear and joy would thrill in me. It would be the most extreme moment of my life. I would walk over an abyss into heaven.

My day would come up. I would leave Mrs Ford's boarding-house and walk into a new world. I would go through the looking-glass.

I began to pack the red suitcase.

I wished that I did not have to take Roy's clothes with me, but, if I left them behind, Mrs Ford would certainly go to the police.

The case that I had come to the house with would have to be left behind. Mrs Ford could give it to her Jack. She could put the plastic bowl to any use for which it was suitable.

When the case was packed I went to the mirror with a comb and a pair of scissors to alter my hair. It proved more difficult than I had expected. In the end I managed to make the hair at the front into a low fringe, but there remained a piece on top that stood up. Nothing I could think of would make it lie down, and I experienced a peculiarly feminine vexation with myself that developed into a tantrum in which I told myself that, if I could not do my hair properly, I could not be allowed to go.

But I had to go. The front of my hair was cut into a fringe. I clipped the piece of hair off—and serve it right. What was left of it still stood up. It would have to be ignored.

It was nine o'clock when I got into bed. I wanted to go to sleep as soon as possible.

I tried to go to sleep. I told myself that, if I did not go to sleep, I would not wake up early enough, and I would have a fringe to explain. I should have bought an alarm clock.

But I could not sleep. I was too excited.

I counted up to a thousand. I squared numbers. I cubed numbers. I said, 'Amaveram, amaveras, amaverat, amaveramus, amaveratis, amaverant, amavi, amavisti, amavit, amavimus, amavistis, amaverunt, amabam, amabas, amabat, amabamus, amabatis, amabant, amo, amas, amat, amamus, amatis, amant, amabo, amabis, amabit . . . amabit . . . amabit . . . amabit . . . amabit . . . amabit . . . amabit . . . amabit . . . amabimus, amabitis, amabunt, amavero, amaveris, amaverit, amaverimus, amaveritis, amaverint.' I recited the names of the kings of England since William the Conqueror. Then I went back to counting.

When I switched on the bedside lamp and looked at my watch I found that it was half-past ten.

109

As is the night before some festival
To an impatient child that hath new robes
And may nor wear them.

I switched off the lamp.

The night would end. I would awake at half-past five and the day would begin. It would come.

I wondered how nasty the police would be with me if I was discovered. They might make fun of me. And then they might become deadly serious and determined to have a list of everything I had on. There might be a frumpish police-woman to assist them with nomenclature.

Sleep brought dreams in which I was running through the streets in scraps of underwear. I could not find anywhere to hide myself.

23

I awoke in darkness. But I knew that it was morning. I switched on the lamp and looked at my watch. It was five past four. I could not go to sleep again.

I switched off the lamp. The bed was warm. It would be cold in the street.

I dozed, and had a morning dream in which I was in an open carriage in bright sunlight. I was wearing a white dress with a long, full skirt. A handsome policeman sat with me. He held a large bunch of flowers, and he was picking the petals and letting them fall from his hand onto my lap. He did it very thoughtfully and slowly, as though he were doing it with special kindness because I had so often been unhappy.

I awoke again and switched on the lamp. It was after five.

The time was come. I had to get out of bed.

I got up and started to dress, careful to make no sound.

I dressed with great care, making sure that everything was right. This time I was not putting on the clothes only for myself but also to be accepted. I would wear these things all day. I would not take them off until I undressed to go to bed in a new place as a new person. Or I might be taken to the police station in them. My stomach seemed to be falling. It was a sensation like going down in a lift. And I had a picture of downfall through the breaking of elastic. I laughed at myself.

It was necessary to put my razor over the sides of my chin.

Then I began to make my face. The concentration stopped my nervousness. My eyes took a long time.

When my face was satisfactory my confidence was increased. I was the girl in nylon stockings and high-heeled shoes.

I combed my hair. The fringe came to the front and all the rest went back. There was the little crossways parting on top of the front of my head, and there was the clipped-off piece standing up. The hair at the back went behind my ears. I wished I had a pair of ear studs. I wished that I had bought a brush so that I could try to make my hair shine. Yet it looked quite pretty. It was not as long as I would have liked it—but it was long enough. The fringe was just above the eyebrows. It made my face an altogether different shape from Roy's face. I wondered if I was really the type of girl to have a fringe . . . It would have to do.

ʻ I went and put my nightdress in the suitcase.

There was over five hundred pounds in the suitcase. The only pockets I had now were the pockets of my raincoat. If I got parted from my money, I would be finished. I thought of making a roll of some of the notes and putting them in the top of my stocking like women used to do in films. I rejected the idea as behaviour unbecoming a young lady from Cottingham. I would have to buy a handbag.

I put on the black coat and pulled the belt tight. The lipstick and the compact and the key of the suitcase and some money went into the pocket. I realised that I did not have a lady's handkerchief.

I was ready.

I studied myself in the mirror.

Yes, I was a girl.

But my knees were feeble and my insides were sinking again.

It was after half-past six. Through a chink at the top of the curtains I could see that it was full day outside. Mrs Ford would be up and preparing breakfast before eight o'clock. I did not want to go out too early because a young woman carrying a case very early in the morning could attract attention

I would set out at seven.

I put the watch in my pocket. The watch my father had given me was in the suitcase. I would not be able to wear either of them.

I sat down in the arm chair.

After I had been sitting a few minutes I began to feel very ill with nervousness. I felt that I could be sick, and I wanted to use the lavatory, but I could not risk going along the landing.

I rocked to and fro and talked to myself. 'You'll be all right, Wendy. You're a pretty girl. There's nothing to worry about. People will think you look very nice. You only have to have courage. You're going to be very happy. And when you've proved that you can live as a woman they'll have to help you. You only have to have courage.'

It did no good at all.

I started retching. I leant forward. My stomach strained. But nothing came up. It stopped for a moment, and then another spasm came. I thought, 'If this doesn't stop, I can't go.' It stopped.

I lay back in the chair and shut my eyes. I was in despair. I would be known for a male at once. People would stare at me. I would want to fall down dead. The police would come. I would be taken to the police station at Queens Gardens and charged with behaviour likely to cause a breach of the peace. I might go to prison, or to Borstal. At best, I would be sent back to the mental hospital. The mental hospital was the right place. I was certainly completely insane.

But I had to go. It had to be done. In a short time from now I had to get along the landing and down the stairs and out of the front door into the street.

I said, 'You'll either go or I'll kill you.'

I was weak with fear.

I opened my eyes and saw my coat and the bottom of my skirt and the tips of my knees in the stockings. It looked like a woman. It did not look like anything else.

I took the watch out of my pocket. It was nearly half-past six. The house was still.

I prayed. 'O God, I have reason to hate you, but you are all-powerful and my hate cannot harm you. Have mercy on me this day as you might have mercy on a fly. Let me go. I know that I am degenerate and loathsome, but, if you let me live as a woman, I promise I won't do anyone any harm. Let me—' I stopped. I said, 'I know you, God, you'll not let me go. I know you of old. You're always on the side of the big battalions. And you're a well-known liar. It says that people only have to ask to receive, but when I was a child I prayed over and over to be a little girl, and you never answered my prayers. You ignored me, just as you ignored my mother. I've not forgotten. I'll never forget. You can do your worst. Go on and destroy me. I'm the sort of person you usually destroy. I'm about your size. I saw some of the people you've destroyed when I was at the lunatic asylum. You must be very proud of yourself!'

I felt better after that.

I went to have a last look in the mirror.

Yes, I was a girl. I was pretty. My lips looked very nice. Perhaps a little more eye shadow? No, of course not.

But what I saw in the mirror might be an illusion.

I got the case and went to the door. With my free hand I turned up the collar of my coat and folded the front closed. Then I had to put the case down to get my shoes off. After which I got myself into position with my case and my shoes in my left hand and my right on the key of the door.

I turned the key. I put my hand on the knob.

I took my hand away from the knob and took the watch out of my pocket. It was ten to seven.

It was now.

I turned the knob and eased the door open. There was a very slight squeaking. The landing was empty. The house was silent.

I started forward, and immediately I became aware of the nature of my clothes. It was a skirt that was open, not trousers that were closed. My legs touched and I felt the stockings catch together. My face felt heavily painted. I was conscious of the lipstick on my mouth. I seemed to myself to be like a great girl doll. I looked down and saw my feet on the carpet. The reinforcement at the toes of the stockings was scientifically complex.

I floated like a Zeppelin to the end of the landing, and there I had the shock of remembering Mrs Ford's dog. It would be asleep in the back room downstairs—or it might be awake.

113

If it heard me, it would start barking.

I began going down the stairs. My skirt limited me. I was afraid that I might fall. I had to be careful that my case did not bump against the wall.

I was at the bottom of the stairs. My heart was running like a machine.

I reached the front door. There was a Yale lock. I put my case down and then set my shoes on the doormat in front of me. The danger of making a noise was considerable as I cockled about to get my feet in, but I had to get my shoes on somehow. When they were on I found that I was panting as though I had been running. There was a pain in the centre of my chest.

I took hold of the knob of the Yale lock and attempted to turn it. It would not turn. I tried to force it to turn. It would not turn. Then I realised that the little catch next to the knob had been used to fasten it. I pushed the catch up. I turned the knob to the open position and pushed the catch down.

I took up my case in my left hand and put my right hand on the door knob. I was panting hard. There was a loud click as the door knob turned. I pulled. The door jerked slightly and stuck. I pulled harder. The door jerked again but remained shut. I pulled as hard as I dared. Again the door jerked. But it was stuck.

I must either get the door open or get back to my room.

There was a bolt at the bottom of the door. I bent down and unslid it.

I put my hand on the knob again. I turned it. It clicked. I pulled. The door came open about an inch.

I opened the door. The morning was cold and clear. The street was as the street had been. A car went past on the near side of the road. In a panic, I started to close the door again. But I prevented myself.

I stepped out and stood on the doorstep. It was the most self-conscious moment I had ever experienced. I was standing in the open in broad day dressed as a woman. All the world could see me. People in London, Paris and Bangkok could see me. A car went past on the far side of the road, and then another. Perhaps the drivers had noticed me. I wanted to get back inside the house. I was disgraceful and grotesque. The door was still open behind me. I could go back. I could

114

do something with my hair so that it would not be seen that I had cut it into a fringe. There was water in the bowl to wash the make-up off my face. I could not go forward, for I was not able to get down off the step.

I put out my foot and stepped down. The sound of my heel striking the concrete was the sound of a woman's high-heel. It's ring was shocking.

I was walking. I wished that I were invisible. It would not be far before there were people staring at me and laughing at me. I was walking in a skirt with my face painted.

There was a man in brown overalls and a jacket coming towards me.

My legs kept moving. My face was a doll's face. I did not blink. I looked straight ahead. The clock in my head stopped.

The man passed me.

I did not know whether he had stared at me or not. I was so self-conscious that I seemed to have hardly any consciousness left over for anything outside myself. What I could see had no solidity. The street was made of lathe and canvas with nothing behind it. There were people moving.

I had a vague understanding that I was walking in the wrong direction. I should have turned left outside the house and gone towards the city centre. But I kept walking straight ahead. I thought that, if I turned round, I would be face to face with a policeman. And I was not sure that I could make a full turn.

They were early morning workers who were passing me. I dare not look to see if they were taking any notice. I focused on objects hundreds of yards along the street.

I thought, 'I may walk along Beverley Road until I'm out in the country.'

The heels made me feel as though I were walking on stilts.

Three women in headscarves were coming towards me. They were talking loudly. As they passed me one of them laughed. The noise almost threw me from my height on stilts. I seemed to reel. There were then some moments in which I knew that everybody could see that I was a boy. I was enormous, I was extraordinary, I was a giraffe. I wished I were a giraffe, I wished I were back in Africa. I wished I could run like a giraffe.

I found myself walking in front of a row of shops. I saw a cheeky boy. He looked at me. I looked at a car that was

115

coming past. The man in the car looked at me. I looked at the radiator of the bus that was coming behind the car.

I seemed to be trying to hurry, and my skirts were dragging on my legs. I began to have a sensation that my clothes were slipping down, except my coat, which seemed to be getting shorter. It seemed possible that all four suspenders would come unfastened at once.

I put my right hand into my coat pocket and dug my fingers into my clothing to hold the things underneath.

I was a fantastic shape. And the ground seemed to to tilting. The fringe on my forehead made me feel like a gorilla with a daisy chain to crown it.

I thought, 'Sooner or later I'll come to a policeman, and that will be the end. I'll be glad when it's over. I can't stand any more.'

There was a middle-aged woman coming past. I thought she had a kind face. I wanted to say, 'Help me. Hide me. Please hide me.' I looked at her eyes. She looked back at me. There was no surprise or contempt in her eyes. We were simply two people meeting each other's glance in the street.

I began to reason with myself. No one was taking any special notice of me. People were not staring at me. The woman who had laughed had done so because of something her companion had said to her.

Happiness was beginning.

I tried to meet the eyes of another woman, but she was looking past me.

I felt afraid again.

A young man looked hard at me. I wanted to put my hand over my face. He looked away. He was shy. I realised that he had not looked at me because he thought that I might be male but because he saw that I was like a female.

I had come through. It had happened. I had always known that I could do it. The lie and stupidity that had gone on for so many years was shown to be a lie and stupidity. I had become myself. They would never make me dress up as a boy again. I would destroy the male clothes that I had in the case. They had no business to be in my case. Mine was a woman's case. I was a woman, a girl, a female, a female animal, a female creature, not male, never male.

In London, Paris and Bangkok the streets were full of

cheering people. In Bangkok people were standing up in their boats cheering. Hull was aware. The whole city was proud of me. Down Hessle Road men stood bareheaded to sing 'My Girl's a Yorkshire Girl' led by the Salvation Army band. On far-flung Bilton Grange there was shouting. There was mighty singing on Wincolm Lea and terrific clog-dancing at Stoneferry. At Pearsons Creek the hornpipe was being danced. There were strange frolics in The Land of Green Ginger. And in White Friar Gate they were putting up a noble Te Deum.

How I loved my city! I was walking along the pavement dressed as a girl in bright daylight.

I covered some distance in a state of marvellous elation before I discovered that I needed very much to get to a lavatory. The public lavatories were in the centre of the city, and I was still walking in the wrong direction.

'If you hadn't been in such an idiotic flap about nothing, you'd have turned left when you came out of the house. What were you so frightened about? Silly bitch! Still, never mind, you've done very well. Now you'll have to turn round and go down to the railway station and lock yourself in the lavatory— like one of the three old ladies—and you can stay there until you've composed yourself. You'll need some for soon. There's your voice to worry about, but we won't get into a heart condition about that until you've got it firmly into your thick head that you look all right.'

I crossed the road, being cautious and waiting until there was a lull in the traffic. I did not want to be knocked down and be discovered for a boy by some Calvinist Scots doctor at Hull Infirmary. Nor did I want to be forced to make a dash in my high-heels and tight skirt. As it was I had to run a few undelicate steps to avoid a car that came up unexpectedly fast.

I would have to pass the boarding house. But it would be on the opposite side of the road from me, and nobody would be coming out until half-past eight. Anyway, if they saw me, they would not know who I had been.

I kept looking, and at last I saw the reflection of a tall, splendid girl in a shop window. I thought of going back to pass the shop again. It was difficult to feel sure that I was the person I had seen. It was not possible to go back because I had to get to a lavatory. The next time I saw the girl I observed that she was tripping along as though she was in a hurry. It looked as though she was hurrying to catch a train. She was tall and exciting. Roy had always been a small, nondescript person when reflected in shop windows.

I skipped in the air quite involuntarily.

But I wanted to get to a lavatory very much. I was so intent on reaching the city centre that I hardly noticed a policeman. He was standing on the kerb looking at the traffic. I passed behind him.

My skirt and my shoes made it so that I could only hurry by means of many small steps quickly taken. My discomfort was increasing. Yet I was glad that I was restricted and only able to hurry like a woman.

By the time I reached the railway station I was too uncomfortable to have any reflections about entering a Ladies' lavatory for the first time. I was almost in collision with a woman who was coming out.

After I had relieved myself and rearranged my clothes I leant against the wall and closed my eyes. I was comfortable and happy. It was as though I was in a shower-bath of happiness. I had survived. I had come through the streets as a woman, and no one had stared at me and no one had laughed at me. And here I was, safe in the Ladies' lavatory. I had done it. My appearance was accepted. The woman who had been going out as I had been coming in had not shown any signs of indignation.

I opened my eyes and took the watch out of my pocket. It was not quite a quarter to eight. I had been out of the house for about three quarters of a hour. It seemed much longer.

Certainly my prayers before setting out had been foolishness, for, if there were a God, he would not have allowed me to be so happy as I was now. But I wished that there was a God so that I could thank him.

I was Wendy Ross. It was exciting. The clothes that I was wearing were real clothes. I was brilliantly alive. The old city had been turned into a place where I was living a dream.

Soon I would set out again and walk about as a girl. It was almost too wonderful to believe.

At the moment I was safe. No policeman could come into a Ladies' lavatory. If a policeman came in, I would scream.

I wondered if I could scream.

My voice was the next danger.

I spoke aloud to practise my new voice: 'This is my case. Actually, it is red. I require tea. A cup of tea, please. Two cheese sandwiches, please. A girl has to eat. A cup of tea, please. Truly, I require tea.'

I heard someone coming into the lavatory. I hoped that she had not heard me talking.

I emerged into the hall of the station. A train had just come in and people were hurrying. I was another person in the morning bustle. People could be looking at me. I kept biting my lower lip.

There were two buffets in the station. When I had gone to Cottingham on the day I came out of hospital I had had a cup of tea in the large buffet near the side entrance. It would be safer to go to the small buffet opposite the newspaper stand this morning.

I walked up and down outside the buffet. The thought of having to speak to someone was daunting. But my suitcase was becoming wearisome, and a young man behind the counter of the paper stand was watching me. Then a policeman came marching from the far end of the station, and I was through the door and inside.

A family of travellers, father, anxious mother, and two little boys, was drinking tea. A thin man was looking at the Daily Mirror. Behind the counter there was a rounded woman, as homely as a brown teapot, and a younger woman who appeared to suffer from something. The older woman looked as tough as she looked good-hearted. No doubt, if there was trouble in the buffet, the older woman would hold the fort while the younger woman ran out to fetch a policeman. I thought that it was not impossible that the younger woman would be running for a policeman within a few seconds.

I presented myself at the counter.

The older woman said, 'Yes, honey?'

The 'honey' gave me an instant of pleasure. It was sympathetic, as though she had a rough husband and five kids and supposed that I had similar experiences coming to me.

My mouth moved and, 'Tea, please,' came out. It was a small rough sound that I made, much deeper than I had intended.

'You'll have to wait a minute, honey. The water's gone off

119

the boil.' She stood with her hand on her fine, capacious hip in an attitude of waiting. 'It's not too warm this morning.'

I nodded.

'Of course we can expect it. It's Hull Fair soon, and then it'll be Guy Fawkes, and then it'll be Christmas.'

The younger woman interrupted the procession of the seasons. 'It's boiling, May.'

I got a cup of tea and took it to one of the tables. It was a good cup of tea and very hot. I felt it all the way down into my empty stomach. When I put the cup down I saw that I had left a trace of lipstick on the rim.

The man with the Daily Mirror glanced at me.

I studied my cup.

Perhaps I would feel more confident after I had had something to eat. 'Cheese sandwich' was not a difficult thing to say. Sibilants should be the easiest sounds.

I went to the counter and whispered, 'Two cheese sandwiches, please.'

'We haven't got any cheese, honey. There's egg-and-cheese and there's ham.'

I whispered, 'Two egg-and-cheese, please.'

'Have you got a cold, honey?'

'Yes.'

'I can hear. It's nasty when you lose your voice.'

She gave me two egg-and-cheese sandwiches on a plate.

'And another tea, please,' I whispered.

I got the plate and the cup and saucer back to my table.

I could not go through life whispering as though I had lost my voice through a cold.

The Daily Mirror man glanced at me again. He was a very ordinary man of about thirty-five. I imagined that he was an electrician or a plumber. He probably spoke with a thick Hull accent.

I concentrated on my sandwiches.

The two little boys of the travelling family began running up and down.

There was danger. Children might see what adults missed. I could almost hear a child's voice exclaiming, 'Daddy, why is that man dressed up as a woman?' I winced. I remembered that I had read that children were the terror of public transvestites.

120

One of the little boys halted and put his thumb in his mouth and looked at me. My mouth stopped munching egg-and-cheese sandwich. Then he took his hand from his mouth and turned away. He was satisfied that I was as I should be. I nearly smiled at his mother.

I was satisfied that I was as I should be. I was still very nervous, but confidence was coming surprisingly quickly.

I would have liked to tell somebody how happy I was. But I was alone. I had to sit with my knees primly together, alone.

The man with the Daily Mirror was looking at me again. I was glad. He was not an interesting man, but he was looking at me because I was a girl. I was glad.

I was glad about everything. I was glad that the world was round and that there was law and order and that I was Wendy. I was glad that I had been born to be alive on this day wearing the clothes I was wearing. Glad rags. Difficulties had been overcome. Despite everything, I had managed to be glad.

The self-satisfied and the secretly jealous might call me a pervert. But what did I care for them? Even when I was a poor thing in trousers I had known that they were contemptible. They were mean, dull, coarse, ugly, vulgar, brutish, ignorant, cowardly and hypocritical. And they were jealous of me. I was a smart young woman. They were mostly middle-aged and disappointed. They had never had as much courage as a rat required to make its way in the world, and their meagre consolation was to hate those who had courage. They might try to sneer at me, but had they done so many things success-fully in their lives that they could rightly sneer at anyone? I was above them. And yet I could tolerate them—so long as they kept their distance. They could look at me.

I wanted them to look at me. I was a girl. I wanted men to fall off ladders looking at me. I wanted to stop the traffic.

It was gorgeous to be alive.

A womanly walk took me to the bookstall to hold up a copy of Vogue and give money for it without speaking. Then I took myself to the Ladies' Room. It was still early in the morning, and I was the only person there. I went to one of the mirrors. The face was surprisingly solemn for a girl who felt so happy. After touching up my lips I sat down and affected to look at the magazine I had bought, but I had to go back to the mirror to marvel at myself.

121

When I next looked at my watch it was after nine o'clock.

I went to an expensive shop behind the War Memorial and whispered to the young assistant that I wanted a handbag. She fitted tightly into a black dress and looked at me as though to show me that she was better at being a woman than I was.

'We have a wide range of hondbogs, modom.'

My mouth fell open when she said 'madam'. I felt as though I could have flown if I had wanted to.

She waggled away down the shop and I waggled after her.

I chose a small bag of soft black leather. It was very simple. It cost me four guineas.

When I got back to the Ladies' Room at the station with the intention of transferring the money from the case into the handbag I found a stout woman in a leather coat standing astride. She had a cigarette hanging from her mouth and she was feeling about in the pockets of her coat like a man. She frightened me.

'Have you got such a thing as a light?' she asked.

I forgot to whisper. I said, 'No, I'm sorry. I don't smoke.' She went out.

As quickly as I could I got the money out of the case and into the handbag.

Then I took the case to the left-luggage office. I could not remember whether the man who took it was the same man who had taken my case on the day I came out of hospital. The case I handed him was as different from the case I had handed in that day as I looked different from the person I had looked that day. Mrs Ford could burn that old case if she liked. I was Wendy, and Wendy owned a spanking red suitcase. The man who took it could not have suspected that it contained male clothing. But there was nothing wrong with a woman having men's clothes. It was not immoral like a man having women's clothes.

I walked in the shopping streets. Whenever I could I observed my reflection in plate glass. I stood to look at clothes in shop windows, which was a welcome new freedom.

I went into a store and was pushed round with the crowds and carried up and down the escalators. It felt like Christmas.

I saw myself in a full-length mirror. I was in a black coat with the collar turned up and the belt pulled tight, tall and dashing. The copy of Vogue was sticking up in the pocket.

The face looked at me detachedly. It seemed the face of a girl who had been going about as a girl all her life. She was a lively, ironic girl. Her legs were handsome.

A woman came between me and the mirror.

I bought a box of pretty handkerchiefs. At another counter I bought a shoe-horn and a set of manicure implements in a blue leather case and a hair brush. I held the things I wanted with my money and got served without having to speak. At another counter I bought a box of powder and a big powder puff and some hand cream and a bottle of nail varnish and a sponge that was shaped like a fish and two bars of special soap and a bottle of bath salts and a bright red waterproof moppet cap for putting on when I had a bath and some shampoos. Then I found a home-perm set that was said to curve the hair but not to curl it. I bought it and I bought some hair lacquer.

I was becoming light-headed, and I almost went to buy lingerie for the sake of buying lingerie, but I checked myself.

I took my parcels to the cafeteria, where I drank coffee and thought a hymn:

'Venus as the morning-star is Lucifer. Chaos is truth. Truth is chaos. Now I am in ecstasy, for I live in the instant. It is the lightening flash that reveals the earth. I am helpless in reality.'

Then I thought that it was not womanly to be rebellious. I must think comfortably. I needed something of special absorbency to put into my head. Through my ear or up my nose? That made me laugh.

What I needed was somebody to talk to.

I went back to the station and got my case and took it to the Ladies' Room and put my parcels in it.

A taxi to The Avenues would be nice, but then I thought that I would like to walk and be seen. It was a long way, but I was a healthy girl.

As I went along I considered the fact that the stout woman in the leather coat had not been surprised by my voice when I had apologised for not having a light for her cigarette. I decided that I would not do any more whispering. A Cottingham accent would be enough.

Before I got to The Avenues my feet were hurting. Every step was painful. I was a woman. It was interesting to be hurt by high-heeled shoes. The pain was more intense than I had

E   123

expected it would be. When my foot struck the ground the ball of my foot felt as though it were going to burst with pain My toes were fiery hot. I tried to put more weight on my heels, but it was nearly impossible to do that. My toes and the front of my foot had to withstand pain. I supposed that I would get used to it. I would certainly go on wearing high-heels no matter how painful it was.

When I reached The Avenues I discovered a Y.W.C.A. hostel. The notion of going in and asking if they had any vacancies had an appeal. I put it away. Even on so successful a day there had to be a limit to audacity.

I found a street that I liked. The fallen leaves were thick on the grass verges and there were drifts of brown and yellow leaves on the pavement. I splashed through the leaves, imagining that they might cool my poor, burning toes.

I picked a house at random and went into the garden and up to the front door. There were three bell pushes, one above the other, each with a perspex covered card giving the name of the occupier of the flat. At the bottom was Mr, Mrs C. R. Biggs. I pressed. There was a burring sound deep inside the house. Then there was silence. I pressed again.

A broad shouldered woman of about thirty opened the door. She wore a green sweater and fawn corduroy trousers. 'Yes?'

'I'm looking for accommodation. Could you help me at all?' My voice sounded well-educated. Well-educated women often had deep voices.

'Oh, well, now then. Well, there's the YWCA. Have you tried there? If you go to the end of the street and turn to your right.' She leaned out of the doorway and pointed. She was a big woman. I thought that, if anyone had to choose the male between us, they might choose her.

I said, 'Well, actually, I'm looking for a flat or something like that.' My voice was doing very well—but I must keep it from becoming too loud.

'I don't know.' She frowned and put her hand to her neck. It was a gesture that many women used to show that they were pondering something. I thought that I must learn to do it.

'You don't know of anywhere where there's a room empty, do you?' My voice was excellent. I wanted to go on talking.

'I don't think so. I'm sorry I can't help you.' She shook

her head in regret, but suddenly brightened. 'Just a minute. Mrs Nelson might know of something.' She pressed the middle bell push.

'Have you just come to Hull?' she asked.

'Yes. Actually, I was living with my mother in Cottingham. She died and —'

'Oh, I'm sorry!'

Someone was coming down the stairs inside. The big woman turned. 'Do you know of anywhere vacant round here, Janice?'

Janice, who was small and fair, arrived at the door. 'I don't really know. There's the YWCA. . . .'

'She wants a flat,' explained the big woman.

Janice did not know of any vacant flats or any vacant rooms.

The big woman suggested that I go to the call-box at the end of the street and ring estate agents.

I thanked them and left them.

I did not know how to use a telephone. I went to another house and rang the bell.

At some houses there was no reply when I rang. At others I had conversations with women. They were all young women. One was superbly pregnant. She had fur-lined slippers and a toffee-paper stuck to her smock. They were all friendly and wanted to help me, but none of them had any information about vacant flats or vacant rooms.

My arm was aching with the case and I was thinking that I was not going to be able to find a place in The Avenues, when I rang a bell and the door was opend to me by a woman of about twenty-four or five with honey-blonde hair. She wore a loose white sweater with a polo neck and a dark green skirt.

'I hope you don't mind my bothering you,' I said, 'but I'm looking for a flat or a room. You don't know of anywhere that's empty, do you?'

'Yes, I do,' she said simply.

Her eyes were blue-grey. She was very good looking.

'Could you tell me where it is?'

'It's up at the top of the house. It's been empty for some time. I don't think the landlady has got anybody for it. I could ring her and see. Would you like to come in?'

I went into the hallway.

Her hair was to her shoulders and curved under at the

bottom.

'It's only one room,' she said, 'but I believe there's a sink and a cooker.'

'That would be all right.'

'She'll want a month's rent in advance.'

'I can manage that. May I sit down while you make the call? I've walked all the way from the station and my feet are killing me. I'm not used—' I stopped myself.

'Yes, of course.'

She led me along the hallway.

'All this ground floor belongs to my husband and me. We've been here since we got married. That's the bedroom.' She indicated a door we were passing, on the opposite side of the hallway from the foot of the stairs. 'We don't use the front room. The Johnsons live upstairs and then there are two rooms above that. There's the empty one and an art student girl lives in the other. The Johnsons are very quiet.'

She opened the door at the end of the hallway and took me into a room that fitted my idea of The Avenues. Neither of the leather arm chairs could be occupied by a husband who washed at the kitchen sink when he came back from work. Nor could a husband in overalls sit at the table. There was a smell of books. And filling the wall between the door by which we had entered and the corner of the room there was a framework packed with books that had high-class modern covers.

I had known that there were such civilized rooms as this, but I had never been in one before.

She asked me to sit down.

I stroked my clothes neatly behind me and sat down in the arm chair near the bookcase and took my shoes off at once. I sighed.

She went and picked up the receiver of a lime green telephone that stood on the sideboard. 'I think I know Mrs Cartwright's number,' she said, and she started dialling.

I was sitting with my legs thrust out before me wiggling my toes. I felt that they had suffered as much as they could be expected to suffer, even in the cause of feminity. But the relief of getting my shoes off and my thoughts about my feet did not distract me altogether from being impressed by the place into which I had penetrated. I looked at the books in the bookcase.

126

The Failure of Myth, The Plays of Bertolt Brecht, An Examination of Education. I decided that the husband must be a school-master.

And they had a television set. I supposed that they only watched intellectual programmes.

She got through to Mrs Cartwright and explained that there was somebody wanting the room that was empty. '—a young woman', she said. She put the receiver down and turned to me. 'She's coming round. Would you like a cup of tea?'

I said that I would.

She went through into the back kitchen and I could hear her filling the kettle.

I sat looking down at my clothes in wonder.

She came back with a tray of tea things.

'How are your feet?' she asked.

'They're getting better.'

She was a complete woman. I wished that my hair was as long as hers and I wished that my hips were as wide as hers. She could have a baby. I liked her clothes. My black raincoat and black skirt and black shoes seemed harshly new. She had been a middle-class person all her life.

'Have you just come to Hull?' she asked.

'Yes I lived in Cottingham with my mother.'

'It's very nice there.'

'It's very quiet. My mother died.'

'I'm sorry.'

'It was an accident with an electric blanket.'

'That must have been terrible for you.'

We talked politely.

My social position was much higher than it had been when I was in trousers. I was now a nice girl from Cottingham, which was considerably more than being an intelligent boy from east Hull. I reflected that it required less hard work for a girl to climb in the caste system than for a boy. One day a Northern novelist might write a book in which the poor lad at the mill climbed to become the Duchess of Golightly.

I told her that my name was Wendy Ross. She told me that she was Marguerite Stephenson and that she and her husband were both schoolteachers.

'It's really lucky that it was today you came,' she said. 'I wasn't very well this morning so I couldn't go to school.

127

Otherwise there wouldn't have been anybody in. The Johnsons both go out to work. I suppose I'll have to go this afternoon and show my face.'

Suddenly she said, 'Would you excuse me? I'll have to go and see if William is about.'

She went through into the kitchen again. I heard her open the back door. She called, 'Puss, Puss, Puss.'

The cat came into the living room proceeding her. It was a grey Persian cat with amber eyes. It came warily on silent paws with tail set high, caring nothing for the world outside itself, so beautiful that it did not need to love anyone. It rubbed itself against my legs, a contact from which we both had pleasure. I stroked it. It raised its back to my hand. I knew how it felt.

William seemed a laughably wrong name for such a cat.

The landlady arrived.

I got my shoes on and stood up.

She was a keen-looking woman. Her suit had been much worn but it had cost a lot of money. I felt that my clothes were cheap—but I did not have crows'-feet round my eyes. Her powder was too thick.

I said, 'Would it be possible for me to have a look at the furnished room you have to let?'

'I'll have to have a month's rent in advance,' she said. 'And I'm afraid I'll have to ask for cash. Is that all right?'

'Yes.'

I hoped that my ability to pay would not make her think that I might be a prostitute.

She was looking me over.

I felt like a large child.

'Where have you been living?' she asked.

'I was living in Cottingham with my mother until she died. Actually, I've come to Hull to look round for something to do. I have some money my mother left me and I'm living on that. I expect I'll have to have some training of some kind. I don't really know what would be suitable. The only job I've ever had was once when I helped at a riding school—though that wasn't really a job.'

I knew that my clothes were not the clothes of a girl who had once been part of the healthy, respectable countryside, and my voice was not at all the voice of a girl who loved

128

horses, but the riding school was an inspiration. It made the old woman content that I was a good girl—she was probably too far behind the times to imagine that I might be a bad boy.

She said, 'Well, you'd better come and have a look at the room and see if you like it. I think you will. It's just comfortable for one person.'

She led the way. I followed her up the stairs. The banisters were painted white. It was all as genteel as I had wanted it to be. She showed me the bathroom and then we went along the first landing. At the end of the landing a flight of stairs ran up to the attics. I thought of the attics at home. All this was more spacious and more substantial and for taller, better educated people. There was carpet and the two doors were painted white.

She put the key in the lock and opened the door to the front attic.

It was a woman's room.

Half the ceiling sloped, but a large window broke out of the slope to overlook the front street. There was a table and two chairs and a comfortable arm chair with a blue cover on it. The single bed had a bare mattress.

'You'll have to get some bedding,' she said. 'Mrs Stephenson might lend you what you need until you get settled in.'

There was a wardrobe and a dressing table with a mirror that had hinged wings. At the end of the room there was a sink and a cooker.

I wanted to live in the room as a young woman. The room was obviously intended for a woman. It was better than I had expected. The wallpaper was yellow and grey in vertical stripes.

I told Mrs Cartwright that I liked the room and that I would take it.

She showed me how to turn the gas fire on and showed me where the gas and electric meters were.

I received the key and a rent book.

When she had gone I took off my coat and my shoes and lay down on the bare mattress.

I stretched my arms. I was happy and I was tired. The day seemed to have been going on for many hours. I stretched my legs out straight and pointed my toes. I had never been more pleased with myself. In half a day I had travelled across

129

millions of light years. I had done what was impossible. I was new-born.

Courage was the best virtue and it was given the best rewards. I liked the grey and yellow wallpaper.

What I had done was correct. It was better to do what one wanted to do than to attempt creepy sublimations. It was better to live as a woman than to be a neurotic dress designer. It was better to live as a woman than to be a miserable hero and rush about the desert like a headless chicken.

I would have to remember to hitch my skirt when I sat down. All day I had forgotten that one should hitch a tight skirt to keep it from seating. I could sit in the blue armchair with my legs crossed, in my room, which was a woman's room. I would buy clothes and hang up coats and dresses in the wardrobe. I would put my underclothes in the drawers of the dressing table. The mirror of the dressing table had wings so that I would be able to see myself in profile. I might leave my stockings in the bathroom on the floor below. There would be my washing on a line in the back garden of the house.

I smiled.

Part Three

———

MY NAME IS WENDY

1

In the Daily Telegraph I read:

'A Baltimore criminal court judge today authorised an operation to change the sex of George Lloyd, 17, who is awaiting sentence on a charge of stealing 15 women's wigs, valued at £400. Two doctors at Johns Hopkins Hospital described Lloyd as a psychic hermaphrodite and said the operation would be in his best interest. The youth said he wanted the operation performed. His lawyer said the request was made so that Lloyd could have a chance for rehabilitation before sentence was passed on the burglary charge.'

But that was in America. If I was found out, I would be sent to a Borstal to march about and play football, or to prison, where there were three men to a cell to prevent sodomy.

I wondered why he had wanted fifteen wigs. I felt happy for him. He was very fortunate. I wondered what he looked like. I hoped he was pretty.

No one who read the Daily Telegraph could be suspected of being a psychic hermaphrodite. I was holding it with hands that had nails that were painted with nail varnish. I thought that nail varnish made me move my hands in a feminine way.

Very often the sane walked about near the edge of madness, like Charlie Chaplins unaware of the abyss. They were sleepwalkers. I had crossed over the abyss. Now there were new dangers, but they were less terrible because they were external.

Through my senses I had pleasant contact with the world. The colours and textures and volumes and densities made sensations that were acceptable to me.

I was part of the world. I occupied space. I did not exist because I thought. I existed because I was a mass, a complexity of molecules. I had reached existence through a series of perversions stretching back in a universe that I had confidence was in a steady state of perversion. Only the void was not a perversion. I said, 'Everyone should change sex at leastonce. It broadens the mind.'

I had not changed sex.

2

They were days of happiness.

I went out shopping, and when I came back I ran up the stairs to try on the things I had bought. I went into shops and bought clothes, and sometimes I went into shops and came out without buying anything. I would have liked to spend afternoons in fitting rooms trying on all the dresses in the shop, but I could not risk that.

It was queenly to sit while a girl put my feet into shoes.

One girl suggested that I had rather a long foot to please. I was not in the least upset. I knew that long feet were fashionable. I left the shop as a lady who has been affronted by an ignorant menial.

Every day I was laughing to myself and thinking how clever I was. I was delighted with myself.

'Madam may find this more suitable. . . . What does madam think? Would modom care to look at these? They are quite the latest thing in panties. . . . I'll just get your change, madam. . . . Yes, madam, we have this style in blue. . . .'

'Would madam care to try it on in our fitting room?'

'I haven't really got the time, I'm afraid. Could I take it away and bring it back if it doesn't fit?'

'Of course, madam.'

They were so respectful that I felt that I really had begun life in Cottingham.

I bought an expensive skirt of orange-yellow tweed and an expensive grey-green jumper, and when I wore them I felt that I must have lived in comfort with a well-bred mother. Certainly I could never have fried chips in a fish-and-chip shop.

I was Madam.

I was tall and slender and making myself more elegant. The

fringe had been a mistake.

Hour by hour and day by day I was pleased.

Those who attempted to reconcile human beings to limitations always maintained that there could only be happiness when the human being lived in a way that is good for others. Thus they would have everybody good to everybody else and nobody good to himself. Their ideal was selflessness and loss of personality. The aim of general moralities was socialization.

I was selfish and I was establishing my personality. I was not living as a social unit. I was living consciously.

I was conscious of the clothes I was wearing. I was selfish. It was an extreme and exquisite selfishness to be wearing women's clothes. To be dressed as a woman, to behave as a woman, that was to be myself. I was not a social insect. I was Wendy, a large mammal that owned clothes. I had bought them. They were mine.

Their effect was so personal that it seemed strange that they had been made in factories that were part of prosaic industrial organization.

Somewhere there were men who cut skirts so that they could get money to buy trousers.

3

It was one evening when I was pushing my hair about in an attempt to get rid of the fringe and wishing that all of it would hurry and grow longer that I began to hear pop music from the back attic.

I had seen my next door neighbour once. She was a small girl of eighteen or nineteen who was coming up the stairs wearing a suede jacket and tight black slacks. She was in a hurry, and she only nodded to me.

She had a habit of getting to one record or another and then playing it over and over again. I had bought a transistor radio. I had to use it to drown her out.

Then one night she was coming up the stairs to the attics as I was about to go down. She wore a heavy blue sweater and her slacks. Under her arm she carried a large black portfolio.

135

She looked up. Her face was round and cheerful.

'Hello!' She grinned up at me.

I smiled and nodded.

She came up on the landing with me. I was taller and I felt much older.

'I say,' she said, 'I've been wanting to see you.'

For a moment I had the fear that she had wanted to see me because the people in the house were talking about the weird monster that had come to live with them.

But she went on, 'It's about my record player. Does it bother you?'

'I can hear it sometimes,' I said.

'I'm terribly sorry. I was only thinking about it today. I'll have to keep it low. Has it bothered you a lot?'

'No, it's quite all right.'

'Are you sure it doesn't bother you?'

'Well, it does a bit when I keep hearing the same record over and over again.'

'Oh, I say, I'm dreadfully sorry!'

'It doesn't matter.'

'No, it does matter. I'll only play it when you're out.'

'I'm afraid I don't go out much in the evenings.'

'Then I'll not play it at all.'

'No, don't stop on my account. You were here first. And I like it sometimes—as long as the same record doesn't keep going on all night.'

'Are you sure?'

'Quite sure.'

'Are you really quite sure?'

'Yes.'

She looked at me intently as though to see whether I was saying that I did not mind in order to be polite. Then she said, 'I must have been annoying you dreadfully. It's been very thoughtless of me. I'm not going to do it again.' She shifted her portfolio from under her right arm to under her left arm. 'My name's June.' She held out her liberated hand.

'My name's Wendy,' I said.

We shook hands with dignity.

'I'm at the art college,' she said. 'I'm going to Hull Fair tonight. Have you been to the Fair yet?'

'No.'

136

'I'm going with a boy from college. He's hopeless—but he's rather good at cricket. I feel sorry for him. I keep telling him that he'll never be a painter and that he shouldn't stay at the college just because of me, but he doesn't take any notice. His name's Mat. I'm not in love with him or anything. He wanted to be serious with me. But I told him that he mustn't be serious because I don't want to hurt him. I had to hurt a boy when I was sixteen, and he said that he was going to jump off the top of the castle—I live at Scarborough—but I didn't believe him, and then he went and got drunk and hit a policeman, and I felt terrible. So I don't want to have to hurt Mat. Do you think I'm being conceited in saying that?'

'No.'

'I'm not really being conceited, it's just Mat. He's hopeless. He's always getting himself hurt by girls. He's too emotional. I don't think it suits a cricketer to be emotional, do you?'

'No.'

'He's played for Yorkshire Colts. Of course I like him a lot, but I only like him for a friend. I don't know how I'd feel about him if he got a Yorkshire Cap. What if he turned out to be another Hutton? It's very difficult. And I don't want to marry an artist. I think it's wrong for artists to marry other artists. Don't you agree? I think I'd like to marry a doctor— a consultant psychiatrist. I was under a psychiatrist for my asthma attacks. He didn't cure the asthma, but I get all sorts of queer feelings about him. Do you ever get queer feelings?'

'Sometimes.'

'I want a professional man for a husband,' she announced, as though she would give herself to a professional man as her contribution to the forces of order in the world. 'A doctor or a lawyer or an architect. I have a boy friend at college who's on the architectural side, but I can't get to like him as much as I like Mat—I feel sorry for Mat. Architects aren't artists, are they? Anyway, I don't think they are. They're just nice, boring people who draw straight lines. Electronics engineers are just nothing. But I don't want to get married for a long time yet. I want to make my name as a painter—if I can. When I finish at the college here I want to go on to the Royal College of Art—that's in London. Don't you think that one should have a career before one gets married? I think so. Don't you agree?'

137

'Well —'

'I definitely think so. If you have a successful career, you don't have to be too dependant on your husband. And if you have to give it up, you can always use it against him when there's a row—though I shouldn't say that. Are you married?'

'No.'

'Where do you come from, if you don't mind my asking?'

'I lived in Cottingham with my mother.'

'You didn't mind my asking, did you?'

'Not at all.'

'Are you sure?'

'Quite sure.'

'I can't imagine your living with your mother.'

'Why not?'

'Well—if you don't mind my saying so—I imagine that you might have been living with a very difficult man—if you don't mind my saying so.'

'No, I don't mind your saying so. It sounds interesting. Do I look like a woman with a past?'

'Not a long past, you're too young. But you do look as though you've had a short past. Something shattering in Paris.'

'Thank you. No one has ever said anything nicer to me.' I smiled.

'I wish I looked as though I had a bit of a past,' she complained. 'I just look what I am. June, who gets asthma.'

'You don't look asthmatic to me.'

'I know. And I'm not tall enough. Sometimes I feel like a rubber ball. In hot weather I feel terrible. I wish I was like you.'

'Thank you.'

'Still, it may help my work later on. One has to suffer if one wants to get anything out of life. Don't you agree? A person who hasn't suffered can't understand the important things. You look as though you understand. The first time I saw you I thought you looked an interesting person. I wanted to get to know you to talk to you. Most people are fools. Don't you agree?'

'I don't know.'

'I say,' she said, 'would you like to come to the Fair with Mat and me tonight? Have you ever been to Hull Fair? It's a preview of hell. Mat and I are going to have a drink first and get a bit tight. I'll probably fall off something and have to be brought back on a five-barred gate. Would you like to come?'

'No,' I said, 'I don't think I can. I'm not too well.'

She made a tender mouth of understanding.

I had never liked Hull Fair. When I had been little and I had gone in daylight with my father and Shirley I had not liked the noise and the crowds. At night, with the blazing lights and the roaring loudspeakers, its garishness and blare was fearful.

4

Marguerite Stephenson had lent me some bedding on the day I had arrived. She continued to be friendly.

From my window I could see the Stephensons come home at about half-past four. She would get out of the red mini-car and come into the house and he would drive away to take the car to where he garaged it.

They did not teach at the same school. She had only been to a training college. He had been at London University. He was tall and dark and moved on long legs with a loping stride. His jaw, thrust out, was clean and angular. I could see that he had as high an opinion of his intelligence as I had of mine.

I thought that he must be in his late twenties, but he tried to be more youthful, like a down-from-the-university television personality, in order that one might admire the boyish ease with which he carried his learning. His greetings to me when we met with each other were gayly patronising.

I quickly developed a hatred of him.

June told me that the Stephensons had decided not to have a baby until Marguerite had got the B.A. degree for which she was studying.

Though she had their confidence, June did not like either of the Stephensons.

'Marguerite's a sly bitch. And she's as miserable as hell. It doesn't show, but underneath she's as miserable as miserable. She knows she's married the wrong man. Of course Philip hasn't noticed. He's too full of himself to notice anything. I should think that when he was a little boy his mother thought he was wonderful, and then he went to the university, and now he's in a world of his own. He thinks if he died the buses would stop running. Haven't you ever noticed that funny look in his face? He makes me sick. That's why I like Frank—have I ever told you about Frank? One night the Stephensons gave a party and Frank came and he got into an argument with Philip about politics. Philip was all goody-goody and righteous about everything, but Frank just cut him to pieces. It was a treat. Philip called Frank a thug and Frank called Philip a pinhead. I thought they were going to have a fight. Frank would have won easily. In the end Philip went off to bed. That's all he could do. There haven't been any parties since then. Marguerite was as nasty as hell with Frank. She hates him because she wants him—you know what I mean. She's like that—sly. Frank looks like Paul Gauguin. You ought to meet him. He was a teacher once, but he got the sack or something. He's a thoroughly bad man. You ought to meet him. He hates Philip because Philip was at university. He says that education in this country is just a racket and that it produces nothing but mediocre people propping up other mediocre people. I believe him. . . . Would you like to see some of my work? I have some life drawings here.'

She took me into her room and showed me drawings of nude women. I was surprised at her skill.

She said, 'You can see, I'm pretty good.'

'They're marvellous,' I said.

Then she talked to me about the technical problems of drawing, pulling out sheets to show me what she meant. She handled the drawings roughly. I thought that, if I had made them, I would have been reverent with them.

June was lively and clever. I liked her, and she seemed to like me. She talked to me, and soon I was saying more in return. I enjoyed showing her things I had bought.

On Friday nights she went straight from the art college to catch the train home to Scarborough and I did not see her again until Monday night.

One Saturday Marguerite asked me if I would like to have Sunday dinner with her and Philip. She told me that on Sundays they had lunch at about two o'clock and their dinner at about seven o'clock.

The next day I went down in the late afternoon when it was time for putting the lights on and asked her if I could help her with the preparation of the meal.

'That's very good of you,' she said, 'but, to be quite honest, I like to do it all myself. My mother used to say that there isn't room in one kitchen for two women.'

'I thought —'

'Well, of course you can help if you want to.'

'I'd like to,' I said.

Philip was sitting in the arm chair near the bookcase reading a newspaper. He looked up at me. 'My wife likes to have all the heat and steam of Sunday dinner all to herself. It makes her feel like a hausfrau.'

'Don't pay any attention,' said Marguerite.

'We always have an up and a down about Sunday dinner,' he went on. 'Marguerite read too much D. H. Lawrence in her youth. It's made her somewhat womanly. All women are fascists. Yorkshire pudding, roast beef with roast potatoes, mashed potatoes, cauliflower with white sauce, rice pudding, and cheese. Every Sunday. It's a sort of gastronomic Nuremberg Rally. And I have to assist in the ritual.'

I supposed that he thought he was being funny. I made a little grin.

He thought that he looked very mid-Sunday lounging in the chair, but really he looked completely awake. He was as bright as a salesman.

Marguerite was soft. She was wearing a dress of pale blue that made one notice the blue of her eyes. I was wearing a navy blue skirt and a red jumper with a polo neck. I thought that I looked feminine in a simple, youthful way, but I felt inferior. There was the weight of her hips.

Philip talked. He was trying to impress me. His many fingers moved about as he spoke. He was talking about something that had happened when he was at university. There was nothing sure about him. My father could sit in his arm chair as though settled for eternity. Philip shifted about. I could see that under his trousers his legs were thin. He was smug. He thought that he was impressing me. He thought that I did not know anything. I did not want him to touch me. He expected approval. No doubt his mother had blessed his existence and told him that he was the best boy in the street.

141

I could see him doing his homework.

I could have been like him. But I knew that it was better to be wearing my clothes than doing the talking.

He was a salesman selling himself.

' . . . Though I am aware that there is a gulf between the sane revolutionary and the ego-maniac Jacobin, I am tempted to do something a mite desperate about the Sunday dinner ritual. . . .'

He had no grasp of how to talk nonsense. His words were like material coming out of a machine that had been built to do talking.

I could tell that I was more intelligent than he was, and there came moments when I almost wished that I was not in skirts so that I could let him know that I was more intelligent than he was. But I pretended to be a baffled girl. And then the circumstance of helplessness was interesting. I smiled and nodded like a fool and enjoyed myself.

Thus I reached a high place of snobbish pleasure. I felt like a brilliant but pretty blue-stocking of Oxford being lectured by a red-brick know-all who was neither brilliant nor female and therefore completely inferior. My brain was better and I was wearing knickers!

Marguerite made a pot of tea, and then the questions began. I was questioned about my social background, my politics, my religion, and my attitude to sex.

My social background I represented as middle-class tending towards bohemianism.

My politics I represented as a loving socialism set upon a sound base of liberal principles. I was in favour of all forms of private enterprise except those forms that led to an accumulation of money—but I liked Jews. I was in favour of the monarchy but against the House of Lords.

My religion I put forth as a respect for the character and life of Jesus Christ that went off into silence.

I put a quaint firmness into my sexual attitude.

In all I was a meek and dainty and fastidious girl.

I tried to help Marguerite with preparing the dinner, but she did really want to do everything herself. She was everywhere in the kitchen, and whenever I picked anything up she took it from me.

It was decided that I should peel the potatoes, but as soon

as I started there was 'Not that knife, Wendy!' behind me and the implement I had found was taken from me and replaced by a blunter knife. I was charged not to leave any eyes in the potatoes, and soon she had the job from me and was doing it herself. I muttered that she ought to have a proper potato knife. I was told to get out the oven dish for the meat. I got out the wrong dish. I was sent to bring a fork from the cutlery drawer in the living room. The fork I brought was in some way the wrong fork.

As the cooking progressed she became more impatient with me. At one point she took me by the elbow and pushed me out of the way. I felt very unmarried.

Later, I was sticking a fork in the potatoes while she was looking at the joint in the oven. She slammed the oven door shut. I found that the pinafore she had given me to wear was trapped in the door. I gripped the pinafore and pulled it out. The oven door flew open. She slammed it shut again. My pinafore was trapped again.

'Really, Wendy, I wish you wouldn't stand in the way!'

'I only —'

'Yes, but don't stand there.'

'Have I to go out?'

'No, Wendy, I'm sorry. I'm glad of your help. Could you go and set the table?'

I began setting the table by finding the wrong table cloth, but soon I was doing the job slowly and deliberately and hoping that it would last until the food was ready to be brought through. I wished that I had not tried to help in the kitchen.

Philip was trying to smoke a pipe.

Marguerite came through. 'Really, Philip, I don't think you had any need to start with that thing before dinner. You're making it absolutely horrible in here.'

Philip knocked the pipe out.

Cooking the dinner had made Marguerite mistress.

He went and turned on the television.

The food was well cooked. I had not had a meal like it since the last time Mrs Wilson had made dinner for my father and me. Marguerite was not quite as good a cook as Mrs Wilson, but she was a much better cook than Mrs Ford.

Philip left the carving of the joint to Marguerite. He toyed

143

with his dinner and did not ask for any second helpings. He ate as though he were critical of himself for having to do anything so animal as eating.

I thought that he ought to have been a monk and lived on lentils and cold water. The memorising of senseless prayers and the writing of books that had already been written would have been suitable occupations for him. His thin legs would have been hidden by the monk's habit, and a complicated system of meaninglessness would have been a fit refuge for his mind.

I hated him because he was better educated than my father.

I tried to imagine Philip and Marguerite in bed together. It was possible that he had read a text book on making love. He would not do anything that would not be passed as normal by an examining body.

After we had eaten he spoke of the rightness of right and the wrongness of wrong like the expensive Sunday newspaper he had been reading. He was the young man who had been to a university and learned well-washed things about the rule of reason.

I would have been like him if I had not wanted to be a woman. Without my madness I would have been as clear-headed as he was. There did not seem to be any darkness in him. There was cause and there was effect, but nothing existed in itself. His mind had been trained in acceptable ways of thinking. There did not seem to be anything contrary or violent. He would never strike a woman. He was not a manual worker. He would never kill with his own hands, but he might agree with other members of a committee that killing must be done because it was necessary. His hands would always be clean. Men like my father blundered into violence. They had rough hands that had been used on stuff. In The Avenues was this man who was trained in abstractions, and had a pure, abstract conscience.

He talked about teaching and complained that he was not paid enough.

Marguerite said, 'If you had to face a class of Secondary Modern girls, you'd know what teaching was like—or rather, what fighting for your life was like. They make me feel about seventy years old and very frail. They know that they're on the short end of the education racket, so they're simply not

144

interested. And they never will be interested. They're not fools.'

'When you've got your degree,' said Philip, 'you'll be able to get away from the impossible to the merely very difficult.'

'When I get my degree.' She sighed. 'You know,' she said, 'I'm getting tired of working. Sometimes, when I wake up on a Monday morning and see all the savage young faces of the week before me, I want to die. I just want to close my eyes and die.'

I said that I was glad that I was not a teacher.

The great explosion of children with wreaths of flowers and cornucopias, blowing on trumpets and playing on harps, was selected from and selected from until it became a few scholars sitting at the High Table of some ancient college, each seeing the other's point of view better than he saw his own, and each wanting to put poison in the other's port.

5

Day by day I was playing my game, like a child playing happily alone. I had my clothes and my paints and powders and creams and perfumes.

I had no prospect of employment. I thought of going to the National Insurance office and telling lies to get a card, but I feared that they might make enquiries until they found out that I did not exist in Somerset House.

In the end my money would run out. I did not like to think about it. I had to be happy in the present. I explained to myself that life was only a temporary arrangement for anyone.

In the meantime my happiness was being alive: washing, ironing, climbing the stairs, waking up and discovering myself in the morning, getting dressed and getting undressed, talking with my Cottingham voice, cleaning my room, cooking my meals, putting on nail varnish and scraping off nail varnish, doing what I could with my hair, making up my face, walking in the street and being seen, being careful not to show too much leg when sitting down, making mental criticisms of the appearance of women I saw in the street, noticing that a man

145

had noticed me.

Sometimes I laughed at myself. 'You poor old thing, you're made out of foam rubber and sticking plaster! You poor lifeless dolly! You're sitting up on the shelf, very pretty, with your hair nicely curved and your face nicely painted, but you're not for sale. Nobody can take you away to play with— you'd soon be brought back and complained about!'

6

One night I asked June if she would like to have tea with me. I made cheese on toast.

'Have you ever been in love?' she enquired.

'No.'

'Are you sure? You look as though you could have been.'

'I promise you I never have.'

'You look as though you could be in love quite easily. You look soulful and all that.'

'Like a cow looking over a hedge?'

'No, not like that. You look as though you have inner conflicts. I should think that you have been in love but you don't want to tell me about it. Why don't you want to tell me? Was it very unhappy? You can tell me about it, Wendy.'

'I can't.'

'Why not?'

'Because I haven't been in love.'

'I don't believe you. Tell me what he was like.'

'Well, actually, I did once have an affair. His name was Arnold.'

'What was he like?'

'Thin and bald.'

'How old was he?'

'About sixty.'

'Good heavens!'

'He may have been older. I never asked him. We would have got married, but his mother didn't approve of me.'

'How old was she?'

'Ninety.'

'You are silly, Wendy!'

'It's all true. His name was Arnold and he was very old and bald and he sagged at the knees, but he had a wonderful personality. Do you know what he did for a living?'

'No.'

'He caught bluebottles and made them into ink.'

'Blue ink?'

'No, red ink.'

'I don't believe you.'

'You can believe me or not as you please, June, but I am most certainly speaking the truth. I always do.'

7

Sometimes Marguerite's femaleness made me feel as though I wanted to rush to my room and attack myself with a razor blade. With June I was always cheerful. She had a boyishness.

She said that I had the figure for slacks.

I told her that I had a pair.

'Why don't you wear them?'

'I don't like trousers.'

'Haven't you ever worn them?'

'Yes. Actually, I used to wear them nearly all the time. I got fed-up with them.'

'You ought to wear them. You're tall and slinky. You'd look good in trousers.'

I said, 'It's a sin to wear clothes of the opposite sex.'

'How is it a sin?'

'It's a sin against God and Nature,' I said with mock solemnity.

'That's silly,' she said. 'If they haven't got a zip at the front, they aren't the clothes of the opposite sex. Anyway, I used to have a pair with a zip at the front. I didn't feel sinful in them. I just felt tough and ruthless.'

'I was brought up with extreme strictness,' I said.

'You weren't.'

'I was.'

'You weren't at all, Wendy. I can tell.'

147

'How can you tell?'

'Because there's something strange about you. It wouldn't surprise me if you turned out to be a Russian spy.'

'Do I look like a spy?'

'Yes. You look a bit dangerous.'

'That's not a very nice thing to say to anyone.'

'I wouldn't mind people saying it to me. I'd like to look like you. And then there's your voice.'

'What's wrong with my voice?'

'It's a man-trap voice. There's a sort of sexy growl in it.'

I was stunned with pleasure. I said, 'I don't think I like being discussed like this.'

Occasionally June and I went to the pictures. Once we went to the New Theatre and saw a play.

June did not enjoy walking along in the street as I enjoyed it. She tended to hurry to get to where we were going.

Walking at night was different from walking in daylight. In daylight I was a girl enjoying freedom. Under the streetlights I was a fragrant woman who had suffered from the world in some subtle, feminine way—though June's good humour sometimes spoiled the mood.

8

The Johnsons kept themselves to themselves. They were both about thirty and both small and dark haired and they both worked at the County Hall in Beverley.

9

Roy's clothes were still in the suitcase. Every morning I took it out of the wardrobe and unlocked it and took out my shaving things. I always shaved at the sink in my room. It was a hateful task. Twice a week would have been enough, but I did it every day. When I had finished I put the shaving things back in the suitcase and locked the suitcase and put it back in the wardrobe. Then I went down in my dressing gown to get washed in the bathroom on the floor below.

I had to be careful because June had begun to examine my cosmetics and sort through my toilet things and handle my clothes. She even opened my handbag. It was not the bag I had bought on the first day but a large one that I had bought since.

'You don't have any letters in here,' she said.

'Should I have?'

'Women always have letters in their handbags.'

'I don't.'

'Then you're an exception. I'm always finding my bag stuffed with letters. I have to sort them out and burn most of them.'

'I'm a spy,' I said. 'I eat all my letters.'

'Haven't you got any family at all?' she asked.

'Not now.'

'And you haven't got a boy friend.'

'No.'

'You must have.'

'I haven't.'

'No family, no boy friends, no job. Don't you ever get sad?'

'I'm very happy.'

'I don't see how you can be. Even Marguerite feels a bit sorry for you. You're so strange. I think there's something very odd about you, Wendy. I don't know what it is, but it's something.'

'Am I a woman of mystery?'

'Yes, you are. You ought to be fretting about not having anything to do, but you don't seem to mind. If I were like you, I'd want to be a model—' She stopped. 'I know what's strange,' she said. 'You're always so well dressed and your hair is always so nice and you always look as though you've just come from a beautician's, but you're never going anywhere. It looks lovely, but it's unnatural. You wear your clothes as though they were the most important things in the world. Everybody does that sometimes, but you're doing it all the time. You're too ladylike. Whenever I come in here you're always as fresh as a daisy. You're too perfect.'

I said that I liked to look nice.

'But you seem to overdo it. You're far too ladylike. And

149

you're so self-conscious.'

'I'm not.'

'You are.'

'I'm not at all.'

'You are. Look at the way you're sitting in that chair.'

I crossed my legs.

'It's no use doing that,' she said. 'I think you're rather strange—if you don't mind my saying so. Did your mother's death have an effect on you?'

'It may have had.' I saw an opportunity to explain my strangeness. 'It made me very anxious about everything. You see, I feel that I have to be neat and tidy all the time or something dreadful will happen.'

'You ought to see a psychiatrist.'

'What for?'

'He might be able to make you more relaxed. Don't you think so?'

'I've never thought of it.'

'Don't you ever think of your future?'

'Not if I can help it.'

10

I attempted to be more casual after June's remonstrance, but it was not easy, for, besides my need to maintain disguise, I always wanted to be as pretty as I could be. My appearance and my freshness were my first concerns. A real woman might sometimes take her femininity for granted. I could never do that. I had to work at being a woman all the time.

Yet there was one way in which I was less self-aware than I had been when I had worn trousers. Now I was not aware of a mind that might take leave of the senses.

I began to think that my chest was developing. It was difficult to tell.

It was quite simple. I wanted to be a woman. The complications were caused by resistance to my desire, not by the desire itself.

Yes, my chest was beginning to develop.

The November mists that rolled on the Humber covered the city. I sat by the gas fire reading a novel. From time to time the fire made a slight clinking sound. I imagined, in the stillness, that I could hear the hootings of ships on the distant river.

I had spent a lot of money on clothes, but, apart from that, I was spending very little week by week. I estimated that I could hold out at least until the summer of the following year. And, before then, something might happen to save me. My lack of a woman's National Insurance card was the problem. I thought that I would be willing to do any sort of work as a woman—as long as it was not anything that would make my hands rough. I might be able to get employment in a shop if I had a National Insurance card. I could serve and give change and be polite. But it would be better to be a typist. I thought of getting a typewriter and trying to teach myself to type. Of course it would be best to be a model—a clothes horse—but that was only something to be dreamt about. And it would be impossible for me to be a model unless I had treatment and an operation.

Early December was very cold. In the mornings the windows were covered with plumes and bursts of hoar frost.

Marguerite spoke about the Christmas holiday. She was looking forward to having a rest from her Secondary Modern girls.

Philip complained of difficulty in starting the car in the mornings.

11

My father would never have had the determination to go to the lengths to which I had gone in order to do something that he wanted to do.

I decided to send him a warm sweater for Christmas, a sweater that would keep him warm when he was cutting the fish on cold mornings. I looked at many sweaters before I bought one that was of heavy but soft wool and was dark blue—but not as dark blue as navy blue.

When I got it back to my room I unwrapped it to look at it, and then I put it away in a drawer in my dressing table.

The next evening June found the sweater and held it up. 'This is miles too big for you, Wendy. You'll be lost in it.'

'It's a present for someone. Put it back. I wish you wouldn't rummage about in my things, June. I've told you before.'

'Who's it for?'

'Mind your own business.'

'I always knew you had a secret. Tell me.'

'I'm not going to tell you anything.'

'There's somebody. I always knew there was somebody. Why don't we ever see him? Is he a married man?'

'Yes. He has a wife and seven mistresses.'

'Are you one of them?'

'That's right.'

'I don't believe you.'

12

June said that I could go home to Scarborough with her for Christmas. I said that I did not want to. She said that I would be lonely on my own and she tried to persuade me. I told her that I did not mind being on my own and that I did not like Christmas.

On the day she left she gave me a pack of two pairs of nylons. I said, 'Snap!' and gave her a pack of two pairs of nylons. She said goodbye and wished me a Merry Christmas.

Then Marguerite told me that she and Philip were going to spend Christmas with her parents in York.

There would only be the Johnsons in the house over Christmas. I did not know them.

I made a sound parcel of the sweater I had bought for my father and took it to the post office. When he saw by the postmark that I was still in Hull he would wonder why I did not come home for Christmas, but he would not know my name and address. On the card with the sweater I had written 'Roy'.

I came back from the post office and lay on my bed and

cried.

After a while I said to myself, 'You can either be a girl or a human being. You have to choose.' I answered myself, 'I've chosen.'

I got off the bed and went to the mirror to see how much damage the crying had done to my make-up. I was pleased to find that I looked quite pathetically pretty with my eyes full of tears.

My detachment made me laugh.

Then I started trying to scream. I was trying as hard as I could and at the same time stopping myself. There was a rattling noise in my throat. I was choking. I knew that I had become hysterical.

I was against the wall, beating my fists on it until I thought that bones must break. The pain was violent, but it seemed to be happening to my fists and not to me.

Suddenly I slipped down and sat on the floor with my legs folded carefully and neatly to the side. My high-heeled shoes were together. They looked very real. It was as though I had never seen them before. I touched them. They belonged to me. My skirt was drawn tight. It curved over my thighs and was flat at the front. It was a grey flannel skirt. It was real. The tears were falling out of my eyes onto the skirt. Where they fell on the grey flannel they made spots of black.

A male head was big enough to live in, but a female had to live in her body. A woman lived under her skirt. Under the skirt was warm darkness. Soldier ants had big heads, but the queen ant in the darkness at the centre of the nest was a belly.

I thought, 'A skirt like this is supposed to mean that one is a woman. But dummies in shop windows wear skirts like this. They aren't women. Dummies in shop windows don't go home for Christmas. They have to stay in the shop windows looking gay and disdainful. While people are eating Christmas dinner the dummies are standing in the shop windows. Only a walking policeman sees them.'

Marguerite had asked me if I would look after her cat over Christmas. That would be company. And I could buy a bottle of whiskey and make myself drunk. I wondered whether I would be able to swallow whiskey. I imagined that it might burn my throat.

The time would pass. I composed myself.

I got to my feet and went to repair my face.

13

Marguerite brought William up on the day she left. She gave
me the heavy creature into my arms and then handed me four
tins of cat-food.

That night I tried to cuddle William in bed. But he did not
want to be cuddled. He wanted to get out. I tried to force
him to be quiet by hugging him to me, but he struggled more
and more as though he had become frightened of me. He
stuck his claws into the front of my nightdress, and for some
entangled moments I was glad that I was made of foam rubber
and sticking plaster. He got into such a state of fear and
annoyance that it was difficult for me to let him get away from
me.

Next morning was the morning of Christmas Eve.

I got through the morning sensibly, but in the afternoon
I heard 'Come All Ye Faithful' on my radio and I started
crying.

After tea I went out and bought a bottle of whiskey. It cost
more than I had expected it would cost.

When I got it back I took off the foil at the top and drew out
the cork. I sniffed. It was a powerful male spirit that made
me think of successful men and five pound notes. I thought
that I would not have to drink much of it for it to have an
effect. There might be enough in the bottle to keep me drunk
until the New Year.

I found a glass and put about a quarter of an inch of whiskey
in the bottom.

If I put water with it, I might not be able to swallow it at
one gulp, but I feared that, if I did not put water with it, it
might burn my throat. I put water in until there was almost
an inch of liquid in the glass.

I held the glass before me in my right hand. I braced
myself. I took a mouthful and swallowed it back.

It did not burn my throat at all.

I made the next dose stronger. It produced a soft, melting

sensation on my tongue and the feeling of it going down was comforting. It explored my stomach and reassured me. I could understand why people like whiskey.

I did not put any water at all with the third dose. It went down, and there was a slow-motion explosion in my middle that made me feel confident and healthy.

I thought well of Scotland. I tried to imagine myself in a kilt and a tight black jacket with lace at my cuffs and neck.

I sat down and set about drinking myself to drunkenness.

After a while I observed myself as a boy dressed as a woman. I felt sinfully German, and I kept starting to sing 'Falling In Love Again.'

The cat was curled up, grey and warm, in front of the gas fire. It had been asleep since tea time.

> *Falling in love again*
> *Never wanted to*
> *What am I to do?*
> *I can't help it . . .*

I stood up, and immediately fell forward to rest my elbows on the table and my head in my hands. I realised that I was more drunk than I had thought I was. To get undressed to go to bed seemed more than I would have the energy and organization to accomplish. It would be an achievement if I could reach my bed and lie down on it. The fire would have to be left burning until the shilling ran out because I could not think how to turn it off.

I raised my head from my hands. The room was moving round at a steady pace.

'You can't make a habit of this, Wendy. Being an intersex is quite enough. Being an alcoholic intersex would be far too much. One has to draw the line somewhere. Do you understand? Degeneracy is one thing, total collapse is another. If you totally collapse on the floor, I won't speak to you ever again. Did I bring you all this way for you to turn into a sunken drut?—drunken slut. It won't do. If you start drinking, you'll stop washing your underwear, and then you'll smell, and then you'll thoroughly deserve to get caught by the police and taken before a dirty-minded, ignorant old magistrate and sent off to prison to have your hair cut. I expect they use carbolic soap in prison. How would you like that? Or they might send you to Borstal and have you playing football. Serve you right. They'd make a man of you—that's all you'd be fit for. Can't you imagine yourself in Borstal having to say "sir" to some stupid bald-head who learns lads woodwork and manliness? Serve you right for getting drunk.

'Drunken showgirls get their pants taken down. They get taken advantage of. But I'm not a showgirl. I'm a nice and genteel—because I have to be nice and genteel. I'm a bitch really. I'm an insane bitch of an animal. I can feel the bitch state in my belly. I can feel it. It's more than I am. I want to be a bitch. I want to be a faithful bitch. I want to be the one that gets her pants taken down. Men can do things. A man can do anything, and you can't stop him. A man should come and shout at me, "Why the hell have you got yourself into this state, you silly drunken bitch!" and hit me across the face. I would be a faithful bitch. We could be happy — and I would never tell him how much I enjoyed wearing my clothes and being the woman. I'd look after him. I'd never let him down.'

I stumbled across the room to my bed and sat down on it. I shut my eyes. Lights were flashing past. It was like standing on a station platform at night as an express train came through. I opened my eyes.

Clumsily and slowly I started to take off my clothes.

I was standing, getting my slip over my head. I reeled and fell onto the bed. I struggled to free myself from the slip and heard a tearing sound. 'Blast!' I got the slip off and sat up.

Now I was in brassière, knickers and stockings, and I still had my shoes on.

The fact that I still had my high-heeled shoes on made me feel like a woman who is paid for extraordinary misbehaviour. I laughed. I pulled at a suspender and let it slap back against my leg. I laughed again.

I kicked off my shoes and snaked myself between the covers. My legs felt nice in my stockings against the sheets.

The light in the centre of the ceiling was still on. I could not get out to go and switch it off. I hid my head under the covers. I had long hair. There was deep blackness. I said, 'Here I am, lewd and drunken and alone.'

I slid my hand to explore the bed, pretending that I might make contact with another hand.

14

I did not feel at all ill when I awoke. I thought that I should have had a headache, but my head was quite clear. My mouth was very dry. I must have a drink. I would have to get up and make myself a cup of tea. As soon as I moved I felt grubby about having slept in my underclothes.

I got up and put on fresh things. The room was very cold. The gas fire had gone out during the night. I discovered that there was only one shilling left for the gas and electric meters.

The whiskey bottle was standing on the table. It was half full. I put it away in the cupboard near the sink.

It was Christmas Day.

I put the shilling in the gas meter and lit the fire and made myself a cup of tea and boiled myself two eggs for breakfast.

After I had had breakfast I got myself ready and went out to get some shillings. There was a cold wind. I wore my grey tweed coat. A few people were walking about to get themselves appetites for dinner. I tried two off-licence shops. At the first I bought a box of matches and my request obtained two shillings in the change. At the second I bought a bottle of lemonade and the shopkeeper troubled himself to go to his living room to find six shillings to give me. I had told myself that he had done it because I was a girl.

I cleaned up the room when I got back.

I managed without trouble until it began to get dark in the afternoon, but then I began to think of my father asleep in his chair on Christmas Day afternoons. He clasped his hands together high on his chest as though any pressure lower down would be unbearable. As it was growing dark he would be as comfortable as an old dog, and the light would not be put on so as not to wake him.

I thought that I was going to start crying. But I remembered the slip that I had torn the night before when I was taking it off. I went and switched on the light and found the slip. The side seam had split near the top. I set myself to sew it.

15

On the morning of Boxing Day I had the feeling that the worst was over and that I had done well.

I would not turn back. I would be accepted as a woman or I would not be accepted at all. I knew who I was.

In the afternoon I sat down to write a letter to Shirley. She ought to be able to understand me.

Dear Shirley, You may have wondered why I was not at home on Christmas Day. I wanted to come to be with you and Dad, but it was not possible. I hope you had a nice time. I hope Dad received the sweater I sent him. I was thinking of you both.

The reason I could not come home was that I am now living as a woman. This may be a shock to you, but I am sure that, if you try, you can understand. I know it cannot be easy, for, although people are aware that there are people who feel themselves to belong to the opposite sex from that which is stated on the birth certificate, they never expect that anyone in their own family will be like that.

I have always wanted to be a female, and the fact that I have been able to dress and live as a female for the last three months without being detected shows that I was never really a male.

I do not know why I am as I am, but I know that my desire to be a woman is so powerful that I can never express it in words. It seems to come from outside of me, for it has much more strength than I have.

People like me are regarded with contempt and sometimes with hatred, but, surely, to feel contempt for me is a sort of contempt for womankind. And, surely, hatred must be a sign of jealousy, for I do not harm anyone.

Please do not go to the police about me. I am not having anything to do with men. I am not a homosexual. I am just living as an ordinary woman. I think that, if what I am doing is wrong, then it must be in some way wrong to be a woman.

Please try to understand my circumstances and do not be upset about what I am doing. Of course you must not tell Dad about this letter. Whatever happens, I do not want him to know what I am doing now. I would only want him to know if I could get treatment so as to be legally a woman.

I would like you to write to me. But, if you hate me very much, just ignore this letter 'and pretend that you never had a brother.

If you do write, my name is Miss Wendy Ross.

Love Wendy

On my way to post the letter I thought about how surprised she would be.

That night I got Roy's clothes out of the suitcase and made a parcel of them with brown paper and string.

I took it, and when nobody was looking, I dropped it over the low wall that surrounded the Y.W.C.A.

I walked back feeling proud of myself.

16

I had boots to wear in cold weather. I had a fringe again. My hair fell across my eyes. I liked tossing my head in order to see what I was doing.

June did not go home one Friday night, and on a very cold Saturday I set out with her to go to a football match in Bridlington. The art college team was playing some Bridlington team, and she had to be there for a reason to do with her extensive and complicated flirtations. She explained it to me, but I did not understand.

That Saturday was one of those days when I was looking my best.

The diesel travelled fast and swayed. June talked.

The land became less flat. There was farmland. We passed through Cottingham station at speed. Soon we could see the towers of Beverley Minster.

The train stopped at Beverley. Beverley was 'One of the best country towns in England'. There was shouting outside in the cold and quiet in the warm carriage. There were many chestnut trees in Beverley. In springtime they were glorious.

As we approached wayside stations the driver sounded two

159

notes on the train's Klaxon. Village platforms made for summer afternoons were left behind in the January cold.

'You look very thoughtful,' said June.

'I'm always thoughtful on trains,' I said.

In a field there were long, low sheds of wood that had been made dark umber with creosote.

June pointed. 'They keep battery hens in them,' she said. 'I think it's cruel.'

Nature was being remade. There was nothing that could not be compelled to do what it was necessary for it to do. Even God had undergone such modifications that hardly anybody knew him anymore.

I laughed.

'What are you laughing at?' June asked.

'Something I was thinking.'

'You are strange,' she said.

Bridlington appeared as the backs of semi-detached houses over the fields. It was supposed to be a jolly seaside place where jolly Northern folk had jolly Northern good times. According to an article I had read in one of the serious Sunday newspapers, miners raced whippets on the beach. I had often been on Bridlington beach, but I had never seen whippets being raced.

The Yorkshire one read about was not the same as the Yorkshire one lived in.

I wondered if I should have called myself Cathy.

The wind met us on the platform. This was no place for a romantic novel. The east wind would shock lovers to decency and blow poor ghosts away forever. We hunched ourselves against the blast.

'Do you think it might be too cold for football?' June asked.

'No,' I laughed, 'men play football in any weather. They have to.'

'Why?'

'They can't think of anything better to do.'

'I wouldn't like to be kicked on the leg on a day like this,' she said.

After enquiring the way of several people who seemed to be stupified by the cold we arrived on an open space of playing fields with a gasworks nearby that was making a smell. There was no football going on. There was nobody there. June said that it was too early, that the kick-off was not till half-past two. I said that I had no intention of staying on the Russian steppes until half-past two.

We found a groundsman in a hut. He wore a high-crowned trilby and had curved yellow teeth.

As though he were talking to two fools he told us that the Hull art college football team was not coming to the playing fields that afternoon and that there were no other playing fields in Bridlington. June argued. He told her slowly and clearly that he knew what teams would be playing football there that afternoon and what teams would not be playing football there that afternoon and that the Hull art college team was in the latter group. June admitted that she must have been misinformed.

When we were coming away from the hut she told me that footballers were mostly unreliable and recalled an occasion when the college team had been defeated by twenty goals to nothing.

I said that, if I did not get food and warmth very quickly, I would die of exposure.

We had to go to the seafront before we found a café that was open.

The sea looked too cold and dark to sustain life of any kind, but, out on the harbour wall, what looked like a bundle of old clothes was fishing with a rod and line. It was impossible to imagine how he withstood the cold, even dressed as he was in the attire of two or three men.

Snowflakes came flying in from the sea.

We ate egg and chips behind tall windows that looked out onto the seafront. We were the only customers. Outside was the sea and the curve of the bay under flurries of snow.

'If this isn't a lesson to me!' said June.

'A lesson about what?'

'A lesson,' she said. 'Never run after men, Wendy.'

'I won't,' I said.

'Fancy coming here! It's like the end of the world.'

I agreed with her.

We contemplated the bleakness through the windows.

I began to think that it was rather beautiful.

June said that there was a train back to Hull at half-past three.

161

The electric clock on the wall showed a few minutes after half-past one.

We decided to go to a pub.

When we left the café the snow was whirling. The wind had dropped and it felt slightly warmer.

We arrived at a pub that looked from the outside as though it might be full of jovial fishermen. It proved to be full of basket chairs. But the holiday makers had gone. It seemed a Marie Celeste of a pub. June had to tap on the bar with a half-crown to make an attractive, thirty-nine year old barmaid appear and say what a terrible day it was.

June bought a pineapple juice and then I bought a pineapple juice.

The barmaid said that there was a fire in the 'snug'.

The snug was a small room at the end of a passage.

There was a man.

June shouted, 'Frank Cracknell!'

He was in his late twenties, fair and strong. There was a lazy-lion ease about him. He sat in a Windsor chair, comfortable, his short grey overcoat open to let the heat from the fire get to him. A cigarette hung from his thick hand. His pint of beer was set on a small table by his side.

The way he looked at June suggested that he regretted being discovered and disturbed. Then he looked at me to see who I was. I remembered that June had said that he was a thoroughly bad man. He was formidable. I took my eyes from his.

'This is my friend, Wendy,' June said, introducing me to him. 'Wendy, this is Frank.'

I smiled and nodded. I thought that he ought to have stood up when we came in.

We sat round the fire. June sat next to Frank and I sat opposite him.

I looked into the fire or looked at June. He was a man. I felt pretty and I felt dressed up. I could sense that he was a clever man. He might see that I was a boy. I tried to go blank.

He was saying something to June.

'Frank!' she exclaimed. 'You're in one of your black moods! I can always tell.' And then to me, 'Frank's horrific when he's in one of his black moods. He says the filthiest things!'

He was smiling as though he thought that June was a joke.

I tried to smile.

I got the thought that he might be able to see up my skirt, which forced me to edge round in my chair so that my knees were towards the fire. I managed a position that was safe but painful. I was too frightened of him to do anything as overt as moving my chair round.

June was bubbling at the unexpected meeting. She evidently thought that Frank was a wonderful animal.

'What are you doing in Bridlington?' she asked him.

'I'm here for the winter sports.'

'He won't talk sense to me,' she told me. 'He despises women. He says absolutely appalling things about women sometimes.'

He was looking at my legs.

I tried to tuck them away under the chair, but my screwed-up position made it impossible for me to do anything with them.

'Are you working nights now?' she asked him.

'I have been. I'll be back on days soon.'

'Frank always works at jobs he hates,' June told me. 'He's a lost soul. Aren't you, Frank?'

'Yes, child. I'm an unloved blacksmith, alone and in need of comfort.'

I glanced into his eyes. He was looking straight at me. There was laughter in his eyes.

I looked into the fire.

He stood up. 'I'll have to go and get a refill. What do you want?'

June said that she would have another pineapple juice. I said that I would like another pineapple juice.

When he came back June told him that I lived in the next room to her.

He was watching me. His eyes were confident. He knew that I was frightened of him. By not speaking to me he was playing a game with me.

I wanted to make a show of not being frightened of him. I spoke to him. 'Have you ever shod a horse?'

He answered me smiling, 'No I haven't. I'm not really a blacksmith. I'm just a factory hand.'

'Do you think you could shoe a horse?' I asked to keep talking.

'I could try.'

'What if the horse kicked you?'

'I'd kick it back.'

'Poor horse.'

He laughed.

'Frank wouldn't kick a horse,' said June. 'He's a soft old thing really. Aren't you, Frank?'

'No.'

'Yes, you are.'

'June likes to think that all men are soft old things,' he said to me. 'She's looking for a weak-willed, feeble-minded man with a lot of money.'

'No, I'm not!'

'What sort of man do you want?' I asked her. I wanted to help with teasing her.

'Not someone who's weak-willed and feeble-minded. I want someone who's kind and good-natured but smart and sophisticated. And I'd like him to have enough money, because security is important. And I want him to be a gentleman of sorts, not a rough-neck. And I wouldn't want him to take me for granted.'

'That means that she wouldn't always be willing to provide entertainment for her keep,' laughed Frank.

'You're horrible, Frank!' she shouted. 'I certainly wouldn't want to marry you!'

He grinned at her.

She grinned back. 'You're a foul beast, Frank. I wouldn't be able to take you anywhere. What would I do if I married you? You're just a common blacksmith.'

'I think he's an uncommon blacksmith,' I said, and looked down at my coat and examined one of the buttons intently. It was grey leather woven into a button. I wondered how they were made. I felt him looking at me.

At three o'clock the pub closed and he left us. He said that he had to see someone, and when he got outside he walked off with his hands set deep in his pockets. The way in which he could be interested in me but still go about his business, leaving me behind, seemed very manly to me.

The snow was beginning to lay.

On the train June pleased me by talking about him. She said that she liked him but that he was moody. 'He's like Paul Gauguin,' she said. She said that one day someone might

164

give him a good hiding to teach him proper manners, but she regretted that such an event was unlikely because he was so big and strong. 'He's terrifically strong,' she said. 'He can crush an apple in his hand and he can lift a chair up by the bottom of one leg. I think that tricks like that are rather cheap, don't you?'

I said that I didn't know.

'Brute force isn't anything,' she pronounced. 'It's intelligence that counts.'

'He seemed quite intelligent to me,' I said.

'I know,' she agreed, 'that's what's so infuriating about him.'

'Why?'

'Because people should be either strong or intelligent.'

'But not both?'

'No.'

'Why not?'

'It's not fair.'

'Why did he get the sack from teaching?' I asked her.

'I suppose because he fell out with everybody,' she said. 'He sometimes pretends to hate women, but he hates men much more. I think he'd like to kill all the men in the world and have all the women to himself. He wasn't suited to being a teacher at all.'

I was glad that he knew where I lived.

But I told myself that, if I ever saw him again, I would have to be determined not to do anything to encourage him. I told myself that I had behaved foolishly in the pub.

He was not happy, I thought. I thought that behind his front he was a bitter and sarcastic man.

17

Towards the end of January I came to the conclusion that Shirley must have decided that the right attitude to take towards me was to pretend that I did not exist. I was relieved, for, since posting the letter to her, I had had times in which I had worried that she might go to the police. There had been moments of anxiety when the doorbell rang downstairs, and sometimes while I was out I had developed a fear that police-men might be waiting for me when I got back to the house.

I suppose I had written the letter because I had wanted help and because I wanted to declare what I had done. There was the desire to tell about what one had done. I realised why—apart from money—people like me sold their stories to a Sunday newspaper. It was to let people know about the adventure; just as, if one had gone on roller-skates from Land's end to John O' Groats, one would have to tell about it—even though the people whom one told might think one a clown.

I was a clown.

I was unhappy sometimes—but everybody was unhappy sometimes.

I had done as well as I could.

Sometimes I wanted there to be somebody to make love to me. Love meant another person. When I thought about love I became restless. It seemed that I would always have to be alone in bed.

Men were very ugly. But they were more active than women. I imagined that their bodies were warmer than women's bodies. And they were comforting because they were confident and cheerful. They were life-givers. I had felt specially sensitive when I had been sitting opposite Frank. But they were very ugly. The thought of a naked man was obscene. It was difficult to imagine how anyone could be happy in a male body. It was quite impossible to imagine being positively glad to be a man. They were so rough. I thought that the truth might be that no man was ever glad to be a man and that men made themselves active to keep their minds off themselves.

I realised that I was thinking of men as the opposite sex. The realisation gave me a pleasant sensation.

I was thinking about Frank one afternoon when the doorbell rang downstairs. I was alone in the house. I did not want to go all the way down to the front door to tell a salesman that I did not need anything.

The bell rang again.

I decided that I would go down if it rang three times. I waited.

The bell rang a third time.

I went out of my room onto the landing and down the stairs.

I was wearing a red pinafore dress with a grey blouse and I had a pair of red, low-heeled shoes that matched the dress. I felt a neat, bright girl going down the stairs. My hair was bouncing. When I reached the hallway the bell rang again.

I opened the front door. It was Shirley. I wished that I had not sent her the letter.

She said politely, 'Does Miss Wendy Ross live here?'

˄She was wearing a dark brown winter coat. For a moment it was like looking at my own face in a mirror, except that her face was plumper and softer and older. I could not say anything. I stood. She was not as tall as I was. She was not as clever with make-up as I was. She was smart but domestic. My appearance was more dashing. I could not speak. I thought, 'It isn't fair that she should be a real woman.' I pictured how her body was different from mine. I wanted to be like her.

'I'm looking for a Miss Ross,' she said.

'Yes,' my Cottingham voice said, 'I'm Wendy Ross.'

I saw her eyes widen. She looked into my face. 'Is it you, Roy? God! what have you done to yourself?!'

'Nothing,' I said foolishly.

'Nothing! I couldn't recognise you at first!'

She saw my embarrassment but she did not spare me. She looked at my face and my hair and my dress and my shoes.

'Really, Roy, I don't know what to say! How can you behave like this? You must be ill. Have you been dressed up like that since you left home?'

I surprised myself by saying, 'Actually, I haven't been wearing this dress all the time. I have other dresses.'

She stared at me as though dumbfounded by my wickedness.

I had taken the initiative. 'Won't you come in?' I asked with feminine friendliness.

She stepped into the hallway.

'I've come to see what can be done about this, Roy,' she said, to show me that her acceptance of my invitation to enter the house did not commit her to any approval.

I said, 'Please don't call me Roy.'

'That's your name. Fancy calling yourself Wendy! How can you be so effeminate?'

As she was following me up the stairs she said, 'You'll have to go back to hospital, Roy.'

I said, 'My name is Wendy.'

When we reached the door of my room she said, 'You go in and get changed, and I'll come in when you're decent.'

'Changed into what?'

'Your own clothes.'

'These are my own clothes.'

'Oh, Roy, they're not,' she moaned. 'It makes me feel queer to look at you. Go in and take them off, there's a good boy. And wash your face. And take that wig off.'

I was annoyed. 'It's my own hair! And these are my own clothes. I'm a girl.'

She shook her head, expressing pity as well as disagreement.

We went into the room and she glanced round. She saw the things on my dressing table. There was a pair of stockings over the back of a chair. I felt myself blushing.

Now she had the initiative. 'Oh, Roy, how can you keep up this ridiculous make-believe? It's disgusting. How can you live like this?'

I said, 'Would you like a cup of tea?'

She said, 'Look, Roy, I've come to get you out of this mess you're in.'

'My name isn't Roy, and I'm not in a mess. Would you like a cup of tea?'

'How can you say that you're not in a mess? You're dressed up like that and your face is painted and—'

'Your face is painted,' I said calmly.

'Yes, but I'm a woman.'

'What do you think I am?'

'You're a young man, Roy.'

'Do I look like a young man?'

'No, you do not.'

'What do I look like?'

'You look like a big, silly girl. Aren't you ashamed?'

'No. Why should I be? I'm not ashamed of looking nice. I like looking nice.'

'But you don't look nice.'

'I do.'

'You look revolting.'

'It's no use saying that. I know what I look like.'

'But it's disgusting. Don't you feel vile in those clothes? I know I would if I were a man.'

168

'We're neither of us men,' I said.

'You could be a man.' Her tone was one of encouragement.

'I don't want to be.'

'But you could wear nice clothes as a man. There are lots of nice clothes for men nowadays.'

'I don't want to wear them.'

'Why not?'

'Because they're men's clothes. I want to wear women's clothes. If women's clothes were made out of old sacking, I'd still prefer them to men's clothes.' Then I said, 'I wish to God I hadn't sent you that letter.'

'Roy—'

'Don't call me Roy.'

'I'm certainly not going to call you Wendy.'

'Then I'll call you Sam.'

'Don't be ridiculous, Roy.'

'Do you want a cup of tea, Sam?'

I went and filled the kettle and put it on the gas.

I must not be too pert with her or she might become dangerous. It would be best for me to play the part of a victim of a problem. The clothes that I was wearing gave me pleasure in the same way that her clothes gave her pleasure, but that simplicity would be impossible for her to understand because it meant accepting that I could feel as she felt.

While I was making the tea she was reasoning with me. She wanted me to go with her to a doctor. She kept saying '—cure,' and '—cured'.

I wanted to ask her how she would like to be cured of being a woman, but I understood that the question would not serve my interests.

To me the situation could be seen as preposterous. I was there in my red pinafore dress with my grey blouse and my red shoes and my fine stockings and she was trying to make me believe that I should be trudging miserably through life in trousers. I wished that I had not sent her the letter. There was the danger of her spoiling everything for me.

But as she talked in what she supposed was a reasonable way she became less excited.

I asked her if she would like to take off her coat.

She was wearing a dark blue jersey suit under her coat. I liked it. She had a good figure. I wondered if she wished that she was as slim as I was. I remembered that she had had a baby. I would have liked to ask her about having a baby. I had heard her talking about it, but I wanted to ask her what the feeling was like just as the baby was being born.

She sat down at the table.

When I handed her the cup and saucer she said, 'This can't go on, Roy. We can't drink tea like this and you dressed like that. It's ridiculous. Couldn't you put your own clothes on and wash your face?'

'I only have women's clothes,' I told her.

'What happened to the things you had when you left home?'

'I got rid of them.'

'I don't believe you.'

'It's true. I don't want to dress up as a boy ever again—I can't help it.'

'What's to become of you, Roy?'

'I want to change sex.'

She made a slight, discreet motion to indicate my bosom. 'That's not real, is it?'

'No. But I think my chest is developing. It's hard to tell.'

'Oh, Roy, you'll have to see a doctor and have it stopped! Do you have a beard?'

'There are just a few hairs that grow at the sides of my chin. I put a razor over the places every morning. I don't really need to do it every morning, but I like to be on the safe side. I have a friend who comes in here a lot, so I have to be careful about keeping the razor locked away.'

'Do you have to shave your legs?'

'No.'

'Who is this friend? It's not a man, is it?'

'No. It's the girl who lives in the back room. She's an art student.'

'Is she pretty?'

'Quite pretty.'

'Don't you ever feel attracted to her?'

'She's just a friend. We get on very well together.'

'Does she know that you're a boy?'

'No.'

'Have you any other friends?'

'There's the Stephensons. They live downstairs. I'm friendly with them. They're schoolteachers.'

170

'Wouldn't you like to be married to some nice girl and have a home and a family?'

'It isn't possible.'

'Why not?'

'I should think it's obvious why not.'

'And do all these people believe that you're a girl?'

'Yes.'

'They don't suspect?'

'No, of course not. How could they?'

'Do you go out much?'

'Quite often.'

'Don't you feel nervous—frightened that people will see that you're not really a girl?'

'I was nervous the first time I went out in the street, but it went off. Sometimes I think that people are looking at me—but a woman often has that.'

'I suppose you could be changed,' she said. The idea was difficult to accept, but she was beginning to think of accepting it.

'It would cost a lot of money,' I said.

'How much?'

'Thousands of pounds.'

'Do you really want to change sex?'

'Yes.'

'Are you sure?'

'Yes.'

'Well, I came here to drag you back home. But I have to admit that you do look very nice—I suppose I shouldn't tell you that. What would they have to do to you to make you into a woman?'

'I'd have to have injections of female hormones—that would make my chest develop—and then I'd have to have an operation.'

'Can you have it done on the National Health?'

'No.'

'Why not?'

'They'd be frightened to do it. Some people think it's wrong to do it.'

'I can understand that.'

'They pretend it's because it's wrong,' I said, 'but it's really because they want you to stay as a male so that you can be exploited.'

'I don't believe that.'

'Perhaps it's just the way I look at things—but there's some truth in it. The country gets a lot more out of the men than it gets out of the women.'

'I think you're badly mixed up, Roy.'

I smiled at what she had said. And then she smiled back.

I knew that my appearance was winning her over. I was no longer sorry that I had written the letter.

I was propounding to her:

'Manliness is always something one hopes to leave to other people. Trawlermen are manly and coalminers are manly. You're quite content to leave your Bill to take care of the manliness in your house, aren't you? Have you ever noticed how people never say "Be a man" about anything pleasant? It's like the other day. I went to Bridlington, and while I was sitting in the train I was thinking that it was a pity that the East Riding accent would die out, but I don't want to speak with an East Riding accent myself. I want to leave it to other people to do that. Manliness is the same. It's an excellent virtue in other people.'

'I'm sure you're wrong,' she said. But she did not tell me why she was sure that I was wrong.

She said, 'When I was little I sometimes wished that I was a boy.'

'That was before you knew what it felt like to be a woman,' I said.

She said, 'A lot of men live very full lives.'

'Full of work and worry,' I said.

She said, 'You wouldn't want to be a woman if you knew what it's like to have a baby.'

'What is it like?'

'I think it might make you change your mind.'

'I'd like to have a baby.'

'You must be mad!'

'Were you mad because you had Gwen?'

'Would you be able to have a baby if you changed sex?'

'No.'

'So you wouldn't really be a woman.'

'I wouldn't be able to have a baby.'

'Then what's the use? Don't you think you ought to have

some treatment to put these ideas out of your head?'

'What treatment?'

'I don't know. But there must be something.'

'There isn't anything.'

'How do you know?'

'Because I don't want there to be anything.'

'You're like a brick wall!' There was a discernible note of amusement in her exclamation.

Whatever she said I had a reply and all the time she could see that I looked like a girl.

Since I had set out from Mrs Ford's boarding house I had been steadily successful. To make Shirley begin to accept my personality was another success.

I told her about the morning I had set out. She was interested and asked questions. I made her laugh when I told her about whispering that I had a cold to the woman in the station buffet.

She said that I might have been different if my mother had lived.

I said that I did not think that my mother's death had anything to do with my wanting to be a woman.

We talked of glands, about which neither of us knew anything.

The talk almost became woman to woman, but she kept remembering who I was. I might be tolerated, but a degree of exclusion would always apply to me. There were positions to which one had to be born.

I was not one of the elect.

I told Shirley that I would be able to believe in God if I changed sex.

She told me with great seriousness that she did not know what she believed in but she believed in something.

I marvelled to myself at how sweet it must be to have thoughts like that, thoughts as soft and warm as one's breasts. One could not feed a baby on intellectual honesty.

My brain had made my breasts, and there was no milk in them.

I wondered if I would go mad in the end.

Yet, whatever I was thinking, my appearance was as I wanted it to be. At least I had got something right.

I could not attend very well to what Shirley was saying to

me because of what was going on in my head. She seemed to be telling me that, if I was determined to be a woman, I would have to be a repressed woman: no men. She expressed herself as though she thought that I ought to wear woollen underwear and not paint my finger nails.

I was sure that she was not wearing woollen underwear. She would never do such a mistaken thing. I had often noticed that the kind of women who wore woollen underwear usually had snivelling colds.

Her finger nails were not painted. They were clean and polished. But she had her house in Cottingham with Bill and little Gwen.

My nails were painted. But I only had a room with nobody to share it.

She put it to me delicately that I ought not to make myself look too nice or I might attract men.

I said that I liked to look nice for its own sake and that I was not at all interested in men.

She said that she understood, and we agreed that one did not wear one's clothes and do what one could with one's hair for the sake of men. Being a woman was being a woman.

I wanted to show her my clothes.

But she remembered who I was and said that she did not want to see them.

'Why not, Shirley?'

'Well, it's no use my pretending that I approve of what you're doing. I can only think that you can't help being as you are, and I suppose you have your own life to lead.'

Thus, not approving but accepting, she left me. She said that she would not tell anyone about me.

At the front door she said that she might come to see me again. She said she hoped that I would find a way through my difficulties. Finally she made me promise that I would never go to her house in Cottingham dressed as a woman.

I was happy. Shirley was a good sister. If she came to see me again, I would manage to make her call me Wendy. One day my father might call me Wendy!

If only I had enough money to have myself changed.

I tried to think if there was a way in which I could get into a bank and get out again with a lot of money. I remembered that a man dressed as a woman had attempted a hold-up in a

174

bank in the North Riding.

I thought of mutilating myself with a razor blade so that an operation to create a vagina would be the only possible repair for the damage I had done. But, of course, I did not have the stark courage for such an act. And I would almost certainly bleed to death before I could be helped. And, even if I did not bleed to death, there was the likelihood that I would do damage that would make it impossible for me ever to enjoy being a woman.

18

June came in that night and said that she had seen Frank in the town that afternoon.

'He asked about you,' she said.

'You didn't tell him anything about me, did you?'

'Yes, dear, I told him all about you. I should think he'll be round to see you tomorrow afternoon.'

'He won't, will he?'

'Yes, he will. Get some pikelets in; he likes pikelets.'

Next morning I bought half a dozen pikelets.

Snow was falling in the afternoon.

He was on the doorstep, huge with his back to the light. His hands were deep in his coat pockets and he was stamping the snow off his shoes.

'Are the Stephensons in?' he asked.

'No. They're both out. They're at work.'

'Damn! You see, I lent Marguerite some records. You don't know when she'll be back, do you?'

'About half-past four.'

He looked at his watch.

'Would you like to come in and wait for her?' I asked.

'If that's all right—'

'You can come up and have a cup of tea, if you like. I have some pikelets. Do you like pikelets?'

He looked down at the doormat. He was abashed. He was not as formidable as he had been in the pub in Bridlington.

I took him upstairs and gave him a cup of tea and gave him

a fork with a pikelet on the end to hold to the gas fire.

'This is where you live, is it?' he said looking round.

'Yes.'

'It's all right.'

'Thank you.'

'I like those curtains.'

'I made them myself.'

'Did you?'

'Well, I cut the material up and sewed it myself.'

'Have you a sewing machine?'

'No. Actually, I sometimes wish I had.'

'My mother used to have a sewing machine, but the needle went right through her finger one day, and she wouldn't use it after that.'

'It must have been a bit off-putting.'

'It was. She wouldn't go near it. We sold it.'

'Shouldn't there have been a guard on to stop you getting your fingers in?'

'There was, but my father had taken it off.'

'What for?'

'I don't know. He's always taking things to pieces.'

I took the pikelet from him and buttered it for him. Then I gave him another one to toast while he was eating the one I had buttered. He seemed to be enjoying it.

I liked him. He was a big, real man, and he had come through the snow to see me. But he did not seem as handsome as he had seemed in the pub. He had become more ordinary—like my father.

I asked him if he had ever been in the army.

'No. I was in the RAF.'

'Were you a pilot?'

'No. I was an electrician.'

'Was it interesting?'

'I used to work on Link trainers. It was all right.'

'What are Link trainers?'

'They're like big boxes. The pilot sits inside and learns to fly by instruments.'

'Did they ever crash?'

He laughed. 'No.' He laughed again. 'No, we didn't have any crashes. We were fortunate. We had a few blown fuses, but nobody was hurt.'

I could not understand why he was laughing.

He leaned forward in his chair. 'There was one top-secret aircraft that I saw when I was in the RAF. It was called the Westland Wump. There were no metal parts in it at all so that it couldn't be picked up by radar. The propeller was turned by a party of dwarfs working a crank.'

'Are you telling me the truth?' I asked smiling.

'Of course I am. You should have seen the party of dwarfs marching alone the runway in their one-piece Air Force blue knitted suits with pixie bonnets complete!'

He drank tea and smoked cigarettes and talked to me.

I kept thinking, 'He came because of me.'

His face was friendly but resolute. There was strength in his shoulders. I wanted to stroke him. His eyebrows were thick and rough. I wanted to touch them with my fingers.

But I began to feel cheap. I felt bitchy. The thought of his touching me was sneaking about.

Men liked to feel girls. If he felt me, he would be sickened. It would be vile and filthy. It would be ugly.

Suddenly I said, 'I'm a rotten person.'

He was taken by surprise.

I rushed on, 'I'm a neurotic. Everybody's neurotic nowadays. It's because there's dishonesty everywhere. We want to get free of other people, but we can't. We can't get free because we can't do without other people. And do you know why we can't do without other people? We can't do without other people because we enjoy telling each other lies so much!' I laughed.

'Are you upset about something?' he asked.

'No. I'm just neurotic and rotten,' I said.

The afternoon was spoilt. I did not know him well enough to talk to him as I had done. He had come to court me, not to have me rave at him.

There was tension.

Then I heard the car outside. I told him that Marguerite had come home.

He excused himself and went down.

I did not go down with him.

I called myself a fool for having invited him up. I could not allow myself that kind of risk.

177

19

To my surprise he was back again the next afternoon. He was pretending that he had come to apologise for upsetting me.

We talked about it in the hallway.

I insisted that the trouble was altogether in me. 'It's because of what happened to my mother.'

'Yes,' he said, 'June was telling me about that the other day. It must have been nasty for you.'

'It was. You see, I found her the next morning. She was very badly burnt. It was horrible. It sent me a bit wrong in the head. I was in a nursing home for a time. And I haven't been properly well since then. That's why I can't do a job or anything. It's psychological. One of the things that I have is that I can't stand to be touched by a man. I can't stand a man to touch me at all—I don't know why. It's part of the illness, I suppose. I'm getting better, but I still have this thing about men. That's why I got into a state when you were with me yesterday. I got frightened that you might touch me. I don't dislike men. It's just this thing about being touched. When I left the nursing home I went to Butlin's at Filey for a holiday, and there was a boy there, and I thought I rather liked him, but I didn't want him to touch me because of my illness. I told him about my illness. But he just grabbed me, and I had to hit him in the face. We had a sort of fight. I was terribly ill after it. I haven't told June about this. I don't want her to know. You won't tell her, will you?'

'No, of course not. And will you always have this thing about men?'

'Well, actually, I need some special treatment, and then I should be perfectly all right.'

'What sort of treatment?'

'Well, actually, I can't talk about it. It's woman's trouble.'

'I thought you said it was psychological?'

'It's psychological and physical. It's complicated. I can't explain it to you.'

'You look pretty fit to me. If you have this treatment, will you be altogether as you should be?'

'Yes.'

'Then why don't you have it and get it over?'

'There are certain difficulties. I can't explain. You won't tell anybody about this, will you?'

'Of course not.'

I wanted to keep him interested in me without letting him touch me. It would not be easy. And it could not last for long. But I wanted it.

I was talking nervously: '. . . That boy at Butlin's was ridiculously conceited. He thought he only had to get hold of me to cure everything. He was a gruesome creep really. I can't understand why I thought I liked him. He was a clerk at a firm of timber importers. Still, he had a car. A girl is supposed to be mercenary and no good if she thinks like that, but when most men are the same as most men you might as well choose the one that has a car.' Then I said, 'You know, Frank, ours can only be a platonic relationship.'

He said, 'Would you like to go down town?'

When we set out we walked side by side but separately.

I felt an excited happiness.

I would have liked to put my neat gloved hand on his arm, but I did not know how to tell him that I was willing to do that.

He was a handsome man. Nobody would suspect that he was a factory hand—anyway, he was only a factory hand by accident. He was well dressed, but he did not give the impression of having his best clothes on. The short grey overcoat suited him. It was a much darker grey than my coat. He was tall. He was nearly six foot. He looked clever. I was pleased to be seen with him. His shoulders were so firm. He was a man. We were a man and a girl together.

We rode on the top of a bus. I had the inside seat and he sat next to me. He paid. People were in the street below and I was riding above them.

We went to a coffee house in Whitefri'gate. I felt like Cinderella arriving at the ball.

An efficient, well-manicured waitress served us. Well-to-do women were drinking coffee and resting from spending money. I discovered that I was the only woman there with a handsome man.

I thought, 'Whatever punishment I have to suffer for my happiness at being here, it is worth it.'

I was telling Frank that I sometimes felt guilty about not working.

179

'Nobody expects you to work overmuch.'

'Why not?'

'You're a woman.'

'It's nice for me, isn't it?'

'Very nice. All you need is a man with plenty of money to take care of you—which lets me out.'

'Haven't you got plenty of money?'

'I have not.'

'I don't care.'

'I do. It keeps me awake at night.'

We had a taxi back to the house.

We drew up behind the Stephensons' mini-car. Marguerite was just getting out. I saw that she brightened when she saw Frank.

'Oh, Frank,' she said, 'I've found that book I was telling you about. Do you want to have a look at it?'

I was angry.

As Frank turned to say something to Marguerite I went past him and up the path to the front door. He called after me. Without turning I called back, 'Goodbye, Frank.' I went into the house and up the stairs. All I could think was that Marguerite was a real woman.

After a time in which he must have been talking to Marguerite he came up and knocked on my door. I kept still and pretended not to be in. I heard him call, 'Are you there, Wendy?' I did not answer. He went away.

I turned on myself: 'What the hell did you think you were playing at, going out with a man?'

20

When June came in I started.

I began by saying that Marguerite was smug and self-satisfied.

June agreed.

'She walks about as though she could do no wrong,' I said. 'She's always so perfect. She's a proper schoolteacher—always so perfect. She's so perfect it's a pity she pees!'

180

June laughed. 'Philip's pretty tedious,' she said.

'Yes, but it's worse in a woman. Women always have a couple of miles start at being too good to be true. It's because they're women. All their lives they've been told that they're superior.'

'I thought men were supposed to be superior?'

'Men are only told that they're superior when there's something unpleasant to be done, so that they have to go and do it.'

June grinned.

'Marguerite's so ladylike and perfect she thinks she's above everybody else,' I went on. 'She thinks she's very much above you and me.'

'I know,' said June.

'They're a pair, Marguerite and Philip. If they were half as good as they think they are, they'd die of it. If Philip got into a fight, he'd write to the United Nations about it. I hate people like that!'

'So do I,' said June.

'Her clothes are always in such good taste, but they're always so dull. She never wears anything that's even a little bit tarty. But you can tell she thinks she's the most gorgeous creature under the sky.'

'She is rather attractive,' said June.

'I don't think so. I think she looks dull. She looks sedate and reasonable all the time. Can you imagine her in bed with Philip?'

'I can never imagine anybody in bed with anybody,' said June. 'I sometimes try to imagine it, but I never can.'

'I can imagine it.'

'What's it like?'

'Philip soon gets tired.'

'I can never imagine anybody enjoying it,' said June. 'Do you think you would enjoy having it done to you, Wendy?'

'Not by Philip.'

'Why not?'

'It would be like having an educated monkey getting up you.'

'Wendy! Shut up!'

'Well, it would.'

'I know—but don't say things like that.'

181

'Why do you think she married Philip?' I asked.

'She had to marry somebody.'

'But why Philip?'

'He has a good job.'

'She'll probably finish up by going round the bend,' I forecast spitefully. 'Unless, of course, she can get her claws into somebody more human to take his place.'

'She wouldn't do that.'

'Why not? There's nothing to stop her. I think she ought to have a baby. That would take her mind off other men.'

'I've never liked her,' said June.

'She's a sly bitch,' I said.

'I've never liked her,' repeated June sympathetically, to sooth me.

'I hate her,' I snarled.

21

My anger only lasted to the end of that day.

The Stephensons were a normal couple. I thought that there must be many thousands of couples like them. As long as Frank was not in sight Marguerite would not feel the need for Frank—Philip would do.

I often thought how very few people who were born as males ever became men—of course there were substantial discouragements. Bluster and noise did not make a man. Men were very rare things. I supposed that a man was a person who could persist in honesty in spite of all necessary lies.

Philip wanted everybody, including himself, to be neuter. He was willing to live in the city that had been built, but he did not want to feel the discomfort of the passion that had built the city. He wanted to be good. He did not even know that there was such a thing as honesty. There would be more and more people like Philip and there would be more and more women in Marguerite's position. Her life was very like mine. She had her clothes. And when she felt that everything had become a swindle she could make herself think about the condition of people in Africa and Asia.

On the Sunday following Frank's visits Philip sneered about him. He called Frank 'The Iron Chancellor' and laughed.

I could tell that Philip did not hate Frank as I had hated Marguerite. Behind Philip's hate there was evil. He wanted to destroy Frank. He was like one of those women who wanted to learn judo to break men's limbs. I thought that he would have made a suffragette. He was prim and much educated, and he hated what was strong and spontaneous. If he had not been taught that Christianity was obscurantist and unscientific, he might have made a determined Christian. He would have liked to substitute eternal boredom for actual life.

I had dressed myself up in order to stay in one piece. He had disintegrated. He was like the Commonwealth. He had become so thinly spread and spuriously high-minded that he was a name that might mean anything or nothing or both simultaneously. But at the centre there was a reality. There was meanness caused by lack of strength, and from that meanness came all his morality and liberal sentiments.

I thought how strange it was that people could drink so many lies and only be sick occasionally. Philip never seemed to be ill—or else he was ill all the time, like the man who was not known to be a drunkard until he was discovered sober.

I observed the Stephensons and understood them.

The way in which I understood them disturbed me. I hoped that, if I was ever able to get injections of female hormones, it would alter my intelligence. I wanted to think nicely. The way I was thinking about the Stephensons was aggressive. I wanted that to be stopped. I wanted to be happy. I wanted my thinking to be as nice as my underwear.

22

When Frank came a third time I admired his doggedness. I began to love him.

He came after tea and said that he was no longer working nights. He wanted to take me out.

I had a new green coat with a high collar. I wore black gloves and a pair of black court shoes with it.

He said that I smelt nice.

I was very happy.

I took his arm as we set out.

We went down town and sat in a pub with seats into which one sank. There was indirect lighting. I liked the feeling of expense.

Frank drank whiskey and I had two gin and limes.

He was talking to me.

Men did not know how graceful they were in their careless yet accurate movements. They were much quicker than women. And men never guessed how mysterious they could look with their faces like big masks.

But, if men knew that they were beautiful, it would be less easy for women to get money out of them.

'Shall we go to The Deliverer and see what's going on?' he suggested.

'Where's The Deliverer?'

'Off Alfred Gelder Street.'

'Isn't it a bit dangerous down there at night?'

'You'll have me to look after you.'

I was protected.

We walked along together. We went down Whitefri'gate to where there was a nautical instrument shop at a corner and turned into Alfred Gelder Street. I enjoyed the thought that I would not have dared to come to this part at night without someone to look after me.

The Deliverer was down an alleyway.

We went into a small bar that was quiet with solid drinking men. They looked like skippers and mates discussing seafaring business. The room was powerful with masculinity. I wondered why Frank had brought me to such a place. But then he took me through into a larger room that seemed livelier. There were women, but I had not time to place them socially or examine their clothes before he was leading me up a narrow flight of stairs. There was pop music coming from above. We reached a landing. There were some talking girls coming out of a lavatory. The noise of the music was very loud. Frank pushed open some heavy swing doors for me. The noise in the room hit me with such force that I could have imagined being knocked backwards and down the stairs by it. We had entered a long, low room that was dense with cigarette smoke. The noise was thought-smashing. At the far end of the room, raised above the crowd that sat at small tables, a group of youths in bright blue suits were tearing at electric guitars and yelling and screaming to a machine-like rhythm. All their noise was amplified and sent out by a loudspeaker much louder than was humanly possible. It seemed amazing that every glass in the room was not shattered by the din. I felt that I would become paralysed.

The room was full of youths and girls, all of them dressed in new clothes. Young waiters in white jackets carried trays aloft that were loaded with drinks. There were great pints for the lads and different shapes and sizes for the lasses.

The girls were brilliant: they had squeezed themselves into tight bright dresses. They had painted their faces without the least timid regard for nature, and their shining lacquered hair was massive.

The youths hid their sharp, cruel blades under dark suits. They were young and hard. They were as smart as metal soldiers in new paint. They looked capable and handy for any savagery.

I saw Frank's mouth making, 'We'll just have one drink.'

I made the shapes of, 'It's hellish!'

We got to a table. Frank wanted to help me off with my coat. I shook my head and made the shapes of 'I don't want to stay that long.' We sat down.

Frank was leaning towards me and shouting in my ear to ask me what I wanted to drink.

I faced him and made the shapes of 'What are you having?'

His mouth made, 'A pint of bitter.'

I made, 'I'll have the same.'

He laughed and shook his head.

I made, 'I want to go.'

He made, 'We've only just arrived.'

I made, 'I can't stand it!'

It was hot in the room. And I felt genteel sitting in my coat. I wished that I could fill a dress as tightly as some of the girls about me. Their ripe-fruit bodies seemed almost in danger of bursting as they sat with their plump thighs squashed together, while my thighs were fresh and white and correctly suspendered but slim. I had to be content with feeling ladylike—but it wasn't a place for feeling ladylike.

185

One of the young waiters set a gin and lime in front of me and a pint of bitter in front of Frank.

It was then that I noticed a young man who was sitting at the next table. He was looking at me. He had fair wavy hair. It was Peter from Mrs Ford's boarding house.

I seized my gin and lime and drank it all at once.

Then I saw that Peter was looking away. He had not recognised me. I told myself that there was no reason why he should have recognised me. I was a different person from the boy he had called Brian who had disappeared. He was looking about at girls or gulping his lager with an up and down of his Adam's apple. He was nothing to do with me.

Frank was waving a ten shilling note to attract a waiter to get me another drink.

I made, 'I don't want any more.'

When we were leaving I went to use the lavatory.

I found that there were two cubicles and that there were two girls waiting. The taller was doing a complicated step-dance while the smaller stood dragging and puffing at a cigarette. One of the cubicle doors was ajar. I went and pushed. There was a shout from inside. I could not understand why some women should have such a fear of being locked in that they would rather be seen in the most undignified of postures than risk shutting the door. The two girls who were waiting stared at me, to accuse me of attempting to go out of turn. I went and looked at myself in one of the mirrors over the sinks.

By the time I had applied lipstick to my satisfaction the two who had been in had come out and the two girls who had been waiting had been in and come out and one of the cubicles had become occupied by somebody I had not seen. I went into the vacant cubicle.

I came out to find that the girl I had not seen was standing waiting for me. She was dark and pale. She was worried.

She wanted to borrow a safety-pin.

I had always wanted to give a safety-pin to a stranger in these circumstances. I always carried safety-pins in my handbag in the hope that I could give one to somebody, and in the act be part of the freemasonry of womankind.

I rummaged in my bag and found what she needed.

She was grateful.

And I went back to join Frank, saying nothing to him of

the woman's world.

The night was clear and cold. Above the street lights the sky was frosted bright with stars. My heels were making smart sounds on the pavement.

'Do you want to go somewhere else now?' Frank asked me.

'No. I think I want to go home.'

He walked me back to The Avenues.

I said goodnight to him at the gate.

'I don't get a kiss, do I?' he said.

'No. I'm sorry. I can't.'

'I hope you get better before long,' he said.

23

Frank told me how he had gone to a training college after he had finished his National Service. He said that it had been a mistake because he had not been suited to being a teacher. He said that he did not know what he could be suited to. Sometimes he said that he would go down to London. I said that I hoped he wouldn't.

It was good to be with him. He was always talking and making jokes. As I got to know him I found him different from what he had seemed in the pub at Bridlington. That day in Bridlington he had seemed rather bitter and sarcastic, but as I got to know him he became more open and cheerful. I could not understand why June had said that he was a thoroughly bad man. He was to me the most worthy person I had ever known.

He often said to me that he had never talked to a girl who was more intelligent. He talked to me about many things. He was very fond of Nietzsche, and when he had had a drink he would quote from *Thus Spake Zarathustra*. At other times he would quote Rilke. One of his favourite pieces of Rilke was:

> 'He who succeeds in reconciling the many contradictions of his life, holding them all together in a symbol, pushes the noisy crowd from the palace and will be festive in a different sense, receiving you as his guest on mild evenings.'

I found that it was easy to let him do most of the talking because he so often said things that I thought were true. It was pleasant to be the woman listening while he was the man talking; for, whatever he was saying, he was saying it to me. There were the two of us.

I loved him. But I could not allow him to touch me. But I did love him.

24

I was wearing a paper-nylon half-slip that made me rustle. I liked rustling.

We were in a pub, and Frank was filling himself with beer and talking. I was beginning to think that he had had enough. There were times when I found it difficult to understand how his ideas were linked. That night I was finding it more difficult than usual.

'Parents don't refrain from cruelty to their children because there are laws against cruelty to children. Human beings don't love one another because they've been told to love one another. They just do it—or else they don't do it. What kind of love is it that is no more than obedience to moral injunction?

'Thought is the rationalization of feeling. To attempt to think clearly by ridding oneself of feeling is to attempt to stop thinking. If you want to think well, you must begin by feeling well, by being passionate and being happy about your passion. But, instead, there are men who count on their fingers. They are ignorant and stupid, so they count on their fingers. There is more to be counted than can be counted on ten fingers.

'Yet mine is the Protestant cause. I intend to continue thinking to the end. The Catholics represent man as either a babe in arms or as hanging dead upon a cross. There comes the time when the baby struggles to be free of its mother's arms. It wants to become a man and walk about in the sun. Hate is necessary. Mary-worship stinks in my Protestant nostrils. Since Luther, man has been struggling to free himself from love. We cannot always be dead, rolled round with rocks and trees and the Board of Education and the Ministry of

Weak Tea. I do not want anyone to take my sins from me. They are my possessions, my private property. I am so much a Protestant that I sometimes feel very like a Jew. When a Jew is clever he is a genius, and when a Jew is strong he is a lion, and when a Jew is a fool he is an idiot. I am an idiot. I want the truth when the people about me are content with explanations. If I go on like this, I shall never have a motor car and a wife to tell me what to do. Would you like to tell me what to do, Wendy?'

'I wouldn't presume. But don't you think you've had enough to drink for one night?'

There were two youths sitting near us. They were brutes with shut-in expressions. I had been aware that they were overhearing Frank. One of them leaned forward and said to me, 'Do you fancy Jew-boys, then?'

I turned my face away from him.

Frank was taking a drink of his beer and had not noticed the youth speaking to me.

The second youth said loudly, 'You'll finish up as a big fat Yidd woman, honey.'

Frank looked at him over his glass and said, 'Is there something the matter with you, son?'

'I think it's you,' said the youth, 'there's a funny smell of olive oil in here.'

Frank was smiling. He said affably, 'Do you think you two make enough of a man to come outside?'

I felt like a lady social worker in the middle of a race riot. I wanted to explain everything. I wanted to say that Frank had not said that he was a Jew and that he wasn't a Jew and that he didn't even look like a Jew, and that, even if he had and he was and he did, there was no need for a fight—and I would get some money out of my handbag and buy everybody a drink.

Instead there was a procession making its way to the door. The two youths went first and then Frank and I followed Frank.

He turned back to me. 'There's no need for you to come. I'll soon clip their lugs.'

'But, Frank, you're drunk. They might have knives, Frank.'

As we went out of the back door into the yard I rushed at one of the youths and threw my arms round him, pinning his

189

arms to his sides. He staggered with me in the darkness. For a moment it seemed that he was too surprised to do anything. Then he tried to get his arms free, but I held on. He kicked me in the shin, but I did not let go of him. Then Frank came and hit him, and he went backwards with me sprawling on top of him. My knee struck the ground. I rolled over on my back. The youth I had grappled with scrambled away.

Frank helped me up. My left knee was in agony. I was hopping about. 'My knee! My knee! I can't bear it!'

'What are you dancing about for?'

'My knee, you great fool, I've hurt my knee! And this is the first time I've had these stockings on. They're ruined. Oh, my knee!'

'Let's have a look,' he said.

'No, get away! Oh, my poor knee! These were new stockings. They must be ruined.' I bent to find out what damage had been done. I could not see, but I could feel that that there was no blood. 'There's a big hole,' I said.

'In your knee?'

'No, in my stocking, you fool.'

'You're in a mess.'

'It's not funny, Frank. If you hadn't have had so much to say, this wouldn't have happened. Did you hit the other one?'

'I thumped him in the guts.'

I reached down and felt my shin where I had been kicked. 'I've got a lump on my shin,' I said. 'He kicked me.'

'You shouldn't have set about him.'

I straightened up. 'I was only trying to help you, Frank Cracknell.'

'I'm sorry, Wendy.' He put his arm across my shoulders. 'Have I to kiss you better?'

'Yes.'

He took hold of me and pulled me to him. I put my head on one side and tried to see his lips in the gloom. He pressed his mouth on my mouth and was kissing me. His lips were strong pressing into me. I felt very weak. It seemed that he was holding me up. There was a wonderful feeling of sexuality in my stomach and my whole body was filled with a sensation of femininity, so that I could have said, 'Yes, for ever and ever I am a woman.'

We were pressed together. He started running his hands

over my back. I wanted to stay pressed to him, but I became afraid. I started to push at him, to push him away.

He held on.

I twisted away from him. 'That's enough, Frank. Let me go.'

'I don't want to.' He held me to him and buried his face against my neck, kissing me.

'I mean it,' I gasped. 'Let me go! I'll shout if you don't let me go!'

'You wouldn't.' There was laughter in his voice.

I was beginning to panic. 'Let me go Frank, or you'll be sorry! Get off! Let me go!'

He released me.

'Thank you,' I said. I was panting.

'You got quite excited,' he said.

'Well, you shouldn't have held me like that. I can't stand it.'

'You liked it.'

'I know. But I can't stand it. I might be ill now.'

'I'm sorry.'

It was over, and I knew that I had done wrong to let him kiss me. The thought that I was not a woman made me feel sick.

I said, 'I do feel ill, Frank. Please take me home.'

He put his arm round my waist and held me to him. 'We'll go to the station and get a taxi.'

'Take me home, Frank. I feel ill. I shouldn't have let you kiss me. Whatever happens, you must remember that I loved you as much as I could. I'd die for you, Frank. I don't mean you any harm. I love you, Frank.'

'Come on,' he said. 'I'd better get you home. You sound like somebody who's had enough excitement for one night.'

'Remember I loved you, and try to forgive me because of that.'

'Shut up and come on.'

25

That night I lay in bed thinking about Frank.

If I could be Frank's wife, I would be so meek. I would let

him do anything he wanted to do to me.

I was in bed with Frank. It was early morning. We were cuddled up warm together. He had made love to me and hurt me, and I had been crying because I was so happy. He was holding me to him to comfort me.

'What's the matter? What are you crying for?'

'Because I love you so much, Frank.'

'I love me, but it doesn't make me cry.'

'But I love you more than you love yourself.'

'Impossible.'

'I wish we could stay cuddled up like this forever, Frank.'

'For ever?'

'Always.'

'Don't you think we might get a little bored after about two hundred years?'

'You might, but I wouldn't. I love you. I'm your woman, Frank. Say that I'm your woman.'

'You're my woman.'

'Not like that. Say it as though you mean it.'

'You're my woman, Wendy.'

I closed my eyes and pressed my face to his shoulder. He was solid and strong.

'What's the matter now?' he asked.

'I'm loving you,' I said.

I raised my head and lo oked into his eyes. I could not tel what he was thinking. 'Do you love me, Frank?'

'Of course I do. Haven't I expended a great deal of energy proving it?'

'Don't be horrible! Say that you love me.'

'I love you.'

'Say that I'm your woman and you love me.'

'You're my woman and I love you.'

'How much do you love me?'

'Enough.'

'How much is enough?'

'It's as much as you're going to get.'

'You're brutal, Frank. But you can't stop me loving you by being brutal. I'd love you whatever you did to me. Nothing can ever stop me loving you. I'd even love you if you went bald. Do you think you ever will go bald?' I put my hand to his head and touched his hair. It was rough hair.

192

'I might,' he said.
'Don't go bald, Frank.'
'I won't if you say not.'
'If you do go bald, you won't wear a wig, will you?'
'Not if you don't want me to.'
'I couldn't stand you to wear a wig.'
'I'll remember that.'
'Just imagine, Frank, if everybody in the world hated us because we loved each other. And we were up here, and we barricaded ourselves in, and there was the police and the army and the fire brigade outside trying to get at us, but we wouldn't come out.'
'It takes a bit of imagining.'
'Say you love me.'
'I love you.'
'Say it again.'
'I love you.'
'Do you remember when we first knew each other and we used to talk all the time and I told you all those lies about having an illness and I wouldn't let you touch me? And all the time I really wanted you to do things to me. I love you to do things to me, Frank.'
He put his fingers to me. I pushed my body to his hand. He just kept his fingers touching me so that I knew that I was a woman.
'That's the best part of me,' I said.
I wanted his something for my nothing.
'Do you want to hurt me again?' I asked.
'In a minute.'
'Are you getting tired of me?'
'Yes.' He smiled.
Now he was not touching me there, and I was wanting him to be touching me. It was a trick he knew how to play on me. I was helpless with wanting him. My mouth was open. He was looking at me, smiling with amusement at my helplessness.
'Oh, Frank, don't torture me,' I sighed.
Then he was touching me again, very gently stroking and fondling. My body was responding. My hips began moving backwards and forwards as though I were doing what I wanted him to do. My legs were going apart. I was empty.
'Shall we get a horse,' he said, 'and harness it to the bottom

of the bed? Then we can go everywhere in bed. What do you think to the idea?'

'Lovely.' I wanted him to stop talking and start on me.

'Imagine going down town on a Saturday afternoon in bed.'

'We'd have to behave ourselves.' I was the woman. I had to wait because I had nothing but longing.

'None of this?'

'We'd get run in.'

'And they call this a free country!'

He started shifting me and pulling up my nightdress. He was going to do it for me. His eyes were smiling and wicked. He was getting on top of me. He was slow. I wanted him. My legs were apart. I was empty. I wanted to feel him in me. I wanted him to hurt me as much as he could. I did not want him to have any mercy on me.

26

Next morning I examined myself carefully in the mirror.

There could be no doubt but that my breasts were developing. It could not be fat because I was not at all a fat person. Compared to a woman my chest was pathetic, but it was not the chest of a boy. Sometimes old men had breasts as I had breasts. I was disgusted. I put my brassière on and put the pads in.

I would have to do something. But it was difficult to know what I could do. I had not enough money.

I must go to see a doctor and ask to see a sexologist. At least I might find out approximately how much money I would need.

I wished that I had ten thousand pounds. I said, 'Cats and women like things beginning with M. Cats like mice and milk. Women like men and money.'

I was not afraid of mice. Perhaps, if I had an operation, I would be afraid of mice.

June was eating cornflakes when I went into her room.

'Are you afraid of mice, June?'

'Terrified. Why?'

'I'm not afraid of mice. I'm going to see a doctor about it today.'

'Do you want to be afraid of mice?'

'More than anything.'

'Are you feeling all right, Wendy?'

'No. That's why I'm going to see a doctor.'

'I think you'd better.'

27

I travelled to Beverley because the doctors in Hull were always busy.

I spent the morning being directed and walking and looking at the outside of doctors' houses. I found that it was difficult to guess what a doctor would be like by looking at the outside of his house. I wanted a doctor who would not insist on knowing why I wanted to see a sexologist. Also, he had to be a doctor who had contact with a sexologist who was naturally understanding. I suspected that sexologists might tend to moral firmness. Some of them might have very angry opinions about people like me. I did not want to be sent to one who would hand me over to the police. I thought that when I went to see the sexologist I ought not to wear a tight skirt and high-heeled shoes. I ought to wear a full skirt and flat shoes so that I would be able to run away. On the other hand, I would like to look my most feminine in the hope of arousing interest in my case and sympathy for my predicament. I decided that I would wear high heels, and, if I had to run, I would take them off and run in my stocking feet.

The thought of taking my clothes off and being physically examined made me want to stop thinking.

But I had not seen the first doctor yet.

It was the first day of March. It was bright and not too cold. I was wearing a suede jacket. I thought I looked smart and competent. The wind caught my hair. I thought that any man could be interested in me. Anyone who thought that I ought to try to dress and live as a man must be a blockhead!

March was a month of winds. I wondered if I would have

to hold my skirts down on some windy day. That would be an exciting embarrassment. Frank might laugh at me.

I wished Frank knew about me and had a lot of money to help me. But, if he knew about me, he would probably spit in my face and punch me in the nose and walk away from me forever.

In the end I rang the bell of a surgery that was attached to a liberal-looking house. Perhaps the doctor would be a Dane. In Denmark they were sensible about people like me.

A twin-set woman of about thirty-five opened the door. By her comfortable manner and her kindness I judged that she was the doctor's wife. She was English. She said that the doctor was out but that I could see him as a private patient at half-past one. She wrote my name on a piece of paper.

I spent some time drinking tea at a café in the market place and then I went to look round Beverley Minster. From outside it was a splendid English building of clean pale stone in the bright air. Its pinnacles were higher than any cooling tower. Inside, I wished that I were wearing a hat so that I could keep it on.

Henry V had journeyed all the way to Beverley Minster to give thanks to St John of Beverley for the victory of Agincourt.

> *Our King set forth to Normandy*
> *With grace and might of chivalry*
> *Where God for him wrought marvellously*

My father had set forth to Normandy. He had not come to give thanks to St John of Beverley.

There was nobody about.

I went to one of the pews and found a cushion. I put it down on the stone floor and knelt on it.

'Thank you for preserving my father in the war. Continue to protect him. He is a simple man. Protect Frank, and let him have a better job than the one he has. Have mercy on me. Please, God, let me be a woman.'

The building was huge and solemn and magnificent. There was no sign that the last part of my prayer would be answered. I felt that my father and Frank would be preserved, but I would never be a woman.

'I can love, but nobody can love me.'

I clenched my fists. I had to suck at the back of my nose to keep tears out of my eyes.

I got up.

I said to myself, 'What the hell are you doing in this place?'

I went back to the café in the market place and ordered lunch. But I could not eat. I was thinking about what would happen when I saw the doctor.

The doctor when I saw him was plump, pink, clean and friendly. He was a Scotsman. It was before surgery hours and his receptionist was not there. He left the door open and just outside his kind wife was dusting about and making golf clubs rattle from time to time.

He asked me to sit down in the chair at the end of his desk and then he sat down with a professional expression on his face that I supposed was meant to show that he was efficient and trustworthy.

'Now, what can I do to help you, Miss Ross? Would you mind telling me first who your usual doctor is?'

'Well, I haven't really got a doctor. I've been a student in London for the last two years, and I never went to the doctor I was registered with down there. I can't remember his name. I only want some advice.'

'I see. And where do you live now?'

'In Hull. I came to Beverley because I've heard that the doctors in Hull are always very busy.'

'I'm pretty busy myself. You want to be a private patient, do you?'

'Actually, what I want is for you to put me in contact with a sexologist.'

'I think you mean a gynaecologist. What seems to be the trouble? Is it something very personal?'

'Yes.'

'Would you like to give me some idea what it is? I might be able to help you.'

'I'd like to see a specialist.'

'You know, Miss Ross, that may not be necessary. In these things a woman can sometimes become alarmed without cause. Are you having discomfort of some kind?'

'No.'

'Are you getting soreness? Are you getting a burning feeling when you use the toilet?'

'No.'

'Is your menstrual cycle regular?'

'Yes.'

'A day of two one way or the other is nothing to worry about, you know.'

'I know.'

'Is there any pain?'

'No.'

'Are you sure?'

'Quite sure.',

'Then can't you tell me what it is that's troubling you?'

'I want to see a sexologist.'

'I think you mean a gynaecologist.'

'No, a sex-'

'Isn't Ross a Scots name?' he asked.

'I think it is.'

'Are you Scottish?'

'No.'

'Was your father from Scotland, perhaps?'

'No.'

'Perhaps it was his father.' He smiled at me. 'I remember once I had a patient who'd got it through his head that there was something wrong with his heart. He used to get pains in his chest. The trouble was he worked too hard, and he suffered from a wee bit of tension—if it wasn't for nervous tension, half the doctors in the country would be out of work.' He smiled. 'There was nothing at all seriously wrong with him, but he was always wanting to see specialists. He was a private patient, and I had to concern myself more with saving his money than saving his life. You wouldn't believe how much a body can frighten himself if he's a mind.'

I said, 'I want to see a sexologist.'

'Do you think you could talk about your trouble to a woman doctor?'

'No. I'm certain I need to see a sexologist.'

'Well, Miss Ross, I can make an appointment for you to see a gynaecologist if that's what you want.'

'No, I want to see a sexologist.'

'What makes you so sure it's a sexologist you want to see and not a gynaecologist? Do you know what the difference is?'

'I think so.'

198

'You see, a gynaecologist looks after a woman's special difficulties, but a sexologist looks after both sexes. I'm sure that, if you want to see anybody, it's a gynaecologist you ought to go to. But there may be no need for you to go anywhere. Do you not think that you might be able to talk about your trouble to a woman doctor?'

'No, that wouldn't make any difference. I would just like you to make arrangements for me to see a sexologist.'

'Is it something that you think about that's worrying you? Are you finding yourself attracted to other women? Do you feel that you'd like to be a man?'

'No.'

'I must say, Miss Ross, that I don't think that you're behaving very sensibly. What am I to tell this sexologist about you?'

'You can tell him I have a sexual problem.'

'Are you sure it's not your young man who ought to be seeking medical advice?'

'I haven't got a young man.'

'Surely you have.'

'No.'

'Is that what's worrying you?' He sat back in his chair like a man who is relieved to have come upon the solution of a mystery. 'Och, you don't want to worry about that! Men are a lot of rogues. Have you never had a boy friend?'

'No.'

'I find that hard to believe. Are you shy?'

'No, it's not that.'

'What do you think it is?'

'There's something wrong with me.'

'What is it that's wrong?'

'Something.'

'Has anybody ever told you that there's something wrong with you? Have you had a medical examination?'

'Yes. I can't talk about it. There's something wrong with me. I know that I need to see a sexologist.'

He leaned forward, looking serious, and said, 'I see. Who was it examined you?'

'I can't talk about it.'

'You've not had anything to do with anybody who's not a properly qualified practitioner, have you?'

199

'No. It's just that I can't talk about it—it's too horrible. I can't remember the doctor's name, but he was a real doctor.'

'I'm glad to hear that, Miss Ross. Now, I think it would be best if I sent you to Dr Goodwin—she's a woman doctor here in Beverley. She's a very nice woman. She can examine you, and then we'll know what ought to be done.'

'No. I need to see a sexologist.'

'You're a very stubborn young woman, Miss Ross. Don't you think you might allow a doctor to know something?'

'I'm sorry. I wish I could explain.'

'Why can't you explain?'

'I can't.' I bowed my head forward and put my hand over my eyes.

'Oh dear,' he said. 'Come, come, now. What is your first name?'

'Wendy,' I told him without raising my head or taking my hand away.

'I'm sorry if I've upset you, Wendy.'

I took my hand away and raised my head. I wished that there were tears in my eyes. I said, 'You haven't upset me, doctor, but I'm in a difficult position.'

'Well,' he said, 'if it's what you want, I'll make an appointment for you to see a gynaecologist.'

It took some more argument to convince him finally that it was a sexologist and not a gynaecologist that I wanted to see.

Then he told me that he knew of a sexologist in Leeds who was an expert and able man. 'It will cost you some money, but, if that is what you want, I can contact Mr Waites for you. Do you want me to do that?'

'If you would.'

'It would be a great deal better if you could give me some information about yourself and your difficulties.'

'I can't do that.'

'Very well.'

He waved away my offer of payment and asked for my address. He said that he would send me a letter to tell me when I could go to see Mr Waites in Leeds.

I thought that, if I could show myself to a sexologist, there was some chance that I could get help to change into a woman.

A sexologist might see that it was necessary for me to be made into a woman.

The doctor had been gentle with me. A less kindly man could have become angry. He was a good man. I thought that it must be very pleasant to be his wife.

On the train back to Hull I imagined Mr Waites as having a fine, masculine face with a beard—like, I soon realised, the face in photographs of Sigmund Freud that I had seen. I imagined his saying to me, 'You will have to endure a truly terrible ordeal. The results cannot be guaranteed in any way. It is not impossible that you may die in almost unbelievable agony. Are you sure that you want to begin treatment?'

'Absolutely sure.'

But I had not enough money for treatment.

I got back to Hull in the middle of the afternoon.

In a shop window I saw a pair of panties that had a pattern of red and yellow tartan. I went into the shop and bought a pair like them.

June laughed when I showed them to her. 'I say, how bloody touching! But really, Wendy, they're not your kind of thing at all. They're more my kind of thing. Give them to me.'

'No.'

'What made you buy them?'

'I don't know.'

'You could wear them if you went out with a Scotsman. Do you know any Scotsmen?'

'No, I'm afraid not.'

'Of course, if you don't wear them, you could turn them into a cover for a set of bagpipes.'

'That's what I may do with them,' I said.

'Did you go to see a doctor?' she asked.

'Yes.'

'What did he say?'

'I have to see a man in Leeds.'

'It's nothing serious, is it?'

'No.'

'Are you really ill, Wendy?'

'No, it's nothing.'

'It must be something. You must sit down, Wendy. You look a bit strained.'

Before she had finished questioning me I was sorry that I

201

had told her that I was going to see a doctor.

28

Frank came on Saturday afternoon, and we went across the Humber on the ferry.

The ferryboats were big white paddle-steamers that trundled back and forth across the river from the Corporation Pier to the landing stage at New Holland on the Lincolnshire side.

We went on the top deck. It was a clear day. We could see right up the river to where trawlers were lying off the fish docks and far beyond out into the country, and we could see down river beyond Saltend. When we got out into the middle of the river we could look back at Hull. I felt a tenderness for the city. On the water the paddles had made a long wake behind the steamer.

A trawler passed astern of us. It was going down river. The name on the bow was *Arctic Eagle*. I said I thought that it was a fine name. I said that trawlermen were brave men.

I told Frank that I couldn't swim.

'Neither can I.'

'What shall we do if anything happens?'

'Sink.'

'Would we?'

'No, of course not. We'd get into that.' He pointed to a lifeboat that was near where we were standing.

'Women and children first,' I said. Then I said, 'You know, Frank, you ought to learn to swim.'

'What for?'

'So that you'd be able to save yourself if you fell in the water.'

'I don't intend to fall in the water.'

'Everybody ought to be able to swim,' I said seriously.

'Some trawlermen think it's unlucky to go to sea with a man who can swim.'

'Why?'

'I suppose they reckon it's a poor seaman that has to do any swimming.'

We did not leave the ferryboat at New Holland. Frank said there was nothing to see there. We watched the passengers getting off and the cars being driven off and then the people coming down and cars coming down to come on board to go to Hull.

When we got back to Hull we had tea in a café that had starched, white tablecloths.

I remember that Frank was an ordinary man that night—but he was more than an ordinary man. I kept looking at him and thinking that I loved him. It was happiness.

29

I went down every morning to see if there was anything in the post for me. I was impatient and nervous. My interview with the sexologist in Leeds might be the most important event of my life. If he said that I could never be a woman, I might decide to kill myself. But, surely, he would not say that. I hoped that, when he had examined me, he would make arrangements for me to be helped even though I did not have enough money to pay for treatment. He might be a socialist.

Obviously, it was unfair that some people could be turned into women because they had money while others had to stay as I was because they did not have money.

I could make a speech in Parliament about it, pointing out that there was a temptation for people in my circumstances to try to get the money they needed by selling themselves for ugly homosexual acts.

The Transvestites' Assistance Act.

There might be opposition to the passing of the bill.

I wished that the letter would come.

The thought of going to Leeds made my hands sweat.

I wished that the letter would come.

30

There was a buff envelope with my name and address typed

on it: Miss W. Ross. It had a Beverley postmark. I took it and went to the foot of the stairs. I sat down on the stairs and looked at the envelope. I dare not open it.

Then I thought, 'Perhaps I have to go to Leeds today!'

I tore open the envelope.

An appointment had been made for me to see Mr Waites at half-past three in the afternoon of the following Tuesday.

31

Frank noticed that I was nervous.

'What's the matter?'

'It's my illness. I have to go to see a doctor in Leeds about it.'

'Will he be able to do anything?'

'I hope so.'

32

I had made my mind up what I would wear on the day. My smartest outfit was a red suit with red high heels and a black jersey. I wanted to look my best. I did not want Mr Waites to think that I was wearing clothes that belonged to my mother or sister.

The red and black suited my fairness.

33

I decided that, if Mr Waites said that I ought to have some kind of treatment to make me masculine, I would pretend to agree with him in order to get through the interview without causing him to lose his temper. He would probably be a man who was used to getting his own way.

If he did say that, it would mean that there was no possibility of my having treatment to be changed into a woman. I would want to die.

34

On the Monday morning I got off all the sticking plaster. I spent the afternoon in the bath to get rid of the marks. Then I fastened myself up with bandages.

I went to bed that night as anxious as I had been on the night before I had left Mrs Ford's.

35

The morning came. I trembled as I got dressed. I could not eat any breakfast. I was ready long before it was necessary for me to set out.

At first the day was cold, so I was standing about in my tweed coat, but then it was warmer, and I put on my suede jacket, but I found that I did not like the dark brown of the jacket against the orangish red of my skirt. I went to the wardrobe and got out my black raincoat. I had worn it on the morning I set out from Mrs Ford's. I would wear it on this day. I put it on. At once my confidence increased. I pulled the belt tight, and I felt much better.

The brown leather handbag that I had meant to carry would not do with the black raincoat. I found the small handbag of soft black leather that I had bought on that first morning. It looked better not to carry a bag with a raincoat, but I had to have a bag with me. It was small. It would go into the pocket.

I had been called madam for the first time when I had gone into the shop to buy the handbag. It might bring me luck.

There was not room in the black handbag for all the stuff

I had in the big handbag. I discovered lipsticks I had bought and forgotten.

'You've got enough cosmetics to stock a shop. You will have to try to get used to being a woman. Why did you buy all these lipsticks? What will you do when you're a middle-aged housewife with a husband who keeps you short of money? Poison him, I shouldn't wonder.'

On the train I worried. A large woman sat next to me and told me about her feet and her son. I wished that I had bought a first-class ticket to worry in peace. I answered her with nods and smiles. After saying many things she stopped talking.

Leeds was noisy at midday. It seemed a more crowded and bustling place than Hull.

A woman I asked told me that the street I wanted was not far from the town hall. She added that she found it difficult to find her way about in Leeds because everything had been knocked down and rebuilt. She pointed in the direction of the town hall.

I found the street. There was a blackened Victorian terrace. I was impressed by the great weight of stone. It looked like a building that could be inhabited by men who knew things that ordinary people were not permitted to know. Everything in Leeds that day seemed to me to be a quarter the size again of everything in Hull.

I found the doorway through which I would have to pass to have my future decided. I saw a number, a wrought iron twelve attached to the grimy stone.

It was not time yet.

I walked back towards the station. Near the station I went into a coffee bar and had two cups of tea and managed to eat a bun. Then I went back to the town hall. I found that the public art gallery was next to the town hall. I was in the art gallery until it was three o'clock. My hands were sweating all the time. I wished that the consultation was over and I was on my way back to Hull.

'If you're like this now,' I said to myself, 'what are you going to be like if you get to an operation?'

When I left the art gallery to go to keep the appointment my legs seemed to be doing the walking for me without my help. I felt too weak to help them. I was in a daze of anxiety. I almost wished that my legs would take me back to the railway

206

station. When I told him that I was a boy he might shout, 'Get out of here, you degenerate tyke!' Or he might get his receptionist to hold me while he phoned for the police. Or he might hold me himself while his receptionist phoned for the police. I hoped that he would be angry rather than officious. Yet he might be neither. He might want to help me.

I was greeted by a middle-aged woman in a white coat. Her hair was grey. She wore spectacles. She said, 'There's no need for you to go upstairs to the waiting room. Mr Waites should be here in a few minutes. He's never late for an appointment. Have you come far?'

'From Hull.'

'Did you come by train?'

'Yes.'

She might have been a teacher at an infants' school receiving a new little girl. The eyes behind the spectacles were practised at being understanding.

'Mr Waites is bound to be here in a few minutes. He says that he never keeps people waiting because, if he did, they'd make jokes about his name. He's a brilliant man. He's very well known.'

Mr Waites came in, tall, striding along in a dark grey suit, boyishly handsome, like a sixth-former who had become steadily more noble as he had grown older. He was about forty. The forelock of his brown hair fell on his forehead. He knew that he was a handsome man. Behind him trotted a young woman in a leather coat. She carried a leather attache-case. I supposed that she would be willing to carry anything anywhere for her master. Her fair hair was taken straight back.

'Miss Ross?' said Mr Waites and smiled a super-doctor's smile.

I put out my hand. He took it between his thumb and forefinger and pressed it and let it go.

The middle-aged woman took a bunch of keys from the pocket of her white coat and opened the door of the consulting room. I thought that the room must be used by different doctors at different times, while the woman was there all the time. It would have been easier to tell her about myself than to tell this handsome, dominating doctor.

Mr Waites strode into the room and I followed him. The girl in the leather coat was behind me. The woman in the white coat was left outside.

The room was furnished like the austere living-room of a gentleman of traditional taste. On the parquet floor was a large carpet with a Persian design. There were two leather arm chairs as well as high-backed Jacobean chairs. There was no desk. In the centre of the room was a long mahogany table. But against one wall there was a medical couch and there was a sink and, in a corner, a hospital screen with wheels. The fireplace was empty but the room was warm.

The young woman went past me and placed the case she was carrying on the table. She took a notebook from the pocket of her leather coat. She took her coat off and put it over the back of a chair. Then she hurried to set a chair for me.

I sat near the table. The young woman was somewhere behind me out of sight. Boyishly, Mr Waites sat on the table with his legs swinging. He was an extremely vain man.

'I received a letter from Dr Murdoch in Beverley about you, Miss Ross. He said you wouldn't discuss your problem with him. Do you think you can discuss it with me?'

'It's very difficult,' I said.

'Then take your time, and try to remember that, whether you tell me the truth or not, you'll still be getting a bill.'

'It's very simple,' I said. 'I'm a boy.'

He did not give any sign that he was surprised.

'In what way are you a boy?'

I did not know what to answer. I was dumb for a moment before I said, 'I am really a boy. I dress up like this because I like wearing women's clothes.'

'Are you sure you're a boy?'

'I think I am.'

'You're not altogether sure?'

'In some ways I'm not sure. When I'm dressed up I feel like a woman.'

'Why did you come here today dressed like that?'

'I've been dressed up all the time since the autumn of last year. I've been living as a woman.'

'I see. Well, then, we'd better make sure what you are. Do you mind getting undressed?'

'No.' I stood up. I felt that I might fall down.

'Do you want Nurse Spencer to go out of the room or would you prefer her to stay?'

'I think I'd prefer her to go out.'

He spoke to the young woman. 'If you could leave us.'

I went behind the screen. There was a chair. I started taking my clothes off. I put them on the chair. I felt ill. My arms were heavy and my hands were weak. I was slow.

When I had taken my clothes off I found that I did not want to take the bandages off. My body looked wretched enough without my poor, unwanted thing being visible.

I came out from behind the screen with my arms across my chest. I was a skinny boy. I thought that I must look ridiculous with my long hair and my painted face. I felt grotesque. It was a woman's head on the top of a boy's body. I was humiliated. I was so foolish and miserable.

Mr Waites had got down off the table. He looked at me without surprise or contempt. I thought that he must have seen people like me before.

He asked me to take the bandages off. I did as I was told. I was a helpless monstrosity. He was methodical and careful. I wished that I could faint. The worst was when he was finding out whether I had two testicles. He examined my chest. He made me put my head back while he examined my neck. He examined my arms and hands. I wished that I was not wearing nail varnish. He stood away from me and looked me up and down. He made me turn about. He made me stand with my legs together. He asked me to walk. I walked backwards and forwards on the carpet while he watched me.

'Do you shave?'

'Yes. Just at the sides of my chin.'

'Right,' he said, 'you can get dressed.'

I went behind the screen and put the bandages back and dressed myself as quickly as I could. When I came out the young woman was back in the room. She looked at me as a patient of no extraordinary interest.

Mr Waites was back on the table. He said to me, 'I have no doubt that you are a male. Do you understand that?'

'Yes.'

'You have an unusual number of anatomical feminine characteristics. However, I'm a sexologist, not an anatomist. I can tell you that I have no doubt at all that you are a male. Even in the best developed men there are often some feminine characteristics. I can tell you that you are not in a position

209

to choose your sex. Do you understand?'

'Yes.'

'What do you do for a living?'

'I used to work for my father. I haven't had any work since I've been living as a woman. I've been living on some money my mother left me.'

'How much was that?'

'Five hundred pounds.'

'Then you're not very well placed?'

'No.'

'You'll have to stop pretending to be a woman or you could find yourself in serious trouble of one kind or another. Have you ever thought of going on the stage?'

'No.'

'I'd advise something like that. If you want to dress up as a woman, you might as well cash in on it. I can't pretend you haven't a very striking appearance. You might do very well on the stage. I believe there are entertainments called drag shows. It's probably not the most wholesome art form—but someone has remarked that it takes all sorts to make a world. Are you homosexual?'

'I think so.'

'Then I think your best bet is to try to get yourself into the entertainment business. I imagine you came to see me because you have ideas about wanting to change sex. Is that right?'

'Yes.'

'Forget it. There is no such thing as a change of sex. You are a male and you will always be a male. There is nothing that anybody can do about it. Do you understand that?'

'Yes.'

'If you were a female who had some abnormality, it might be possible for you to be given medical help. But you're a male. You'll just have to make the best of a bad job—which is what we all have to do.'

36

I threw away the return half of my ticket and bought a first-class ticket to go back to Hull. I had a compartment to myself. I cried.

Dwarfs joined circuses. I was expected to go on the stage. Sabina had killed herself rather than go on the stage. What could I do on the stage? I could not sing or dance. I would have to pose and mince about and let people look at me and know that I was a boy dressed as a woman. Drag.

I was a pervert. I was a thing twisted out of shape. I was expected to creep into corners where there were other perverts. I would live to be a middle-aged man dressed a as woman. I would grow soft-bellied, soft and white all over like a skin filled with lard, a loathsome, soft slug of a pervert lusting for hard young men. Now I was pretty, but I would become old and fat, full of lies and gin and sniggering jokes. It might be possible to buy young men to do things to me, but it would not be possible to buy a man like Frank.

Frank was a good soldier.

There were stories of girls who had dressed up as boys to go to the war with their sweethearts. I would dress up as a boy to go with Frank. I would march along by his side all day and at night I would sleep on the ground with him.

'O grenadier, let me be your mouse. Put me in a little tin and carry me with you.'

I might save his life in a battle, and he might say, 'Because you have saved my life, I must forgive you everything.' But he would not be able to forgive my being a boy. I would have to put my gun in my mouth and kill myself. I would be better dead—like my mother.

'Why can't I have my mother's body instead of its being dead and rotten in the ground? Mother, I am a woman, like you. Your suffering is over, but mine goes on and on.'

Frank was a good soldier. He was strong and healthy. He had nothing to do with drag. He had nothing to do with peanuts.

I was a peanut.

Or was a peanut a transvestite who was not a homosexual?

I had told Mr Waites that I was a homosexual. But if I were not in a male body, I would not be a homosexual. It was not my fault.

Yes, it was my fault. I was what I was, and the fault was in me. I was rotten. I had a cancer of masculinity.

Mr Waites had said that I must forget about wanting to

change sex. How could I? If I forgot that, I would almost cease to exist. Apart from that desire there was not much of me.

I stopped thinking and cried.

Then I had a phantasy about a kind surgeon coming into the carriage and finding me crying and asking me what the matter was and, when I had told him, saying he would help me.

But then I came back to reality again and cried again. There was no hope for me. My life was stopped.

I decided that I would have to kill myself.

I saw myself as from a distance. I was sitting hunched up in a railway carriage. Other people's lives were possible, but the life of that creature was not possible. It was a queer, miserable, hunched up little perversion. It should not have been born. It was an obscenity, a filthy thing. It should have been put down the lavatory and flushed away.

37

Frank came that Tuesday night. I told him to go away. I told him that I could not see him again.

38

He came three times after that Tuesday night. Each time I told him to go away. He tried to question me, but I did not tell him anything. He was angry when he left me the last time.

39

I still had my clothes.

I had been happy before I had known Frank. I told myself

that I ought to be able to get back to being happy.

But I would not wake up in the morning and think, 'Frank will come.' I could look nice, but I would not feel Frank looking at me. I would not listen to him again as he talked confusion into temporary order.

40

One night I drank some of the whiskey I had bought at Christmas and brooded on injustice. Some time after midnight I wrote a letter to Shirley.

Dear Shirley, I know that you think that my behaviour is altogether selfish. But I am twenty-one. Fifty years ago I would have been sent to be killed in France. What happened in 1914-18 gives a clear picture of the attitude of Society to its young men. Society seeks to exploit its young men, and in that exploitation there is no thought of justice and no thought of mercy. Young men are only educated and trained so that they can be exploited. Society is Woman. Woman is Society.

I should be selfish. I should take what I can and give as little as possible in return. The clock cannot be put back. One cannot regard history as an abstraction that does not affect personal attitudes. The many dead of the Great War are with us. We are always stepping over their bodies. Their vile smell makes us dislike the sunshine, and they ask us questions with their rotted mouths that are so simple and so unanswerable.

When there is the blowing of bugles in November the women can think beautiful sad thoughts, but men should feel bitterness.

If I had gone to France and been turned into manure, I would have been one of the selfless dead. But I am alive and selfish. How wicked it is not to be dead! Wendy

I read over what I had written. I could not understand why I had written it. Shirley would not be able to understand it. I tore the sheet of paper to pieces.

41

It was morning. I lay in bed looking up at the ceiling.

I could lie there forever, but Frank would not come. I could go out and spend all my money buying clothes, but Frank would not come.

And yet I still loved clothes.

My nightdress was pretty. It was deep blue, decorated with lace and net at the top and with a band of lace at the hem. June had said that it was a nightdress fit for a ball.

I wondered if I ought to buy a smart umbrella.

Or I could buy a bottle of gin.

The ceiling was rather grey. It needed distempering.

Frank had been in this room, but he would never be in this room again.

I pushed back the covers and swung my legs out of bed. I sat on the edge of the bed.

It was a lovely nightdress, but I was not a real woman.

I said, 'Frank.'

There did not seem any reason to get up. I got back in and pulled the covers up. I closed my eyes. I thought that I would like to stay in bed for the rest of my life.

I slept.

When I awoke I felt hungry.

I got up and got dressed.

I put the kettle on.

I buttered a slice of bread. When I had it buttered I held it on the palm of my hand and threw it upwards. It stuck flat to the ceiling.

42

I spent much of the time in bed. It was easy to sleep.

June noticed the difference in me.

'What's the matter, Wendy? You do look miserable.'

'I'm all right.'

'But you look miserable every day. And what's that slice

214

of bread doing up there?'

'Where?'

'Up there. There's a slice of bread stuck to the ceiling.'

'I threw it up there.'

'What for?'

'I got bored with it.'

'Are you going crazy?'

'I went crazy long ago.'

I climbed up onto the table and peeled the bread off the ceiling. A rectangle of butter remained.

June, looking up at me, said, 'There'll be a mark. The grease will have gone right into the plaster. You won't get it off. You'll have to paint the whole ceiling to cover it.'

Next day I bought a large tin of emulsion paint and a brush and painted the ceiling pink. It made my arms ache, but I kept working, and when it was finished I felt better.

June came in and said, 'It's superb, Wendy! I wonder what Mrs Cartwright will say about it.'

That night June and I went to the pictures. We brought fish-and-chips back with us, and we sat up until late agreeing that money was an important test of a man.

'That's the trouble with Frank,' I said. 'He hasn't any money. He talks a lot, but there's nothing to show for it. That's why I've finished with him.'

'Have you finished with him, Wendy?'

'Yes.'

'He's very good-looking in a barbaric way,' she said thoughtfully.

'There's no such thing as a good-looking man,' I told her. 'They're all ugly.'

'You have to think of security,' said June seriously. 'After all, Wendy, you are alone in the world.'

'As alone as a leper on a desert island,' I said.

When I got into bed that night I told myself that it was possible to go on living. I was not as happy as I had been with Frank, but I had myself. Most women had to be content with themselves. There were not enough barbarically handsome men to go round.

I must lie still and alone in my pretty nightdress. It was a white, waltz-length nightdress. There was an embroidered yoke at the top and then it was very full and there was a flounce at the hem. I must lie still like a gentle girl.

Even if there were no Frank, I would still want the operation more than anything. I would give up Frank to have the operation.

Two things in my mind would not meet. There was a gap that stopped my thinking. My mind was a woman. My body should be made the same. The difference between mind and reality made me sweat and yearn to be a woman. I could not understand. I could only want and want to be a woman. My desire made me strain my body forward. I was in madness.

I was glad that I was suffering. It was a woman's suffering. I was a bitch.

And then I lay still again. It was right that I should be stopped and frustrated. I was female.

I was Wendy lying still in her nightdress, secret in the darkness. I could not do anything to get Frank back. I was a girl. There were many actions that I could not do.

I wished that I had no choice but to be a girl. An operation would make it so that one had no possibility of choosing; one would always have to sit down when one used the lavatory. I always did sit down, but I had the possibility of choosing. If I were bound to one way, I would be one person. I would be a woman.

43

I sat in my dressing gown eating breakfast.

Happiness was contentment with symbols. But when one knew a split between symbols and reality one was in trouble. I must try to get back to being content. After all, I was in the same condition as many others. I could handle symbols but I could not touch reality. Most human beings were fetishists. They had to believe that money was wealth and that words were thought and that mind was God. If one was not content to be a fetishist, one went mad. I must try to be content. The sticking-plaster forced me to sit down when I used the lavatory. I was cunning at imitating.

But there was only one truth, and that was being a real

woman. Men were branches from the tree. Women were the stuff of the central trunk.

Before I could paint the walls of the room pearl-grey I would first have to get the wallpaper off. Perhaps my landlady, Mrs Cartwright, would not want the walls painted pearl-grey. And she might not like the pink ceiling. She would come for the rent at the end of the month. Time was getting into gear again. Time could go on even though it was not divided into sections by Frank's visits. As long as something was happening somewhere, there was time. Once I had believed that time was taking me forward to happiness. Now it was eating into my money and making me older. Time might be taking me forward to a place where I would be middle-aged. But I must kill myself rather than be a middle-aged man. I would not be able to live in the body of a middle-aged man. My mind would go out of my body and cling to the pink ceiling. The body could be taken away and put in a mental hospital, but the mind would remain in this room clinging to the ceiling.

44

I was going to have Sunday dinner with the Stephensons, but when I went down Marguerite said that she was not going to cook a dinner. Philip was sitting reading a Sunday paper with resolution. Marguerite seemed distant, as though she was thinking of herself as a beautiful woman who had married an uninspired man. I could tell that there had been a row.

Marguerite had a tang of red, green, yellow and blue raffia on the table. She was pulling out strands from it and trying to untangle them.

'It's for raffia work,' she said to me. 'I've got pushed into looking after an extra class on Monday afternoons. They're supposed to do art, but the art mistress is away. I'm going to make them do raffia work. I could have them drawing, but I'm going to make them do raffia work. And if that silly cow of a headmistress doesn't like it, she can get somebody else to look after them. She can give me the sack if she wants.'

I helped her with the raffia. When a strand could not be

217

untangled she cut it off with a pair of scissors. Her temper was short, and consequently some of the pieces of raffia were short too.

Not much was said because of the row there had been before I came in.

The clock ticked on the mantelpiece. We were on a mountain of futility. Clouds of ennui rolled round the room. Far below there were rocks and streams and woods where tough bears lived, but we were high on the mountain in pure white snow. The crystals were symmetrical and mathematical. They had been made in heaven. Bad bears that loved hunting and honey and rolling with their mates and playing with their cubs were of the earth.

I thought that, if I were Marguerite, I would go down. I would reach the earth and be a mother bear. On the television I had seen a mother bear teaching her two cubs to catch salmon in a stream. Salmon were quick, but bears were clever.

In the high place the snow was perfect white and smooth. The earth below was many-coloured and tangled, like the raffia.

I wondered how many people finally slipped away to insanity on Sunday afternoons. Sunday was a high day. It was making me dizzy. For the insane, every day must be Sunday. All my days were becoming Sundays. Being with Frank had been Saturday. Now here I was, high and stranded on Sunday, like Noah's Ark. I imagined a door opening out of my belly and animals coming out two by two—two of everything. The room was crowded with my innocent creatures. I must die that they might live.

When tea time came Marguerite boiled eggs.

I thought of making a joke by asking who would get the custody of the Encyclopaedia Britannica. But that would have been cruel to Marguerite—and they did not have an Encyclopaedia Britannica.

I was not playing gooseberry and preventing them from getting to a fight they wanted to have. Marguerite did not love Philip at all. He was perfectly unlovable. He ate his egg intelligently. One could imagine that the food went up into his skull instead of down into his stomach.

45

The day I tried to kill myself was a Friday.

In the morning I was feeling reasonable and fairly cheerful. I went to the city centre and stepped about and admired my reflection in shop windows. But when I got back I suddenly felt tired. I felt heavy and I wanted to close my eyes. I went to bed and slept.

When I awoke I felt refreshed. I got up and dressed myself. While I was dressing I thought, 'There is no purpose in being alive, but it is interesting to be alive and it is pleasant to be putting on these clothes.'

It was late afternoon. For some reason I went downstairs.

In the hallway I found Philip. He was wearing his overcoat. He was standing like a man who has gone to fetch something and forgotten what it is he intended to fetch.

He said, 'Marguerite isn't here. She wasn't there when I went to pick her up. She's been back here and taken her things. She's left me a note.' He took a folded sheet of notepaper from his pocket and handed it to me to give proof. It was only when I noticed the blank look on his face that had replaced the usual smugness that I realised that he was telling me that Marguerite had left him.

I unfolded the notepaper.

Dear Philip, I have left you and I am not coming back. I am going away with Frank Cracknell. There is nothing to be said. Marguerite

'It's very short,' I said.

He took the piece of paper out of my hand and put it back in his pocket—perhaps he wanted it to show to his mother. He went down the hallway and out of the front door.

I stood in the hallway. I did not seem able to think.

Then I went and tried the door to the Stephensons' living-room. It was open. I went through into the kitchen. The clothes horse was leaning against the wall, but there were no clothes on it. I went back into the living-room and started searching the drawers and cupboards. In the top drawer of the sideboard I found a pair of stockings. They were an old pair. There was a large hole in one of them. I got out of my shoes and unfastened the stockings I was wearing and took them off.

I put on Marguerite's stockings. They were short for me. I had to lengthen my suspenders. The hole was at the side of the right calf. I went on searching, hoping to find other clothes that she had left behind, but I could not find anything else in the living-room.

I went up the hallway in stocking feet. The door to the Stephensons' bedroom was locked. I went back to the living-room and got the poker.

The bedroom door resisted me. I lost my temper. I kept splintering the wood but not doing anything to unfasten the lock. In the end I managed to get the poker between the door and the frame and lever on it. The lock broke. I went in. The wardrobe doors were open and the drawers of the dressing table were pulled out. She had not left any cosmetics behind on the dressing table top. I looked in the drawers. There were no clothes. But at the bottom of one of the drawers I found some rose petals. I gathered them up with my fingers. I put them into my hair.

Lying at the bottom of the wardrobe was an old dress of blue worsted. I took it out and held it up. The zip at the side had been taken out. There were loops for a belt, but the belt was missing. I took off the skirt and sweater I was wearing. I got the blue dress over my head and struggled into it. When I had it on I found that one of the sleeves was torn. They were three-quarter sleeves and the one on the left was ripped along the seam. It hung off my arm. I remembered seeing a safety-pin at the bottom of one of the dressing-table drawers. I found the safety-pin and pinned the sleeve together.

The dress did not fit me very well. It was too short, so that my slip showed all the way round. And the side gaped open where the zip had been.

I went back to the living-room and picked up one of the stockings I had taken off. I tied it round my waist as a belt. Then I got into my shoes.

I stood facing the books in the bookcase.

'Now children, I am your new teacher. My name is Mrs Cracknell. Do you like my dress? You can tell that I am Mrs Cracknell because this is Mrs Cracknell's dress. I always wear women's clothes, because I am a woman. Always remember, children, that it is wrong and wicked not to wear the right clothes. You can get shot for not wearing the right clothes.

There are boys' clothes for boys and girls' clothes for girls. That is how it should be: two of everything. Everything is divided into two—down the middle. Consider the black horse and the white. I'm the girl who rides round the circus ring with a foot on each, and for that one needs two legs. I remember that Nero used to go to the circus with his wife Sabina. A man who had studied philosophy remarked that it would have been well if Nero's father had had such a wife. Sabina was married in a pink wedding dress. I would prefer white. I do not know whether Sabina's father was invited to the wedding. Actually, Mr Cracknell is not at all like the Emperor Nero. Nero was like Humpty-Dumpty. Impenetrability—and it looks as though I'll have to stop here all the rest of my life. But today I am not like Alice. Today I want to travel at great speed through the sky. I want to stream over all the land like a great empty angel. And the people would look up and cry out of a great wonder. And the joke would be that I would be an empty angel; an empty white angel, meaning nothing, an emptiness in the sky, my long hair streaming and my great white wings beating, all meaning nothing. Men work hard all the day to make meaning out of nonsense, but nonsense is the truth. How can they think their way to being women? How can they think their way to existence? It is impossible. One can only exist by loving and being loved. Without love one cannot understand. One's head gets split in two. I cannot understand how men can live and women can go mad. A woman should not go mad; she has her clothes. The black horse and the white are galloping at full speed in opposite directions. It is difficult to keep a foot on each. Do you wonder I gave it up and became a schoolteacher? Actually, I'm really too pretty to be a schoolteacher, but it was either this or dragging myself about on a stage. I chose schoolteaching. At least you don't have to be showing people your knickers. Knickers must be kept secret, or else they lose their power to hold things together. My father, the Emperor Charlemagne, who rules over both France and Germany, would not approve of my showing people my knickers. It is by no means private to show people your knickers. I like being private. The grave's a fine and private place. I think that I would like to be in a grave—like Juliet—shut in with the door locked. Putting a shilling in a gas meter is like putting a penny in a lavatory door. You get in and shut the door after you and then you're private. My mother's dead. She's been dead all my life. She makes quite a fetish of being dead. Your son, my lord, has paid a soldier's debt—a penny to get into the ladies' lavatory. We did Macbeth at school. I wanted to be Lady Macbeth, but I didn't tell anybody. Lady Macbeth doesn't have to show her knickers. But, if I'd been Lady Macbeth, I wouldn't have been allowed to wear any knickers. They hadn't got to Method acting at the grammar school. I wouldn't have felt I was a woman without knickers. I'd rather be Juliet than Lady Macbeth. Lady Macbeth is all heavy curtain material and no knickers. . . .'

I could hear myself talking. It went on and on. It was not easy to stop it. When I did manage to stop it I said to myself, 'It's happened. You've gone round the bend. Look at the mess you've made in here!'

I started putting things back in the drawers and cupboards.

When I had put everything back and made the room tidy I took off Marguerite's stockings and rolled them up and put them back in the drawer where I had found them. I untied my own stocking from around my waist, but then I could not find the other one. It had been lying on the floor where I had taken it off. I thought that I must have put it away in one of the drawers. It did not matter.

I went back to the bedroom and took off the blue dress and put on my skirt and sweater. Without stockings my suspenders were dangling.

I inspected the door. There was nothing I could do to repair the damage I had made with the poker.

The poker was lying on the floor near the dressing table. I went across to pick it up and remembered putting the rose petals in my hair. I brushed them out with my hand. I picked up the poker and took it back to the living-room.

I went upstairs to my room and locked the door behind me.

I did not like the feeling of my suspenders dangling. I found a pair of stockings and put them on.

Now I was going to gas myself.

It was Friday. June would have gone home to Scarborough.

The room would have to be sealed as well as possible.

One of the top windows was open a few inches. I pulled it shut. I took the mat that was by my bed and laid it against the bottom of the door.

I felt behind the gas meter where I kept a pile of shillings.
There were no shillings.

I did not want to go out to the shops.

Aspirins.

I had a bottle of aspirins. I found it. It was half full.

I shook the tablets out into my hand and set them on the
table to count them. I set them in rows of five. When I had
them all out there were nine rows of five and a row of three.
That was forty-eight tablets.

I went and turned the gas fire on but did not light it. I came
back to the table and held a cupped hand at the edge and
pushed the tablets into it with the other hand. I went to the
sink and put the tablets on the draining board. The gas was
hissing from the gas fire. I found a glass and filled it with
water. Then I began swallowing the tablets, one and then the
next and then the next. I thought it was a humourless way to
kill oneself. It took some time. Before I had swallowed the
last tablet there was a poisonous smell of gas.

I went to the bed. I sat on the bed and took my shoes off.
I got into bed and pulled the covers up. I had to do some
tugging and pulling at my skirt to make myself comfortable.
I closed my eyes.

I was glad that I had not left a note. It did not matter that
they would find out about me. It did not matter what they
thought. All the clothes I was wearing were clean.

It might be a long time before they broke into the room and
found me dead. My eyes would be open. It did not matter.

There would be an inquest.

'Suicide while of unsound sex.'

I would be dead. Mine had not been in any way an important life.

'A white slip with a six-panelled skirt with matching panties;
a white mini-slip with matching briefs for wearing under suits;
a white bra with contour cups in satin-covered forma with
wired undercups and wide-set shoulder straps; a suspender
belt in white taffeta; a white waist-length girdle with a front
panel of lace and satin; a white half-slip trimmed with slotted
lace. . . .'

I became unconscious.

46

My body seemed to be jerking. I was lying on my side. My mouth seemed to be full of soup. It was running out of my mouth at the side. The pillow was slimy wet. I opened my eyes and saw that it was blood that was coming out of my mouth. The jerking was vomiting. There was sick and blood on the pillow.

I tried to raise myself up, but I could not. I had no strength at all. I could not even raise my head. My stomach kept jerking and the blood kept coming up into my mouth. I could only lie there and slaver the blood out onto the pillow to keep myself from choking.

I was sure that I was dying.

By the light I judged that it was early afternoon. I was lying on my right side facing the door.

The vomiting stopped.

I lay with my mouth open. The blood on the pillow frightened me. I wanted somebody to come to help me.

I started trying to shout for help, but the noises I made were only soft moans.

My head began to hurt. And I had a feeling like diarrhoea.

But with the discomfort there came a slight increase in strength. I rolled onto my back. The movement made me aware that the feeling of diarrhoea was accurate. I was foul.

I put my hands up to my head.

I lay with my hands fixed on my forehead for a long time. I became less sure that I was dying. I began to think that, if somebody helped me, I could survive.

I shouted, and it was a louder noise than I had made before, but the effort caused my head sudden pain that I did not want to happen again. Also the shout hurt my throat. I was very thirsty. I wanted somebody to come and give me a drink of water.

I lay listening. There was no sound in the house.

I had to have a drink of water.

I began to struggle to get myself up. I was so weak that I could hardly move my body. I was as heavy as a whale. I got to the edge of the bed and fell out onto the floor.

I lay still on the floor with my eyes shut. I was cold. I was bloody and filthy. There was a stink.

I began to crawl. My hair hung forward at the sides of my face.

I got to the sink.

I waited, preparing myself. Then I reached up and got hold of the top of the sink. With all the strength I had I pulled myself up.

The glass was standing on the draining board where I had left it. There was some water in it.

One hand held on to the edge of the sink. The other hand went out and took hold of the glass. I got the glass to my mouth and swallowed the water.

I wanted more. I had to put the glass down in order to turn on the tap. Then I got hold of the glass again and started drinking. The water seemed to make me stronger. It spilt out of my mouth onto my sweater. There was blood on my sweater. There was blood swimming in the water at the bottom of the sink and going down the plughole.

I remembered about the gas. There did not seem to be a smell of gas. Perhaps I could not smell it because I had been in it so long. But I could smell myself. But there must be a lot of gas in the room. If I wanted to live, I must get out of the room.

I wondered if I could walk.

I let go of the sink and stood.

I was taking tottering steps and going towards the door.

I reached the door and turned the key in the lock and opened the door. It was as though the sea were outside on the landing. The air was fresh and strong. My stomach started jerking. I did not want to vomit again. I clenched my teeth and held my mouth tight shut. It seemed that there was no more to come up from my inside. I held on to the banisters. The jerking stopped.

I got along the banisters to the top of the stairs. I did not know how I was going to get down. The stairs looked too steep.

Perhaps I should stay on the landing and shout until the Johnsons heard me.

I would be found filthy and stinking.

And that was the truth about me. It was right that I should have shit running down my stockings. That was the truth.

225

I had never been strong enough to hold heaven and earth together. I would have to go to London. I would get myself to Le Carousel in Paris. They would give me champagne to drink.

I fell down the stairs.